**Jordan took a step closer, close enough to read the headstone that said,** *Tricia Bishop, beloved wife and mother, gone far too soon.*

He hesitated there. Didn't look at the next marker.

As if not looking at it could make Eddie's grave not real.

He closed his eyes for a long moment, searching inwardly for at least some little bit of courage. Then he felt a touch, Emily's fingers brushing against his. She said nothing, but somehow the touch was enough. He opened his eyes and looked. His gaze zeroed in on the dates, and he was grateful it was only the years of birth and death, although that was bad enough. That the final date was this year still knotted up his gut.

*Edward Steven Bishop*

*Beloved son and brother*

*With Mom at last*

He was barely aware of going to his knees.

"It should have been me," he said hoarsely, staring at the metal plaque.

Dear Reader,

I've always found the idea of military dog tags both logical and grim. I'd read about how soldiers in the American Civil War used to write their names on a piece of paper and pin it to their coats or scratch their names into the metal buckles of their belts. But I had no idea that the concept went all the way back to the Spartans, who wrote their names on sticks that they tied to their arms. Or the Roman *signaculum*, a metal tag on a string, which was close to what we have today. The need for such a thing is obvious, if unpleasant. And the need for two really pounds it home, introducing the idea that the soldier may lie where they've fallen for some time. Even now, today, with all our science and technology, it's still the simplest way.

I've met some veterans who served years ago yet still kept those tags. I'm sure there are many who couldn't wait to put them away, never to be seen again, but some keep them and even wear them after their service is done. I understood that. And it got me to thinking about the origin of the term *dog tags*—which of course led me to Cutter and, finally, wondering what would happen if he found a set of those tags and brought it home. That's all there was, the idea of Cutter finding these tags and bringing them to his people. It's been a note on a list for a very long time. Until one day...

Well, I'll let you read and find out the story behind these particular tags.

Happy reading!

*Justine*

# OPERATION TAKEDOWN

**Justine Davis**

HARLEQUIN
ROMANTIC
SUSPENSE

### HARLEQUIN®
# ROMANTIC SUSPENSE™

Recycling programs
for this product may
not exist in your area.

ISBN-13: 978-1-335-59383-2

Operation Takedown

Copyright © 2023 by Janice Davis Smith

For questions and comments about the quality of this book, please contact us at CustomerService@Harlequin.com.

Harlequin Enterprises ULC
22 Adelaide St. West, 41st Floor
Toronto, Ontario M5H 4E3, Canada
www.Harlequin.com

**Printed in U.S.A.**

**Justine Davis** lives on Puget Sound in Washington State, watching big ships and the occasional submarine go by and sharing the neighborhood with assorted wildlife, including a pair of bald eagles, deer, a bear or two, and a tailless raccoon. In the few hours when she's not planning, plotting or writing her next book, her favorite things are photography, knitting her way through a huge yarn stash and driving her restored 1967 Corvette roadster—top down, of course.

Connect with Justine on her website, justinedavis.com, at Twitter.com/justine_d_davis or at Facebook.com/justinedaredavis.

### Books by Justine Davis

### Harlequin Romantic Suspense

#### *The Coltons of Colorado*
*Colton's Dangerous Reunion*

#### *The Coltons of New York*
*Colton's Montana Hideaway*

#### *Cutter's Code*
*Operation Homecoming*
*Operation Soldier Next Door*
*Operation Alpha*
*Operation Notorious*
*Operation Hero's Watch*
*Operation Second Chance*
*Operation Mountain Recovery*
*Operation Whistleblower*
*Operation Payback*
*Operation Witness Protection*
*Operation Takedown*

Visit the Author Profile page at Harlequin.com for more titles.

Recently, my beloved dog became seriously ill. During the late hours spent in the emergency veterinarian waiting room, I observed many things. One, the overwhelming pressure of worry when it's someone you love hurting. Two, the dedication and devotion of the staff, from the vets to the techs to the front desk people, who handled the incoming calls of worried pet owners with grace and kindness. And three, the love between other pets and their people.

Now that my girl is home safe and well, the one image forever burned into my memory is of the woman who emerged from the examination rooms in heartbroken tears, choking out the words to her family: "They can't save him."

The world seemed to stop, and I wanted to hug this total stranger who was facing the moment all pet owners dread. I thought of the candles I had seen in two other vet offices with the request that if they were lit, you kept your voice down because someone was saying their last goodbye to their beloved companion.

I'm taking this space to ask that all of you who have a beloved creature in your life take an extra moment to let them know how much you love them. Their lives are so much shorter, which I suppose is why their love for us seems boundless. But it's also why we should never assume we will have tomorrow with them.

Make sure they know today how much they are loved.

And when the time comes, if you have to make that decision, never let them face it alone. No matter how much it hurts, they need you by their side. It's a small price to pay for the pure love they've given you.

# Chapter 1

Hayley Foxworth heard the slight jingle the moment her dog, Cutter, came through the doggy door. They had long ago made his tag noise-free, for both sleep-related and tactical reasons, so she knew it had to be something else.

"And what have you brought us today, my fine boy?" she asked as the distinctively colored dog approached. His dark head was up, his reddish tail up and wagging at the sight of her. The jingle got louder as he trotted toward her, his amber-flecked dark eyes fastened on her intently.

There was nothing of the goofy, bouncy dog she and her husband, Quinn, had played fetch with this morning. Now Cutter wore an expression she'd grown quite familiar with since he'd tumbled into her life.

"Tumbled into it and probably saved it," she murmured to Cutter as he came to a halt and sat in front of her. It was true—the animal had appeared on her doorstep at a time when she'd desperately needed distraction, after her mother's death. She'd never felt so lost. She would have thought that after months upon months of caring for her dying parent she would have not wanted the responsibility for another living being for a good long time. But Cutter blew that out of the water.

*And brought you to the man you love more than anything in the world.*

On that thought she heard footsteps in the hall as Quinn left their office headed this way.

"Too much to hope for a vacation, huh, dog?" she said as she reached for what he was holding in his mouth.

"What's he up to now?"

Her husband's deep, resonant voice gave her the same shiver of delight it always had—even when she'd only known him as the man who'd unceremoniously kidnapped both her and her dog and spirited them off in the proverbial black helicopter. So did the way he was looking at her, as if he'd like to carry her back to their bedroom and resume the activities they'd been indulging in until just a few hours ago.

"Dog tags," she said, her brow furrowed as she stared at the metal tags dangling from a chain.

That got Quinn's full attention. "What?"

She held them out to him. As he took them his fingers brushed over hers and lingered just that extra second that told her she'd been right in her guess about his thoughts.

Quinn studied the tags that would be very familiar to him, given he'd had more than one set of his own as he'd moved through the Army before he finally left the Rangers a few years ago.

"No social security number," he murmured as if to himself, "so post-2015."

"I didn't get that far," Hayley admitted. "I got hung up on his name."

He shot her a grin. "Yeah, I noticed that."

"Both tags are the same," she said. "Not from different units."

He nodded. "So he likely came back alive, did Mr. Jordan Crockett."

"He'll probably want these back."

Quinn smiled. "Guess we'd better find him, then. I'll make some calls."

Hayley knew her husband still had a lot of military contacts, and if none of those panned out, Foxworth had their own. They would find Corporal Crockett and return this memento, and that would be that.

Unless, of course, Cutter had once more brought them something…complicated.

Emily Bishop sat staring at the calendar page on her phone. Wondered if she would ever remove the entry that marked this day annually. She doubted it. She'd loved her brother too much to ever erase the date of his birth, even if it brought on waves of pain now, after his death. She'd vowed she would not dwell on or mark that other grim date but celebrate she'd had him in her life at all.

*Easy to say, hard to do.*

Moisture welled up in her eyes at Eddie's oft-quoted maxim. It was part of her psyche, that saying. They'd said it and laughed over it so often. She wondered when she would stop crying. Decided that if her tears were a measure of the love, the answer was never.

When she got to work at Bishop Tool, it was the usual morning chaos. Boxes being loaded, phones ringing, orders shouted across the big garage that housed the trucks.

Upon entering her office, she saw three messages waiting for her, for which she was almost grateful. Otherwise she would have felt compelled to walk to the office down the hall and see her father, which she wasn't quite ready for yet on this particular day. But he would put business first, and this was why Bishop was surviving tough times in the industry. That and all the goodwill her father had built over the years that had landed them on a "Take care of them first" list with many providers.

She had handled only two of the messages when there was a tap on her open door. She looked up to see her father standing politely in the doorway. It was typical of him that, despite being the CEO of the business, he never barged in unannounced or without knocking. He was respectful of the time and position of everyone who worked for him, which was probably why the newest of their employees had been there four years.

"Morning, Em," he said as she stood up. "Glad I caught you before I have to head out."

She walked over to him. "I hope the meetings with Mountainview go well." The signing of a major contract with a regional construction business was due the middle of the month, and it was one that would carry Bishop through the next three years at least, along with expanding their reach in the region. It would involve a flight to Boise and a couple of weeks spent schmoozing, but they both counted it well worth it.

He nodded. His smile didn't quite reach his blue eyes, so like her own, although she got a more genuine version than anyone else. Because the pain he felt was one she shared, especially today. The ripping, shredding pain of loss, hammered home by the empty spot in both their lives. She'd lost the little brother she adored and helped raise, and her father had lost the son he loved and had such great hopes for. They would take over Bishop someday, that had always been the plan. She and her brother would run the business their grandfather had begun and their father had built into a major concern in the region.

She noticed again the new gray that threaded through his dark hair. She and Eddie had gotten their late mother's pale blond, although Emily kept it shoulder length rather than Tricia Bishop's luxuriant middle of the back, for convenience. It hurt to see the change. They'd both lost so much…

"I just wanted to drop this off. It was in a stack of mail I picked up two or three weeks ago. It got mixed in with a bunch of flyers and junk, so I didn't see it until now. Sorry." He held out an envelope that appeared to be something she hadn't seen in a while—an actual, physical letter.

"Snail mail? Wow."

Her father grimaced. "Sad, that that is a novelty these days."

She knew he sometimes bemoaned the loss of what he called the personal touch. She took it, saw that it was hand addressed to her here, but with no return address. Even as she noticed, her father commented on that.

"No return name or address. Anything I should know about?"

She looked up at the man who had single-handedly raised two kids after their mother had died, never stinting on either love or understanding despite being left alone to do it by a cruel, vicious disease. But luckily for her—and Eddie—Benjamin Bishop had definitely been cut out for fatherhood, and he'd done it well. And now he was looking at her with a trace of concern.

"No," she answered, glancing at the envelope again, and the handwriting. It was a rather nice looking mix of cursive and printing that seemed masculine to her, but beyond that it wasn't familiar. "I'm sure it's fine."

"Let me know if there's a problem."

"I will. Now, you need to get to the airport."

"Going," he said. He hesitated, looking down at her, and she had no trouble reading the emotions in his face because they were the same ones roiling inside her. It was Eddie's birthday, the first one without him, and today life was hell.

"I know," she whispered to him.

"I know you do," he said, and pulled her into a bear hug that she returned with all her strength. "I love you."

"And I love you."

And then he was gone, leaving her thinking about how they had both, without discussion, adopted the habit of expressing that before parting, no matter if it was for an hour or days.

Because one day it just might be the last thing they said to each other.

She went back to her desk, in a way grateful that this trip had been unmovable. She was afraid if she and Dad spent the day together, they'd slide into a morass of grief and mourning that would be debilitating. She sat, finished the memo she'd been writing about the change in deadline for the delivery to the county, then picked up the envelope she'd set to one side. She looked at the front again, at the distinctive writing. It was appealing enough that she looked for repeating letters, wondering if it was not handwritten but a handwriting font. The slight differences in both shape and the thickness of the ink told her it was indeed handwritten. The stamp was, oddly, an image of her favorite wild creature, a kingfisher. She felt a stinging in her eyes once more; that was the kind of thing Eddie would have done, picked that stamp for that reason. She blinked rapidly and shifted her gaze.

The postmark was Tacoma, July 17. She didn't know anyone in that city, but she knew it was a processing center for the postal service so the piece could actually have been mailed from any number of places. She gave an inward laugh at herself for avoiding the obvious answer of simply opening the thing. She turned it over, peeled back the flap and pulled out several pages of lined paper, the kind that came in writing pads for just this purpose. They were covered on both sides with more of the same handwriting.

Her breath caught when she unfolded the pages and saw the salutation.

*Dear Emmie.*

Only one person besides her father had ever called her that. Had ever been allowed to. Her brother had done it from early childhood, when the middle syllable of her name had been too tricky for his toddler tongue. And later he insisted they were "Eddie and Emmie," to her delight.

She began to read, her gaze racing across the pages.

*Dear Emmie,*
*I know you don't know me, but please, please read this. I was a friend of Eddie's, I was there when he died and you need to know the truth.*

*My name is Jordan Crockett. Eddie may have mentioned me. We served together the entire time he was there. We sort of connected from the day he arrived, because we both loved sailing but were stuck in the desert. We found other things in com-*

*mon, like losing family young. He told me how you took over for your mother and were always there for him. He talked about you so much I almost feel like I know you.*

*The day he died was my last day deployed. I was due to be transferred stateside and discharged—honorably, I promise you. The detail we'd been sent on was to be my last, my airlift out was due in a couple of hours and Eddie and I were making plans to stay in touch. He even wanted me to come see you, meet you in person, because he'd told me so much about his amazing sister.*

*We groaned when we saw who was leading the check to see if there were salvageable parts in a truck that had been hit by an RPG, but we didn't have much choice. We just figured there'd be a lot of eye-rolling between us as the cake-eater lieutenant preened his way through what should be a routine task, making it seem like the fate of the world depended on it and that's why he was in charge.*

*I know what the official report says. That there were three or more insurgents in the area. That they spotted us away from the encampment and decided to attack. That one of them hit Eddie before we could take cover. That the lieutenant bravely risked himself to fire back. That he hit at least one of them. That he didn't pursue because Eddie was so badly wounded. That I tried to save Eddie, tried to keep him alive until we could get help. That last part is true. I did try, everything I knew and then made up some. But the rest... It's lies. All of it. I swear to you, Emmie, that is not how it happened.*

*There were no insurgents. No attack. Eddie was not shot by the enemy.*

*What really happened: an old, barely running vehicle from the local village backfired. I'd seen it earlier and had heard it before. We all had, but our idiot lieutenant panicked and grabbed his weapon. Sent out a wild spray of rounds without even looking. Two of his shots hit Eddie.*

*If you've reached this point you probably think I'm crazy. If you contacted the Army, they'd back that idea. PTSD, they'll tell you. That I finally cracked. And how sad it is that I lost it on my last day of deployment. That they got me home as soon as possible for treatment, since I was obviously having hallucinations. That what I remembered wasn't true.*

*I almost believed them. They were convincing, and I started to doubt myself. It took me a while to put it all together. To figure out the reason they were so determined to convince me I'd imagined it all. Once I did, I cooperated enough to get free of them, long enough to do some research. That's when it all came together.*

*Eddie was shot by Lieutenant Hartwell Lyden. Yes, of those Lydens, the power brokers from your neck of the woods. That was the piece I didn't have, before. How famous and powerful they are, and not just there. Powerful enough to bury this whole thing. Powerful enough to have me classified as crazy with PTSD so no one would believe me. And to cover themselves if they had to take that last step, and get rid of the one witness. They could make it look like I'd committed suicide and nobody would question it much. Lyden promised me as much, if I didn't keep quiet.*

*I'd like to tell you I stood up to them then and there, but I didn't. I needed time to think, to figure out what to do, and I couldn't do it with Hart Lyden on my tail. He was already using Eddie's death to build his myth, and I was afraid if I ran into him I'd...well, I'd pay him back in the way he deserved.*

*But I also realized I needed to get the truth written down, and to someone I could trust. At least, to someone I trust would care as much as I do about the truth of what happened to Eddie. Part of me didn't want to dump this on you, but it had to be you. Eddie's sister, who loved him and helped raise him and deserves to know the truth. And I needed to tell someone the whole of it, just in case Lyden got to me. They've got the power to hack, to intercept, to erase—virtually and in reality—so I had to do it. And via this snail mail, for those reasons as well.*

*So there it is, the truth. I'm sorry for the pain reading this must have caused you, but from what Eddie told me of you, you're likely still in horrible pain over his death anyway. I'll write again once I have a way for you to contact me. I'm headed your way, so I'll let you know when I'm in the area. Then it's up to you. If you've decided you agree I'm crazy, I'll understand.*

*One last thing, something no one else can tell you because they weren't there. Eddie died in my arms, and his last words were of you and your father. You meant the world to him, and he made me promise that if you were ever in need, I'd help. So regardless of whether you believe what I've told*

*you here or not, if there's ever anything I can do,*
*reach out.*
*Respectfully,*
*Jordan Crockett*

When she was done, Emily sat staring at the final page.
It rattled slightly, because she was shaking. And breathing hard and fast.

Everything, absolutely everything, had changed in an
instant. Just as it had when they'd learned about Eddie's
death.

Only this was almost worse.

A wave of nausea swept over her, and she had to run for
the bathroom. Barely made it. And for a long time after it
had passed, and there was nothing left to leave her roiling stomach, she sat huddled on the floor. Still shaking.

For the third time in her life, her world had been ir-
revocably altered.

## Chapter 2

He'd done the best he could.

Jordan Crockett put his head down on his arms, crossed and resting on the small table in his camper van. He felt the edge of his watch digging into his forehead, but he didn't move. He both wished he could doze off and feared he would. He needed the sleep, but was afraid if he did he'd dream, and so far that price was too high.

He still wasn't sure if what he'd done was the right thing, but he'd felt he had to do it. Still, the moment he'd dropped that letter through the slot the day before he'd headed here, he'd wanted to climb into the mailbox and get it back.

Hard to believe there had been a time when the biggest annoyance in his life had been people calling him Davy. Hard to believe he'd once said if only that would stop, he'd be happy with life. And he couldn't quite shake the notion that he'd brought it all on himself with that idiocy.

*Right. Think about yourself, Crockett. Not Eddie. Not Eddie, who has no problems at all anymore. Because he's freaking dead!*

He erupted into motion, up from the table so fast he upset the plate of eggs he'd fixed and tried to eat this morning, thinking he might fool himself into believing he was hungry. No such luck. He stared down at the mess, feeling numb. Mechanically he scraped up the salvageable food and put it back on the plate. He carried it outside and tossed it at the underbrush, a treat for the various furred and feathered locals. He'd seen a few, and was glad he'd chosen this site that was offset a bit from the others, surrounded on three sides by tall trees.

He went back inside and cleaned the table, then the dish. All mechanically, without thought, simply because that's what had to be done.

*Like sending that letter?*

He didn't know the answer. He didn't think he knew the answer to anything anymore. Especially things like how the hell he had ended up being more worried about being killed back home than he had been overseas.

*It's the difference between the uniform you're all wearing being targeted and having the big red bulls-eye painted only on your back.*

He heard the now familiar whistling as Sarge approached. They all still called him Sarge even though he'd been out of the service longer than many of them had been alive. It was out of respect, for the hero he'd been to his country then, and the hero he was to them now. He'd taken this bit of small-town acreage he'd inherited from his grandfather and turned it into the kind of refuge he'd wished he'd had when he came home from his war. And any honest veteran now would admit their homecoming was better than his had been. At least they hadn't been spit on when they came home.

*No, you just have someone the same ilk as those spitters hunting you.*

He'd told Sarge about it, when he'd first arrived—had it really been three weeks ago? His sense of time seemed to be a bit messed up. But he had told him. He couldn't—wouldn't—have moved here otherwise.

It had happened after some mutual commiseration about their names, his usually bringing on comparisons to the historic icon—or occasionally, depending on the age of the other person, a character from an '80s TV series—which had led to Sarge bemoaning that his own last name, Rockford, brought on the same comparison to an even earlier television character. Sarge had said Jordan had it tougher—the older they got the fewer people remembered a TV character, but Davy Crockett would live on.

He'd relaxed a little after that, and it had been easier to say what he had to say. "I saw something happen, something no one else saw. And now the guy who did it may be after me, Sarge," he'd told the grizzled vet. "I'm not sure if he'd care about taking down others on the way, if it meant he got to me in the end. And he's got a lot of money and power behind him."

"Seems like all it takes these days," Sarge had mused aloud. "I know the type. Think they're better than the rest of us, smarter, so they should be in charge and we should snap to when they tell us what to do." Then the thoughtful look vanished, and Jordan knew he was seeing the man who'd come home from that jungle with a chest full of medals. "But he might find us tougher to take than he thinks."

"His family could make your life hell," he warned. "They're beyond rich and they own a lot of people in power."

"And what family would that be?"

He remembered now the moment when he'd hesitated, when he hadn't wanted to answer, when he'd been certain the crusty old guy would change his mind when he heard the name. This was the only place he'd found where he thought he had a chance of successfully hiding out until he'd finished the task he'd set himself, and he didn't want to lose it.

But as he looked into those steady eyes that had seen so much, he'd found he couldn't lie to him, even by omission. "The Lydens."

One brow quirked upward in that way Jordan had never been able to manage. "Well, now," Sarge said. "If you've crossed them, then you're welcome here, son. I never had much use for any of them, with their backroom dealing and front room lies. Not to mention how people who do cross them tend to go away, one way or another."

"I didn't cross them, exactly," he'd told Sarge, feeling compelled to give the whole truth. "It was one of their sons. Hart."

The single brow shot higher. "Hartwell Lyden? Future president, if his father has anything to say about it?"

Jordan's heart sank. "Yeah."

To his shock, Sarge had burst into laughter. "Oh, now, you're even more welcome. Anybody who's ticked off that pompous young prick is welcome on my property."

Jordan had smiled despite his now seemingly constant state of unease.

"You look surprised," Sarge said.

"I am, a little."

"Shouldn't be. It's obvious that he was only in the military to pad his résumé for his political future. It's not stolen valor, but it's not all that different, either." Sarge shrugged Lyden off contemptuously. "Now, let's get you settled in."

Sarge was exactly what Jordan had heard he was—a tough old bird who took no guff off anyone, and if he accepted you he would back you to the hilt. And remembering that initial exchange now, Jordan smiled again. Life couldn't be hopeless with guys like Sarge still around. The guy was practically running an employment agency here, knowing which of his tenants had what kind of skills, and having enough friends in the area that people turned to him when they needed this or that odd job done.

"Self-interest," he'd answered when Jordan had asked. "How are you guys gonna pay my exorbitant rent without work?"

Since what he charged them for the space and the use of the showers, laundry facilities and pump-out station was minimal, Jordon knew he was joking. He suspected Sarge's goal was more about keeping them all stable and away from that helpless, lost state that enveloped too many. He knew the man had just recently turned down a generous offer to buy the property—"When anybody offers more than it's worth, you can be pretty sure you won't like what they'll do with it," he'd said—because he believed completely in what he was doing.

When the tap came on the van door now, he had himself pretty well in hand. He opened the door and stepped down to the ground.

"Barbecue night tonight," Sarge said. Jordan blinked. "Once a month, first Friday, seven o'clock. Everybody welcome. Meat provided, bring your own sides and

drinks. Usually optional, but for you this one's manda-
tory. Folks need to officially meet you."

"I… Okay." He was in no mood for socializing, but
he wasn't about to argue with this man.

"And," Sarge added in a stern tone, "they deserve to
know the guy they're accepting some risk for."

He couldn't argue that, either. They did deserve to know.
"Maybe they'll vote me off the island." He said it with a
grimace, wondering where he'd go if they did.

But Sarge only laughed. "I think you'll find they're a
tougher bunch than that. Some of them would probably
relish a fight. Blow off some steam."

"I don't want anyone getting hurt on my account,"
he said.

"That's their choice to make." Then came the thoughtful look again. "You know, I know some people who might
be able to help you with this."

"No. I don't want anyone else involved. Bad enough
that I'm a target, and now maybe you. I don't want somebody else trying to help and getting hurt on my account,"
he repeated.

To his surprise Sarge had laughed. "You can be for-
given for not knowing, being as you've been downrange
until recently, but trust me on this, it would take a lot
more than that little wimp to hurt these folks. They've
taken down bigger fish. Including one who had the same
aspirations as your little punk."

Jordan frowned. "And they're friends of yours?"

"They helped me set up this place, when I ran into
a little fuss from the city bureaucrats." Sarge grinned.
"Their name can open doors and shut up idiots like nothing I've ever seen. They suggest a course of action, but

unlike some, they let the person they're helping have the final say."

"That's...unusual."

"As are they. A lot of their crew are vets, so they'd have a special empathy for your problem. Can't hurt to at least consider, right?"

"Maybe," Jordan said, reluctant to say a flat no to this man who had already helped him out so much.

Sarge knew when to walk away, and did so. Whistling cheerfully again. And Jordan once more silently thanked the other veteran he'd met at the post office where he'd mailed the letter he hadn't wanted to write, for mentioning this place, and this man.

*Stop shaking and think!*

She had to think, had to work through this, decide what to do. Emily sat in her office, trying to calm herself, glad that her father had gone. She didn't know what he would do if—when—he found out what she'd learned in this letter.

Because it was the only thing she could think of to do, she pulled up the folder with all of Eddie's old emails. She felt the urge to read them all again, but didn't think she could bear it just now. So instead she did a name search. She'd recognized the letter writer's name right away, but couldn't remember specifically everything Eddie had ever said about his best buddy, Jordan Crockett. She did remember Eddie saying a couple of months after he'd first mentioned him that Crockett was the kind of guy you wanted on your side, and that he knew that he would always have his back.

She also knew from what they'd been able to pry out of various sources that it had been Jordan Crockett who had tried so desperately to save Eddie's life but had ended up being the one to hold him as he died. It had been the one small comfort she'd had, that Eddie hadn't died alone, that a friend had been with him.

She sat back in her chair and pulled the handwritten letter out of the envelope again. Read the truth in it. She had no doubts that it was true, both because of what Eddie had told her about this man, and because she remembered what else Eddie had said in his emails, observations about the other men he was serving with. One in particular, the one mentioned in this letter. Observations that fit with what she and most people from here knew.

She didn't know where to start. She knew that she would—she wasn't about to let this go, let it be swept under a rug that already hid so much. However, she didn't have the slightest idea how to navigate the waters ahead. But somebody must.

Something tickled at the edges of her memory. Something Eddie had mentioned. Some organization or website…

She shifted forward, pulled her keyboard closer and began to search again. And if she didn't find it that way, she'd do what she both desired and dreaded. She'd read every one of her dead brother's emails again until she found what she needed. Because she wasn't about to quit until she'd done everything possible. It was the last, best thing she could do for him.

It was nearly half an hour before she found it, that throwaway mention in a comment of an online forum where many vets posted and communicated. A forum built by a woman who had lost her SEAL husband to treachery, from within. A woman who had had the courage to do what Emily must now do. Even when it meant going to the nation's capital and facing down people at the highest levels.

She opened her browser and typed in the name of the forum the poster had mentioned.

*Accountability Counts.*

And she vowed as the site loaded that she would have the same kind of courage. For Eddie's sake.

Emily found the contact number quickly, and dialed. She hadn't expected the woman she already admired, who had taken her fight for her KIA husband straight to the top, to answer the phone; it was clear *Accountability Counts* had grown into a sizable operation and she'd expected to have to wade through some gatekeepers first. But Sloan Burke, now Sloan Burke Dunbar, had answered on the third ring. She also hadn't been surprised by the woman's immediate and fierce reaction to her story; Emily had thought it might strike a powerful chord with her.

No, the real surprise was her reaction when, almost in passing, she mentioned Eddie's friend's name.

"Jordan Crockett? That's the second time I've encountered that name today."

Emily blinked, then her brow furrowed. "What?"

"Someone else is looking for him."

Emily gasped. Could Lyden be that hot on his trail? "Who?" she asked, a little sharply.

The woman was obviously both smart and quick, because she immediately answered, "No one connected to the Lydens. In fact," she added in a thoughtful tone, "the polar opposite. The best people I know to handle situations like this, given the Lydens are a local…phenomenon. I'll put you in touch."

She said it as if the family was an infestation of sorts,

which made Emily decide then and there she liked her. "These are people you know?"

"Yes. So does my husband, who's a detective for the county sheriff. He has the utmost respect for them, and he's a hard sell."

Love and pride echoed in her voice as she spoke of the man she was now married to. Emily found it even more admirable that this woman continued her work even though she had found love again, that she hadn't tried to forget her first love. And she also felt admiration for the new man in the woman's life who understood and clearly supported this.

"Do you remember what happened with the governor here, about a year and a half ago?" Sloan asked.

"Of course," Emily said. The question called up the memory of her father, watching the reports on the news with satisfaction. He'd never had a high opinion of the man, and finding out he was, among many other terrible things, a murderer had satisfyingly proved him right in his judgment.

"That was these people."

Emily blinked. And finally connected Sloan's new husband's name. "Wait…your husband's that Detective Dunbar?"

"He is," Sloan answered, that pride in her voice again. "And the people who helped him in that effort are also the ones who called about your Mr. Crockett. The Foxworth Foundation."

She remembered that name from those news reports, too. Remembered feeling heartened that there were still people like that in the world. But right now, she was merely puzzled about why they would be looking for Eddie's friend Jordan.

Her stomach plummeted at a sudden thought. Was Jordan a fake, a liar? Had that letter he'd sent, that had upended her fragile equilibrium, been a fake, or part of a ruse perhaps? Would he suddenly appear, demanding money or something? She hadn't caught any of that in the tone. The outpouring in that letter had seemed utterly genuine, but she was hardly an expert.

"—connect you. Give me a couple of minutes to contact them, and then they'll call you, if that's all right."

It only took her a moment to decide. She herself might not be an expert in spotting fakes and scams, but from what she remembered of the case that took down a sitting governor and put him in prison where he belonged, she was willing to bet these Foxworth people were.

# Chapter 3

Quinn Foxworth hung up the phone and turned to look at the dog sitting beside the big table in the meeting room of Foxworth headquarters. Cutter was looking at him expectantly. "You," he muttered, "are too darn smart for your own good, dog."

The animal tilted his head almost comically, as if to say, "Finally figured that out, did you?"

Quinn chuckled. He'd quit trying to fight the habit he'd fallen into, translating the dog's numerous expressions into human terms. At first it had felt absurd, but as he'd gotten to know the impossibly clever animal it had become second nature.

Moved by an unexpected upswell of emotion, he leaned over and stroked the dog's head.

"Thanks, buddy. For the best three years of my life."

It wasn't really three years until next month, but Quinn wasn't going to quibble. Three years since the day this

furry troublemaker had dragged—almost literally—
Hayley into the middle of a crucial op. And what had
seemed like a serious complication at the time had instead changed his heart, his soul, his life, forever.

And Foxworth. The Foxworth Foundation was what
it was today because of what this creature had done, in
more ways than one. The dog brought them, in his own
unique way, case after case that was exactly suited to both
their goals and the way they operated. The network they
had now, with people from all walks willing to help, was
in large part due to Cutter's instincts.

But more importantly, he had brought Quinn the missing piece, the person who could read other people better than anyone he'd ever known, the person who had
changed everything, including himself, down to the core.
The woman he loved more than his own life.

Who had just appeared at the top of the stairs.

"You'll never believe the call I just—" he began.

"Weird, I just got a call from—" she said at the same
time.

They both stopped. Grinned at each other.

"You first," Quinn said.

"I just got a call from Sloan. A woman contacted her
today about some information she got from another vet
about her brother, who was KIA overseas a few months
ago. You?"

"And I just got a call from Douglas Rockford, that tough
old bird Rafe found who was having trouble setting up his
campground for vets a while back, about a new arrival."

They stared at each other. Then simultaneously shifted
their gaze to the dog watching them both.

"I'm guessing," Hayley said, "that neither of us has to
ask who this new arrival is?"

Quinn gave her a wry smile. "No. Thanks to this guy—" he nodded at Cutter "—who, as usual, is ten steps ahead of us."

"The dog tags," Hayley said.

Quinn nodded. "Hits from three sides. Sloan, Sarge and our chief case finder."

Hayley sighed, but she was smiling as she did. "I guess we're in, then."

"Guess we are."

And Cutter let out a satisfied little woof.

Based on what she'd already known, plus her research on the Foxworth Foundation and their accomplishments, Emily had expected some sort of grand headquarters. Certainly not the discreet building hidden from the road by thick trees, and painted nearly the same color as those trees, making it even less conspicuous. Quinn Foxworth had told her on the phone how to find them, had said they weren't obvious, but that had been an understatement. There was no signage, no indication at all of what the place was. This could easily have been a large, private home, carefully masked from the outside world.

Then she realized that it was the perfect fit for the organization she'd read and heard about. And fit what she'd read about its founding, after the Foxworth siblings had been orphaned by a terrorist attack. It fit that almost everything she'd found was not them blowing their own horn—their website was pretty minimal—but others they'd helped doing it for them.

She could only hope they could—and would—do the same for her. For Eddie.

She would convince them. She had to. She couldn't let this go and live with herself.

She fought down the urgent anxiety that wanted to flood her every time she thought of what Eddie's friend had said in that letter. She didn't doubt the sincerity of what he'd said. She knew simply from reading it that he utterly and completely believed what he was telling her.

*He doesn't talk much, sis. Part of being on his third tour, I guess. But when he does talk, smart people listen up, because there's no BS in the man.*

Eddie's words from one of his last emails home rang in her head as she drove the winding gravel driveway. When she got clear of the trees and into the open space around the building, she saw the broad expanse of meadow leading out to a thick stand of trees on one side, a large, tall outbuilding on the other, and what appeared to be a helipad, judging by the windsock close by, in between. And what perhaps should seem an anachronism instead made sense to her. The beauty of the surroundings seemed indicative of their mission, to help, and the helipad indicative of their ability to do it—to the tune of exposing corruption and murder at a high level. So who better to take this on?

If they would, of course. This might be too small for an operation like Foxworth, although Sloan had assured her the size of the case had nothing to do with whether they took it on or not. That seemed almost too noble to be believed in this day and age, but she had to try. For Eddie she had to.

Before she'd even come to a halt in the gravel parking area, the door to the main building swung open. She saw a dog—and only a dog—coming through. The animal headed for her at a run, but didn't look in the least threatening. In fact, it looked almost welcoming, head, tail and ears up. She barely had time to register that she liked his coloring, black head to shoulders shifting to a reddish brown over back to tail. His longish fur looked soft and fluffy, although as he got closer and she saw his eyes, dark and flecked with an amber color, fluffy was the last word she would use for this dog. That gaze was anything but.

He sat at her feet, looking up at her intently. She held out a hand, letting him sniff. He nudged her hand, and instinctively she stroked his head. The moment she did, her worry eased up a little, the knot in her chest loosened. She even smiled a little. The wonder of petting a dog.

She leaned down to look at the tag hanging from his collar. It was in the shape of a boat, which amused her when she saw the name stamped on it. Cutter. Maybe his owners were connected to the Coast Guard. Or were sailboat aficionados.

After a moment the dog got up, turned and headed back the way he'd come. After about ten steps he paused and looked back at her. Emily wondered if there was anyone in the world who didn't understand that signal. And she was smiling again as she followed. The smile became a slight chuckle when they reached the building, the dog rose up to bat at a silver metal square beside the door and the door swung open. It felt odd—it had been so long since she'd laughed. Since the day they'd found out about Eddie, in fact.

There was a man standing just inside the door. Not as if he'd been about to open it himself, but just waiting.

Eddie had talked about what he'd called command presence, that ability some people had to project authority without saying a word. The ability to make people realize he was the one in charge before they even knew who he was.

This man had that in spades.

She tried for a smile as the dog went inside. "I like your butler."

"Cutter?" Quinn smiled back and quickly went from imposing presence to approachable guy. Approachable, extremely good-looking guy. "He's a good one."

"And trustworthy, obviously, since no fence."

"We've learned that if he ever takes off, he's got a darned good reason. Come in, Ms. Bishop. I'm Quinn Foxworth."

That didn't surprise her in the least. This was exactly the kind of man it would take to run an operation like this. And the woman who was coming toward them now had her own kind of presence, a warm, welcoming kind.

"And this," the man said, in an entirely different tone, so full of love and pride that her throat tightened, "is my wife, Hayley."

"Emily," she said and sighed inwardly at the way they casually touched, as if they needed the contact, or as if they simply couldn't be that close without touching. She'd always longed for that kind of relationship, but so far it hadn't been in the cards.

"Come, Emily, have a seat," Hayley said. "There's coffee on, or something else if it's too late for caffeine for you."

"Coffee would be wonderful," she said, knowing that sleep likely wasn't going to happen for her tonight anyway.

Quinn headed for the compact but sleek kitchen she could see in the far corner of the spacious room they'd come into. And for her next surprise, it looked like the great room of a pleasant home rather than any kind of an office.

Hayley led her over to where two long couches and a couple of comfortable-looking armchairs flanked a large, square coffee table and faced a gas fireplace she imagined was quite cozy in the winter. But today was a warm—well, for the northwest anyway—summer day, and instead she breathed the fresh air coming in through open windows as she took a seat on one of the couches.

Quinn arrived moments later with three mugs of coffee and a restaurant-style holder with cream and sugar. Then he sat on the couch opposite her, and Hayley took a seat beside him. And again Emily felt that twinge that wasn't quite envy, but more longing. She tried to stifle it, and was glad when the Foxworth dog came to sit at her feet. He gave her that steady gaze again for a moment before he rested his chin on her knee. She couldn't help but smile, and when she stroked the sleek fur atop his head, she felt that same easing of tension she'd felt outside. Dogs really did have a knack.

"We're so sorry about your brother," Hayley said quietly. "Believe me when we say we know how hard it is."

Emily nodded, then flicked a glance at Quinn. "You were military?"

He nodded, then said wryly. "It still shows?"

"In a good way, yes," Emily said.

"Sloan said your brother was younger?" Hayley asked.

Emily nodded. "Three years. Our mother died when we were kids, and Dad never remarried. So I tried to step up for Eddie, although I'm sure I annoyed him back then, trying to act like his mother."

She blinked rapidly as moisture brimmed in her eyes. What she wouldn't give to hear Eddie yelling at her to act like a sister, not his mother again. She swallowed and went on, grateful that the Foxworths seemed willing to let her go at her own pace.

"When he signed up for the Army, I was...so torn. I was proud of him, but afraid for him."

"Understandable," Hayley said, with a glance at her husband. "I consider myself lucky Quinn was already out when we met."

"It's a special kind of hard on those left behind," Quinn said, surprising her. "In many ways, they have to be tougher." He shifted to a businesslike tone. "Sloan gave us the basics. Something about a letter from someone who was in your brother's unit?"

Emily drew in a deep breath. It was difficult, deciding to trust these strangers. But she had no idea how to deal with this herself. How to do what had to be done. All she knew was she simply couldn't let this stand. And from what she'd been able to find, these people and their foundation might be just the ones to help.

"After...it happened, they told me about Eddie's buddy, who risked his life trying to save him. I tried to contact the man, to thank him, but that had been his last day in and he was already back home. And he'd...vanished. No one seemed to know where he was. And now, months later..."

She couldn't seem to find the words, or her voice to speak them with. So instead she pulled out the envelope holding the letter she'd read so many times that she had it practically memorized. She closed her eyes for a moment, and the pages seemed to materialize in her mind.

Emily gave a shake of her head, snapping out of the painful reverie. She stared at the envelope for a moment as if that could change it somehow. But it didn't—nothing could.

She handed the letter that had blasted what had been left of her life to Quinn Foxworth.

# Chapter 4

Jordan went through the pockets of his faded jeans once more before he threw them in the washing machine with his T-shirts. They were empty, as they had been the last time he'd checked. There was no denying any longer that he'd lost the damn tags.

He could blame it on the season. It was the sun and the heat of summer that had made him peel off his shirt while working at the various jobs Sarge had lined up for him last week. When he did that, the chain and tags moved freely and got in his way, so he'd taken them off and shoved them into his right front pocket. Or thought he had.

He wasn't even sure why he still wore them, other than it felt odd to be without them after so long. He kept reaching for them reflexively, and it was always a jolt when he remembered they weren't there.

*You don't need to be wearing them, so don't. The Army's behind you now.*

He thought eventually the frequent self-lecture might take and he might stow the tags away. But he'd wanted it to be his choice, and not because he'd done something stupid like lose the damned things. Besides, maybe he did need to be wearing them. If Hart Lyden had his way—and when didn't he?—the tags might just have to fill their intended purpose. That of identifying his body.

He grimaced, shoved the jeans into the washer and started the cycle. He was being ridiculous. Lyden probably assumed he'd been cowed into silence, as he knew others had been, by the power of the man's family if nothing else.

"Hey, Crockett! Somebody here for you."

He froze at the call from someone behind him. The voice was familiar, he'd picked up on the slight drawl last night at the barbecue. When he'd been introduced by Sarge, he'd asked, "Any relation?" assuming Jordan would know what he meant. He'd been used to the question since he'd been a kid, but this was one of the few times it hadn't irritated him, mainly because the man had explained he was asking because he himself hailed from Tennessee and claimed a distant connection to the famed frontiersman.

"Other than being called Davy half my life? No."

Marcus Arroyo had grinned at that. "Funny how people assume."

But at the moment, Jordan had fixated on the fact Marcus had tossed out. Someone was here for him...

He should have known the Lydens would find him. They had connections everywhere in the region, probably even over here in the more rural side of Puget Sound. Maybe they'd decided to cut to the chase and sent someone to take him out. He doubted it would be the first time; if he'd learned nothing else since he'd started looking for information, it was that problems for the Lyden family had a habit of magically disappearing. Usually to be found later, dead in an "accident" or, more likely in his case, from apparent suicide. It was horrible enough that the statistics on veteran's suicide would make it so believable, but to use it as a cover for murder was… He had no words bad enough.

He turned around slowly. Marcus was grinning at him.

"Up at Sarge's. And I'd hurry if I were you."

"Somebody…important?" That fit. The Lydens would roll in in a way that made it clear to all in the vicinity just how special and important they were. And Marcus wouldn't know any different; the former Navy submariner hadn't lived or been stationed here at Bangor so he wouldn't know the locals. Wouldn't know how slimy that family was.

Marcus's grin widened. "Would be important to me. Any woman who looks like that…"

Woman? A woman was here looking for him? Now he was utterly confused. He hadn't had any female contact since he'd gotten here, other than Sarge's wife and the elderly woman who'd hired him to fix a few things around her home, where he suspected he'd lost his tags.

"C'mon, Crockett, unless you want me to stand in for you with the hot blonde."

That only confused him more. He didn't even know any—

His brain locked on a remembered image. But it was impossible. He hadn't told her where he was, hadn't told her how to reach him yet—there was no way she could have found him. Was there? He muttered a thanks to the lanky Tennessean and headed toward the house.

Sarge had left the door open on this bright, sunny day,

and when Jordan got within ten yards, a dog came out. It looked like a longer-haired, fluffier version of the Belgian Malinois he'd encountered in the service, and the animal had the same alert, intense look about him. He jumped the two steps down from the porch and trotted toward him. There was no threat in his manner, but Jordan didn't assume anything; he'd seen what Mals could do when motivated.

The dog stood looking up at him intently. Not with the "Lemme go get 'em" stare he knew from those military K9s, but more of an "I can see your soul" kind of stare. Jordan gave a quick shake of his head at that silly thought.

Then the dog stretched out, nosing his hand. He meant to only give the animal a quick pat, but ended up stroking the soft fur instead, puzzled at the feeling it gave him. A feeling not quite of calm, but definitely an easing of tension.

"Come on, kid," Sarge called from where he now stood in the open doorway. "Some folks you need to meet."

Jordan straightened to look at the man. Folks, plural? Marcus had left out that little detail. Or maybe he had only noticed the blonde he'd mentioned.

He felt a gentle but definite nudge at the back of his legs. Startled, he looked down at the dog who had made the move, as if to herd him. "I'm a lot of things, dog, but I'm not a sheep."

The dog just looked up at him intently, and he noticed some almost golden flecks in the dark eyes. It was oddly difficult to look away, even to speak to his landlord.

"Taking in canine strays now, Sarge?" he asked as he walked to the foot of the steps, the dog close on his heels.

Sarge laughed. "That's no stray. But he is persistent, so you might as well give in now."

He didn't want to. He didn't want to step into that room and face emissaries of the Lyden family, no matter if they were here to try to buy him off or kill him if they couldn't. If it was going to happen, he didn't want it to happen here, at Sarge's place, when the man had done nothing but help all of them.

As the dog nudged him again, something belatedly struck him. "Wait…you know this dog?"

"I told you about the folks who helped me. He's theirs."

He blinked. "You called them? I only said maybe."

"You didn't say no," Sarge pointed out. "And besides, someone else contacted them, too."

The dog nudged again. Jordan sighed and gave in. That it was the people Sarge had mentioned before eased his mind a little, but he still wasn't looking forward to this.

He stepped through the door just as another man was reaching to open it from the inside. Jordan stopped in his tracks, staring into a pair of icy blue eyes that reminded him of the special ops guys who had come through on their way to a mission now and then. The guy was as tall as he was, so the effect was straight on and powerful. Command presence, Eddie used to say. The kind of guy who could get you to follow an unspoken order merely with a flick of those eyes.

Jordan's mouth quirked wryly. "Let me guess. Sarge said Army, so… Ranger? Green Beret?"

"Ranger. Once upon a time."

"You've still got the look."

"Comes in handy now and then," the man said, with a trace of a smile. Then he held out a hand. "Quinn Foxworth, Corporal Crockett."

He grimaced at the rank, but took the offered hand. The shake was firm but not challenging, nor did it hold even a trace of arrogance. Just assuredness—the confidence of a man who knew who he was and why.

*I envy you that. Because I haven't got a clue anymore who I am, and I'm not sure there is a why.*

"I feel like I should salute," he said, aware that his words were coming out sounding a little sour.

"You served as much as I did."

"I," he said flatly, "was a mechanic."

"Then you made what I did possible," Foxworth said, and there was no doubting his sincerity. "Could have done with a little more breaking down of the brass's transport, though."

Caught off guard, Jordan laughed and his tension faded. "Point taken," he said.

Foxworth stepped to the side and gestured him into the room. Jordan took two steps and stopped in his tracks. Because there was a woman standing just a few feet away, staring at him.

A woman he recognized on sight.

She was even prettier in person than she'd been in the video calls he'd caught glimpses of, the calls with Eddie that had told him just how close this brother and sister had been. The teasing, the familiarity, the unhidden love had made him feel oddly tight inside, since it was something he'd never known.

She was staring at him. Her eyes, a deeper blue than Foxworth's ice, were oddly shiny. When he realized it was with tears, he felt a sensation he could only liken to a kick in the chest. He'd thought when he'd glimpsed her image over Eddie's shoulder that maybe after Eddie got out and went home, he could introduce them.

*But Eddie went home in a box.*

His jaw tightened. "Emmie." He whispered it, because

at the moment he seemed incapable of any more volume than that.

"Jordy," she whispered back, using the name only her brother had ever used, laughingly saying his name had to fit in with Eddie and Emmie.

Then she was running to him, and the next thing he knew was the impact of her as she threw her arms around him in the fiercest hug he'd ever gotten. As he looked down at the top of her head, at the blond hair the same golden shade as her brother's, because it seemed the only thing to do, he hugged her back.

And tried to ignore the simple fact that nothing in his entire life had ever felt so right.

# *Chapter 5*

Eddie's description of his closest friend had been decidedly lacking. How very like her brother to say he was cool, liked the sea and sailing and hated the desert just as he did, and that he played a mean game of poker and an even better one of baseball.

*He could have gone pro, I swear, sis. He's got a swing the size of Texas. He drove a ball clean over the camp fence line once.*

And through all that he'd failed to mention that Jordan Crockett was drop-dead gorgeous, with thick, shiny brown hair and a fascinating pair of hazel eyes. Of course, that wasn't the kind of thing Eddie had ever cared about. Unless it was whatever woman he was attracted to, and even then he'd looked beyond the surface.

She remembered, as she sat studying the man now, the first time she'd told Eddie she'd like to meet the guy he'd bonded with so quickly. Get to know him.

*He's kinda shy about that kind of thing. I don't think he's used to family much.*

*He doesn't have family?*

*Not that I know of. I asked him once, and he just said his grandmother raised him, and he had no idea where his bio parents are. Don't think he cares.*

At the time she'd thought it very sad. But as Eddie continued to mention him often—and okay, sometimes she'd asked—it seemed he was pretty well-adjusted.

But now, all she could think of was how good it felt to hold him, to feel him alive and warm and breathing, this man who had tried so hard to save her brother. And after a startled moment—was a hug so strange to him?—his arms came around her. And then she heard him, softly, saying "I'm sorry" over and over again, until finally she pulled back to look up at him.

"It wasn't your fault. You tried to save him."

"But I couldn't," he said, and when she looked up into those eyes, the hazel blend of green and brown, she saw pure misery there. For the first time she fully realized that there was someone besides her and her father who had a gaping hole in their life where Eddie used to be. She'd been sunk so deep into her grief, she hadn't been able to look beyond it. But in the face of his, her battered heart fought back.

"It should never have happened. It's Lyden's fault, Jordy."

He went very still. For a moment he just looked at her, lips parted. Then he swallowed visibly and said, in a tone of wonder, "You…believe me?"

Her brow furrowed. "About what happened? Of course I do. You wouldn't lie about something like that."

"How can you be so sure? You don't even know me."

She smiled, albeit sadly. "I know what my brother told me about you. He said you didn't talk much, but when you did it was pure truth. That you told him you never bothered to lie because you didn't like having to keep track of what you'd said to who. And that he trusted your opinion more than anyone else's because he usually had to pry it out of you."

He looked oddly embarrassed. "Did he…always talk about me so much?"

It seemed as if the idea was utterly foreign to him, that a friend would share what they admired about him. Or maybe it was more that he didn't expect to be admired at all.

"You were his best friend, Jordy. Of course he talked about you," she said softly.

He let out an audible breath, and for a silent moment his eyes closed. She wanted to hug him again, because it meant so much to her that he shared her pain. But a tiny woof from the Foxworth dog reminded her abruptly that they weren't alone, and that this was not the time to pour out her emotions.

She glanced at the other man in the room—the owner of this place had tactfully departed, leaving them in private—Quinn Foxworth. He nodded toward the living room, and she nodded in turn.

"Let's go sit down," she told Jordan. "We need to talk about what to do next."

His eyes snapped open and his brow furrowed. His gaze flicked to Quinn, then back to her. "What?"

"Quinn's here to help. But we have to decide how."

He looked uncertain, but when she walked over to the couch before a wide, brick fireplace and hearth, he followed. He looked a little startled when she sat right next to him, but it had been an accident; the Foxworth dog had gotten in the way and she'd almost lost her balance. And it would seem rude now to get up and move, so she stayed. When she looked up again, at Quinn, who had taken a seat in one of the armchairs, she found him watching his own dog thoughtfully.

As if he'd sent some silent command, the animal turned and sat at Jordan's feet, but facing Quinn. The two seemed to stare at each other for a moment, before Quinn said quietly, "Got it, dog."

Emily had no idea what that meant, but obviously it was what the dog had been waiting to hear because he got up and walked over to Quinn and plopped on the floor beside him. Then Quinn looked at Jordan.

"As she said, I am here to help." His mouth quirked. "And I'm not from the government."

"Well, that's a point in your favor," Jordan said dryly.

Quinn flashed a disarming grin, and Jordan seemed to relax a little. "What we need to know is how far you want to push this."

"Push…what?"

"The case against Hartwell Lyden."

Jordan drew back, staring. Then he glanced at Emily, and she felt a qualm. "I showed them your letter, because I trust them."

"Just like that?" he asked, as if she'd betrayed his own trust.

But this was too big, too important, so she pushed on. "Not just like that. I did a lot of research before I went to them." She laid it all out for him, contacting Sloan Burke and her organization—whose name he apparently recognized—and the other things she'd discovered about Foxworth, including their sizable part in the downfall of

their murderous governor. Quinn just let her say it, as if
he thought it would be more convincing coming from her.
Jordan listened, his face expressionless now. And when
she was done, he didn't say anything to her, but looked
back at Quinn.

"There is no case. Just me, and my word means nothing against the Lydens."

Quinn met his stare unwaveringly. "Which means
this is exactly the kind of battle Foxworth was founded
to fight."

"Take on impossible odds, do you?"

"Frequently."

Jordan grimaced. "Look, I've had my fill of fighting.
Now I'm just trying to stay alive."

Quinn's gaze sharpened. "Have they tried anything yet?"

Emily wasn't sure what he meant, but Jordan obviously was. "I…don't know for sure," he said.

"But you suspect," Quinn said. "What happened?"

"It was just a near miss when I first got back. At the
storage lot where I kept my camper. A truck swerved
toward me as I was about to climb in and head out. It
could have been accidental. He might not have seen me."

"But?"

He grimaced again. "If I hadn't been able to dodge
behind the boat parked next to me, I would have been
smashed into a very solid wall. As it was, he took a chunk
out of that wall."

"And the truck?"

"In the wind."

"You report it?"

Jordan gave him a sour look then. "Without knowing
exactly which locals the Lydens might own? No. I told
the storage yard owner and got out of there."

To her surprise, Quinn nodded. "Probably wise." That seemed to surprise Jordan, too. But Quinn just went on in businesslike tones. "It's likely the Lydens would have been able to find out what flight you were on and its arrival time, and had you followed. So, for the moment at least we're going to accept that was an attempt on your life."

"We?"

"Yes. Anything since then?"

"No. But they'd have no way of knowing where I was headed. I wasn't even sure. At that point it was totally random. I...wandered for a while."

"Good. Decent chance they don't know you're in the area, then. Yet, anyway. I assume the storage yard has security cameras?"

"Yeah, but—"

"What's the address of the yard? I'll have my tech guy get hold of video from them, see if we can get more on that truck," Quinn said, pulling a phone out of his pocket. "Traffic cams between there and the airport, too, to see if we can spot the truck."

Jordan blinked. "It's in Missouri. You can just make a call and get that?"

Quinn was already speaking into the phone so Emily answered for him. "They have five regional locations, and their main headquarters is in St. Louis."

He turned his head to stare at her, clearly startled. "They're...that big?"

"They are. I told you I researched them before I decided to talk to them." She smiled encouragingly. "And I told you they were good."

"If they're that big and that good, I can't afford them," he said flatly.

"You don't—" Emily stopped, unoffended, when Quinn interrupted.

"Date, time and airline, and the time you arrived at the storage yard? And all you can remember about the truck?"

Jordan gave him the information, although she could tell he was far from convinced. Quinn repeated it into the phone, ended the call and looked back at Jordan.

"As for affording Foxworth," Quinn said, "that's not your problem. We don't charge a fee for fighting for justice."

"Justice," Jordan repeated, almost in a laughing tone, "is open to interpretation these days."

"True enough," Quinn said easily. "So isn't it nice that the interpretation we act on is our own?"

"The Lydens think they're immune," he warned.

"Which will only make it sweeter when you win."

Jordan's expression made it clear he'd never really considered that, the possibility he might win. It made Emily's eyes sting again. Then she realized she'd been wrong. Not just he, but *we* might win. If he did, she did, because winning meant Eddie's death would be, in a way, avenged. Justice would be done, as Quinn had said.

That it would be against someone like the Lydens was even more appealing. They truly did think they were above it all, that they were better than what they'd call ordinary citizens. Or the little people. The people who tried to keep things running while people like the Lydens reaped the benefits.

Yes, they were a living example of a two-tier justice system.

That word again. Justice.

And from what she'd learned, no one was better at getting justice for the little guy than Foxworth.

## Chapter 6

Jordan stood staring out of Sarge's window at the campground down the hill. He was feeling a bit numb. Just as had happened after watching the life fade from Eddie's eyes, there was a faint buzz in his ears, in his head, a hum that seemed to hold him a step back from what was going on. The counselor they'd made him see told him it was the brain's way of putting a buffer between him and things that were too difficult to process yet. And that it would fade with time. And it had.

Until now.

He felt as if it had all come rushing back full force.

"Jordy? Are you okay?"

Emily's quiet voice came from so close behind him he nearly jumped. He scowled inwardly, thinking it was a good thing he'd left the actual fighting to guys like Quinn Foxworth, because he got lost in his head too often and too easily. Eddie had always said that was his strength, that he could get so totally focused on a problem with some system or machine that he didn't let go until it was solved. Which was all well and good—until someone started shooting at you.

"About as okay as you are, I'm guessing," he muttered.

"Actually, I'm…doing better. Knowing we're doing something about what happened to Eddie, that Foxworth is on our side now, makes me feel better."

He turned his head to meet her gaze, looking into those blue eyes so like her brother's. Eddie had once called her pretty cute. He'd grossly understated. She was lovely, with those eyes, that silky sweep of blond hair just brushing her shoulders, that delicate face, and above all that sweet, kissable mouth.

He instantly quashed that. His thoughts were out of line, he knew that. So he grasped at something that had occurred to him before. "I'm still not clear on exactly how that happened. I mean, I know the woman from *Accountability Counts* recommended them, but you said they'd already called her yesterday?"

"Yes. She was startled when I gave her your name, because she'd already heard it from Foxworth."

Wariness stabbed through him. "And how did they know my name before you told her?"

Her brow furrowed. "I don't know." She apparently read his look—seemed she was good at that, but then Eddie had always said she was very perceptive—and quickly shook her head. "It's nothing bad or suspicious, I'm sure."

"I'm glad you are. Because if they're as big as you say, how do we know they and the Lydens aren't linked?"

"Quinn and his sister started Foxworth with insurance money they received after their parents were killed in a terrorist attack when Quinn was a kid. They built it into something that helps people they feel are in the right but beaten down, by people just like those we're up against. And they do it all over the country. Does that sound like someone the Lydens would be connected to?"

"No," he admitted. What he didn't want to admit was how much he'd liked that "we" part.

"Do you really think that of Quinn? That he'd lie to your face like that? That he's no better or different than the guy who killed Eddie?"

When she put it like that, the answer was obvious. "No," he said again, feeling the suspicion fade away.

"Then trust your own judgment, if you don't trust mine."

He almost smiled at that. "Eddie always said he trusted your judgment more than his own. That's good enough for me."

She did smile, although it was clearly bittersweet.

"All right," Quinn said briskly, crossing the room toward them. "We should have what we need from Ty— he's our head tech guy—within the hour. He'll send it to our headquarters here."

"Quinn," Emily said, "Jordan has a question. About how you knew his name before I called Sloan."

Quinn smiled at her before he shifted his gaze to Jordan. With a smile that looked more than a little wry, he nodded toward the dog, who Jordan only now noticed had gotten up from his spot on the floor and padded quietly over to stand beside him and Emily. "Cutter found something of yours and brought them to us."

"Found some—" He cut himself off mid-word when it hit him. He stared down at the dog, who was looking up at him with an expression he could only describe as proud. "My dog tags."

"Yes."

Quinn's tone was completely neutral, yet Jordan still felt the need to explain. He looked away from the clearly self-satisfied dog and at his owner. "I took them off at a job I was on last week because they were getting in the way." He wondered if the man still had his, too. Given his progress through the ranks he probably had a few sets. "I thought I had them safely in my pocket, but I guess not."

Quinn nodded. "We'll get them back to you."

He almost said don't bother, thinking this might be the way to break himself of the habit of wearing them. But then he remembered his earlier thought, that they might be needed for their original purpose if Lyden ever caught up with him.

And the way Quinn had said they'd get them back to him made him think the man understood completely. Jordan turned back to the dog. "Guess I should thank you, huh?" Cutter woofed softly. Jordan reached down and gave the dog a scratch behind the ears, which put what he'd call a smile on the animal's face. What it did for him, he didn't have words for. It was just that same strange sense of calm he'd felt before when he'd touched that silken fur.

"So…thanks, dog."

"Scary part is, I'm sure he's only just begun," Quinn said, and now his voice had taken on the tone he'd heard sometimes from the K9 operators he'd known, one they'd described as that of trying to keep up with a pup too clever for his own good. But when he went on, it was to business. "It would be easier to pull all this together and work out our plan of action at our headquarters, if you're okay with that. It's not far. We're just outside of Redwood Cove, about three miles north."

Jordan hesitated, glancing over his shoulder toward

the campground again, thinking of the hassle of pulling up stakes here and getting the camper ready to roll. It had taken him nearly half an hour to get ready to head to the job he'd lost the tags on, but he'd needed all his tools there. For other things he usually used his bike, his only other means of transport. Three miles wasn't a bad ride, but he didn't know the area that well yet, and the roads were narrow and required caution, so it could take him fifteen or twenty minutes.

Then, as if he'd read Jordan's thoughts, Quinn spoke. "You can ride with us. We'll bring you back."

Jordan studied the man for a minute. That was exactly what he should have expected from someone with his experience. He had probably assessed the camper, seen the bike and guessed at the rest.

"I'll bet you were hell on wheels as a Ranger," he said.

The grin flashed again. "I've been accused."

For a moment he just looked at the man, picturing him in uniform. And he knew Emily was right. If this guy had arrived when he'd been serving, by now he would have already classified him as one of the good guys.

"All right."

They headed out to the big, dark blue Foxworth SUV. When they reached it, Cutter stopped so abruptly Jordan almost ran into him. The dog was looking from him to Emily then back to the car. To his surprise, he heard Quinn chuckle.

"Figure that one out, dog," the man said.

Jordan had no idea what he meant. But a moment later he was startled again when, as Quinn opened the front passenger door for Emily, the dog jumped in instead, ensconcing himself on the seat. Emily looked as surprised as he felt, especially when Quinn burst out laughing.

"That'll teach me to dare you," he said to his dog. Then he looked at them. "There's a reason, but I'd just as soon let Hayley explain. You two mind sitting in the back seat?"

As they did, Quinn fished a harness out of the side pocket of the door. Cutter let out an unhappy sounding half bark, half whine.

"You know the rules, dog. Front seat means the harness." Emily and Jordan laughed at the dog's put-upon air as Quinn fastened the harness around him and then ran the seatbelt through it. "Oughta make you wear it in back, too," Quinn said, ruffling the dog's fur.

If Cutter had an opinion about that—and Jordan suspected he would—he didn't express it.

"He's quite something," Emily said.

"Yeah," Jordan said, looking at her sitting next to the opposite window, behind the seat the dog had commandeered. He stared out his window of the vehicle, embarrassed at the thought that had just struck him, that he'd liked it a lot better inside when she'd ended up sitting right next to him. Which had, in a way, happened because of the dog as well.

"Did he sit there on your way here?" he asked her as Quinn walked around to get into the driver's seat.

"No. He was back here."

"Weird."

"Quinn said he's a very different sort of dog."

"Hmm," was all Jordan said as Quinn got in and started the vehicle. He had more important things to think about than the vagaries of canine behavior.

Like dodging the powerful Lyden family and that little problem of staying alive.

## Chapter 7

When Quinn had said Foxworth headquarters, Jordan had pictured some kind of office, maybe in a row of them along the main street, such as it was in the little village on the sound. What he hadn't pictured was the secluded drive through thick trees, unmarked by signs or street name, as if anyone headed here would already know where they were going. Nor had he pictured the two buildings set in a big clearing that they reached after a few turns on a gravel drive. One was three stories tall and painted the same green as the trees, the other about a story and a half set off to the right.

And in between…

"Yes, it's a helipad," Emily said when she saw him looking at it. "I asked when I first got here. And apparently there's a plane at the airport, too."

"That must have been a hell of an insurance policy," Jordan muttered.

"Apparently Quinn's sister is a financial genius. She built on that payout until they had the funds to start Foxworth, first one office and now five."

Places like this, times five? Helicopters and planes? "More like financial wizard, maybe."

Emily laughed, and the sound of it made him feel better than it probably should have.

He glanced at the other cars parked here—an older, slightly battered silver coupe parked over by the second building, a dark gray SUV slightly smaller than the one they'd arrived in next to where Quinn had parked and, directly in front of the green building, another of the same model smaller SUV in a bright, cheerful blue.

But then he was distracted by the sight of Cutter who, freed from the front seat harness, was racing toward the front door.

"Watch this," Emily said with a grin. And he did, as the dog rose up on his hind legs and batted at a silver square beside the door with a front paw. The door started to swing open, obviously on an automatic opener the dog had triggered.

"That," he said, "is a scary dog."

When they stepped inside he was surprised all over again; despite the rather industrial exterior, this looked and felt more like a home than an office. It was furnished like one, with couches, chairs, a big coffee table, a gas fireplace with a big flat-screen TV above, and a colorful rug setting it all off.

He wondered if this was how they got people to relax and cooperate. If so, he guessed it worked better than a hard push, although he suspected Quinn Foxworth was capable of that, too.

Then two other men entered the room. The first one

came down the stairs at the far end of the room, and was greeted with a rhythmic little bark from the dog. The other, a bare minute later, came in the back door from outside. He got an odd combination of long barks and short yips. Jordan wondered for a moment if that was typical. He would have expected a dog to greet people he knew differently than strangers, but this was a step beyond.

Jordan focused on the new arrivals. The one from upstairs was a sandy-haired guy with clear blue eyes who moved with a light, easy grace and the kind of confidence that only came from knowing what you could do and that you were good at it.

The one coming in the back was a totally different picture—tall, rangy, dark hair and eyes, and an entirely different kind of grace. The lethal kind, that went with the look in his eyes. Jordan had seen that look before, in the guys who had come through his camp overseas, usually after a mission. This man had been there and back, as he and Eddie used to say.

"Emily, Jordan, meet Teague Johnson," Quinn said with a nod at the light-haired guy, "and Rafe Crawford," he finished with a nod at the taller one. "They're both former Marines," Quinn added with a crooked smile, "but don't hold it against them."

Jordan eyed the two newcomers warily. Especially the tall guy with eyes the color of a Missouri thunderstorm, and whose name sounded vaguely familiar, like he'd seen it somewhere. "Even if I did, I don't think I'd be mouthing off about it."

Teague laughed and said, "Good call," while Rafe just looked at him, assessing.

Jordan thought he had given up worrying about what other people thought of him long ago. But somehow it was different with these guys. Quinn definitely, but these two as well. Not just because they were former military— even Marines—but because they had that air about them that he recognized. He'd seen it before. That air of good men fighting the good fight. And it did matter what they thought of him.

And Emily. Oh, yeah, it mattered what she thought of him. A lot.

In the manner of the commander he suspected Quinn had been, he gave the other two men a sitrep. And his report on the situation was both concise and precise.

Teague's eyes widened at the mention of the name involved. "Lyden? Of *the* Lydens?" Quinn nodded, and Teague let out a low whistle. He looked at Jordan. "I grew up around here, and they've been big wheels as long as I can remember. And spreading."

"I know that," Jordan said. "Now. Back in the Army I just thought he was one of those rich guys with a blown-up image of himself on the wall." Teague laughed again.

Then the other man spoke, and his voice was as deep and innately intimidating as he would have expected. "And you witnessed Hartwell Lyden take out Ms. Bishop's brother with friendly fire?"

Jordan grimaced. He was hesitant to go through it again, but maybe, just maybe, these people, this Foxworth organization, might be able to actually do something. Or at least try.

If they, unlike those who had chalked his story up to trauma, believed him.

*Roll the dice or walk away.*

He glanced at Emily, who was watching him steadily. He sighed inwardly and rolled those mental dice.

"It was more like panicky, stupid fire, but yes. It happened right in front of me."

He told the story again, and when he was done Teague was no longer laughing, and Rafe wore an expression that brought the word *lethal* to mind once again.

"Look," he said, "I'm not surprised no one believed me, now that I know how powerful they are, so I don't expect him to ever pay for what he did."

"What did Lyden do, when it happened?" Quinn asked.

Jordan grimaced. "You mean after his molasses brain figured out that he'd shot Eddie? First thing he did was turn that gun on me, and tell me I'd better never tell anyone what had really happened. I half expected him to shoot me, too, as the only witness. I told him to eff off, because I was trying to save Eddie's life."

He heard Emily make a tiny sound.

"But he didn't," Teague said, his tone grim.

"If I had to guess from what I know of Lyden Senior," Quinn said, "I'd say he's been trained to do nothing and phone home so daddy can handle it."

"That figures," Rafe muttered.

"And by the time he was able to do that," Quinn mused aloud, "you were already gone. Lucky timing."

After a moment Teague asked, "Why did you come here? Rather than stay home in Missouri?"

He hesitated, then went with one of the true answers. "It…took me a while to decide. I kind of wandered for a couple of months. But I knew Eddie had been buried here. I wanted to visit his grave." The other true answer was sitting beside him on the couch. And then she reached out and put her hand over his, and the rest came pouring out. "And I wanted to meet his sister, to tell her how sorry I was. Am. And…tell her the truth about what happened, in person. I only wrote that letter in case…"

Her fingers tightened over his. He didn't dare look at her, but squeezed her hand back.

"In case they killed you before you could." Quinn's voice was cool, but underneath it Jordan thought he heard a steely sort of anger.

"Yeah," he admitted. "I know it sounds crazy, but…"

Teague and Rafe looked at Quinn, each giving a barely perceptible nod. Quinn returned the gesture, then looked at Jordan and said flatly, "Adjust your expectations. He will pay. One way or another. Foxworth will see to that."

He couldn't quite believe it. Could even an operation like this one take on a family so powerful they had governors on speed dial?

"I heard yesterday that it's already started," Jordan said, remembering what Sarge had mentioned, in a tone of utter disgust. "That he's going to run for the Senate next year. That he'll be running for president within a decade."

Quinn nodded. "Playing largely off his 'heroic military service.' Which we now know is a lie. We'll look into that. And I'd hold off on that visit to the grave. They'd probably be expecting that."

He heard Emily gasp. "You really think they'd come after him…at Eddie's grave?"

"I know their type," Quinn said flatly. "And I don't put anything past them." He shifted his gaze back to Jordan. "We're not doing this just for you, or you, Emily, but for Eddie and anyone else who has been, or might be in the future, sacrificed on that altar of Lyden power."

Jordan held the man's gaze and found himself unable to doubt he meant every word of what he'd said. What he couldn't be sure of was whether they could truly pull this off.

But if they'd helped bring down a murderous sitting governor, as Emily had said…

Quinn began assigning tasks to the two other men. As if Jordan had already agreed to go along with this. But then, maybe they didn't want or need his help. They had his story, maybe that was all they'd wanted. Maybe he should get the hell out of there right now, while he could. He could walk back to the camp. It would take him a while but he could do it. He could—

Jordan felt a nudge and looked down into a pair of intense canine eyes. Once he had his attention, the dog rested his chin on Jordan's knee, bringing on the automatic move to pet the silky fur. And there it was again, that feeling of calm, of reassurance, as if the animal was telling him everything would be all right. And he began to understand the theory behind therapy dogs; if they all had this effect, there must be something to it.

"He makes you feel better, doesn't he?" Emily said softly. He could only nod. "Have you ever had a dog?"

"No. My grandmother was allergic, and after she died…it wasn't possible."

He wasn't about to explain his sorry childhood to her, especially not here in front of this group. It didn't matter anyway, not anymore. Not to him at least. Eddie had found that hard to believe, that he really didn't care about his biological parents, even after he'd told him—

His gaze shot to Emily's face. And somehow he knew. Knew that she knew. Something in her steady, warm gaze told him that Eddie had shared with her what he'd shared with him about his life. He'd suspected it at the time but had never worried much about it since he wasn't likely to ever meet her. Of course, the first time he'd glimpsed her on one of those calls, those bright blue eyes, her smooth sweep of blond hair half falling over her face as she laughed uproariously at something her brother had said, he'd thought he'd like to change that likelihood.

And now here he was, beside her, and it felt so wrong because Eddie wasn't here with the sister he'd loved.

*She saved me, man. When our mom died I was a wreck. She's only three years older, but that was twelve to my nine, and she stepped up.*

"Maybe you should get a dog now," Emily said. "They're a lot of company." She let out a tiny laugh as Cutter leaned over Jordan's knees and nudged her hand. "Maybe I should take my own advice."

"Eddie said he always took your advice seriously."

He almost regretted saying it when he saw that sheen in her eyes again, but changed his mind when she whispered, "Thank you. For telling me these things he said."

"He loved you, Emmie. And more than that he admired and respected you. Don't ever forget that."

"I won't," she promised. "And if I ever do, well, you'll have to remind me."

He smiled, but it was a lopsided one. Because that would require he be around to do so. Be in her life, to some extent.

And he didn't think that was going to happen.

# Chapter 8

Emily knew Jordan wasn't happy about this. But he was the only one who could do it. Foxworth could help, and it seemed they were going to, and she would do what she could wielding the Bishop Tool name, but without him it couldn't possibly happen. Yet it would make him the front man, as it were, the leader of the mission, the one who would take all the incoming fire from the Lydens.

She wondered when she'd started thinking in military metaphors.

She didn't know what to say to him. They were alone in the downstairs of the Foxworth headquarters—except for the dog, who seemed to have attached himself to Jordan. Maybe the obviously clever animal had sensed Jordan's uncertainty about all this and was trying to sooth his worry. Or convince him it would be okay, that it would work. To trust his people.

She nearly rolled her eyes at herself. He might be

clever, well trained, and empathetic, but Cutter was still a dog. She let out a compressed breath at her own silliness.

And tried to think of the right words to say to Jordan.

Quinn and his crew had gone to work upstairs. He'd told them Foxworth believed in doing all the in-depth research they could do before they tackled something, because they never knew what tiny bit of information might eventually be the key to solving everything. And, he'd added, they'd be doing it without their resident tech expert, Liam Burnett, who had just gotten married last week and was off on his honeymoon.

"We're falling like flies," Teague had joked happily to Quinn. "First you, then me, then Brett Dunbar, then Hayley's brother, then Liam, and now Gavin's engaged."

"Gavin?" Emily hadn't heard that name yet.

"He's our consulting attorney," Quinn had answered.

"Gavin de Marco," Teague supplied with a grin.

Both she and Jordan had gaped at him. She doubted there were many in the country and a lot of the world who hadn't heard of the once notorious big-case defense attorney who had walked away from a career envied by millions. She'd never heard where he'd ended up, but helping Foxworth do what Foxworth did was certainly a switch.

"And that's not to mention that darn near every other case ends up with some new couple together," Teague added.

Emily remembered staring at them, brows arched upward.

"Don't blame me," Quinn had said, his mouth quirking. "It's his fault."

When she'd realized he was nodding at Cutter, who tilted his head comically as if he knew he was being talked about, she was puzzled.

"Our resident matchmaker," Teague joked. At least, she thought he was joking. But something in the way the man's gaze had flicked speculatively from her to Jordan and back made her wonder.

But then they set off to do what they do, and she was left alone with Jordan. Who was now pacing the spacious room, with Cutter watching his every step as if the dog were ready to jump if he needed help. Not likely, since he was moving in a big circle around the room. He moved slowly, as if he were just curious, instead of back and forth in a straight line, as her father sometimes did when he was worried about something or trying to solve some problem.

Her father.

She sucked in a deep breath, trying to quash the nervous tension that wanted to build. She'd made the decision, but still had doubts. She knew perfectly well what Dad would consider most important, but he couldn't do anything from where he was, and he'd worked toward this deal for nearly a year, so—

"Emmie?" She gave a little start. Jordan had stopped right in front of her, and now crouched down so he could look her in the eye. "You look like you just... I don't know what."

"My father."

He blinked. "What?"

"Dad. I haven't...told him."

He pulled back slightly. "About your brother's crazy friend and his crazier theory?"

Her gaze locked on his face. "Stop it. You're not crazy, and it's not a theory."

"But you haven't told your father. Eddie's father."

"Because he's out of town on business and won't be

back for two weeks." If she sounded a little snappish, she didn't care, because it was clear he thought she hadn't told Dad because she doubted his story. "Not because I don't believe you." Her mouth twisted downward at one corner. "I wish you'd stop doubting me. But most of all stop doubting yourself."

"Easy to say, hard to do."

Her breath caught at the old, familiar words. And this time when her eyes began to sting she couldn't stop it. The tears came too fast and too abundantly, and she felt them tracking down her cheeks.

Jordan's hands shot out and grabbed hers. "Damn, Emmie, I'm sorry, I should have thought, never should have said that."

"No. Don't… It's just that…you said it exactly like Eddie used to."

"That's where I picked it up."

She blinked fast, clearing her vision enough to look at him. "And that's why it hit me like that. Because in a way, it came directly from my brother."

"And it hurt you."

"But it was good, too," she insisted, turning her hands to grab his now. "Good to know he was important to someone else, too. That someone else misses him."

"I do, Emmie. I know we weren't like childhood friends or anything but… I miss that danged son of a gun every day."

"Sometimes it isn't length of time. Not when two people click like you and Eddie did. I sensed that when he first told me about you. He said he'd found his brother from another mother."

Jordan's worried expression cleared a little at that. "He

told me that, too. And that…since I'd never known my father, I might as well borrow his."

Her throat was so tight she could barely get words out. "That so sounds like him."

"He said your dad had plenty of heart to spare."

The tears welled up again. "He does. And he will, when he meets you."

His expression changed again. She wondered if it was at the idea that he would even still be around when her father returned. Which made her wonder if he was already thinking about bolting, regardless of Foxworth's offer to help. Which made her think about what life would be like, knowing what had really happened to her brother but unable to do anything about it.

"Emily," he began, but stopped when she shook her head. She couldn't let that happen.

She wouldn't.

"Don't mind me. I'm just building worry castles, as Eddie used to say."

He went still. "He…had a way with a phrase."

"He did."

She could see his discomfort, his worry at causing her pain. Maybe soon she'd get a chance to really convince him she meant what she'd said before, that it felt good to know Eddie had been so important to someone else, too. Because she wanted to hear more, more about the Eddie she hadn't really known, the Eddie he'd been around his buddies, especially his Army buddies.

But for now she went with something else as distraction.

"Teague seems like a nice guy. Even if he is a little silly about him," she said, nodding toward Cutter, who was watching them both intently.

"I think everybody here is a bit silly about him," Jordan said, but he was smiling.

"That Rafe, though," she said hesitantly.

"Yeah. He's a different kind of scary." Jordan's brow furrowed. "I swear, I've heard that name before. Can't remember where, though."

"Maybe he's famous, somewhere. I mean if they've got Gavin de Marco working with them…"

"Good point," he said and smiled. That he'd managed that made her smile in turn.

He started to straighten up, and she was just thinking about how long he'd spent crouched before her, trying to comfort her, when he seemed to wobble a little. She thought it was his legs protesting, but then realized Cutter was right there and had apparently run into him. He reached for the back of the couch she sat on, but Cutter, clearly intent on getting by, nudged him again and he ended up sitting abruptly beside her.

Very close beside her.

"Sorry," he said hastily.

"It's all right. He just got in the way. He seems to do that. Or maybe he thought you needed to give your legs a break."

"As long as he didn't break one of them," Jordan said dryly.

She laughed, all the time hoping he wouldn't get up and move farther away. Because she quite liked him being close enough that she could feel his heat. It felt good, comforting and yet…tempting.

Which was a thought she hadn't had about a man in a very, very long time.

# Chapter 9

He should never have agreed to this.

Jordan knew that, now. But who'd have thought a simple ride home, such as his home was at this point, would turn into something so…unsettling?

It had seemed only logical at the time. After the Foxworth crew had come back downstairs with their initial report—which consisted mostly of discovering just how far, wide and deep the twisted Lyden roots went—Quinn said this was going to take a little more time. So when Emily said she could drop him off at the camp since it was practically on her way home, he'd accepted to save them the trip back out there.

She'd driven as he'd expected—carefully, aware, but not single-mindedly. And smooth. No herky-jerky stop-and-go with her. Which made him think of Lyden, and what a lousy driver he'd been. Now that he knew the truth about him, Jordan realized he was probably more used to being driven than driving himself.

He felt the usual jab of pain as the fact of Eddie's death surfaced yet again. They'd told him it would get better with time, but he wasn't sure he believed it. And he could only imagine how much worse it must be for Emily.

Emily, who was sitting just inches away. Which brought him back to the here and now.

The problem was that he'd expected her to just drop him off at the gate and then leave. But it was clear the moment they arrived that she'd had no intention of keeping it that simple. No, she'd driven right in, and he'd had no choice but to direct her to his spot. And then she'd gotten out of the vehicle, clearly intending to look around.

He scrambled out of the passenger side. At least the van was fairly tidy. No dirty dishes in the small sink, or clothes strewn—

"Damn," he muttered under his breath.

"Problem?" she asked, her voice determinedly light.

"I had laundry in the washer when we left."

"Well, let's go get it."

She said it so energetically there was no denying her. When they reached the small laundry facility that Sarge—well, more likely Sarge's wife, the ever-efficient Lydia, known always as Mrs. Sarge—had had installed, he stood wondering where his wet clothes had ended up, because someone else's were in the washer. Nor were they in the basket left there for just that purpose.

"Very organized," Emily said, looking at the schedule posted on the wall. Every space had its corresponding laundry time, with weekends being a free-for-all.

"That's Sarge," he muttered, looking around.

"Maybe whoever needed the washer put them in the dryer," she suggested.

He should have thought of that. Would have, if he wasn't feeling so unsettled. Just because Emily was here? Or because doing this, dealing with laundry of all things, seemed too damned domestic?

*Or because doing domestic things with Emily felt too damned good?*

His clothes were in fact in the dryer, and dry but still warm. He pulled them out in a tangled armful and turned to head back to the camper.

"Shouldn't we fold them here, on the table? They'll be even more wrinkled if you just wad them up like that."

*We* again. Domestic again. That good feeling again.

A feeling he had no right to be feeling. Not with Eddie's sister. Dead Eddie's sister.

"They'll be easier to carry, too," she went on. "I'll help."

Desperation shot through him. "If you're so eager to get your hands into my underwear, you should have said so." She looked at him in a way that made him wish he could pull the smart-ass remark back. "I didn't mean—"

She cut him off in an even tone that had no inflection for him to interpret—or misinterpret. "When I am, I will."

It took him a moment, by which time she had turned away and grabbed a T-shirt to fold. *When?* Had she really said *when?* Not *if*, not *no chance, jerk*, but…*when?* Did she mean she'd say so, or that she just would?

That led him down a mental path that had his jaw clenching against a wave of heat that he couldn't blame on the dryer in here or the summer outside. He grabbed up the pair of jeans and folded them, sloppily. Emily said nothing, just folded another shirt. When he hastily grabbed up the discussed underwear—the only thing he had more than three of—she gave him a sideways look that had him holding his breath, sure she was going to zing him. And rightfully so.

But she only said, "Do you always wash things all together, dark and light?"

He was so relieved she hadn't gone for the throat, as she could have, that he admitted, "Don't have enough to make it worth two loads." He tried for a smile and made it about halfway, which echoed his half shrug. "Besides, kind of fits life these days. Dark and light mixed up together."

"Hmm." Her smile was better than his, but still not the bright thing he'd seen before. "Yes, that fits."

"Jeans are faded enough it's not a problem anyway." Probably the most inane thing he'd ever said. But safe.

She only nodded. He grabbed up the almost pitifully small pile of clothes that truly were almost every item he owned, and they headed back toward the camper. He thought about apologizing for his crude, snap remark, but decided against bringing it up again. Besides, he didn't trust himself not to ask exactly what she'd meant with that "When I am…"

Emily was still chastising herself as they walked back to his campsite. He'd been embarrassed at the thought of her pawing through his underwear, and she guessed that was why he'd said something he was probably sure would back her off.

*And what did you do instead? Immediately start imagining the very thing he'd said…*

That—imagining hot, sexy things—was not something she did. Not now, still deep in grief. In fact, not ever. And especially not with a man who was practically a stranger.

But was he? Didn't she know him, or at least know the Jordan her brother had known? All the emails and calls… Had one ever gone by without a mention of his best friend?

*He's smart, sis. He could be running this operation.*

*He fixed it, Emmie! That part I broke, he rigged a replacement, so I'm not in a jam. Boy, do I owe him.*

*He's a hell of an athlete, which isn't fair because he's got that engineer mind, too. I swear he could build anything out of anything.*

*He's been alone a long time, but he doesn't whine about it like the other guys do.*

*We lost Mom, but he never had his, or his father.*

She stifled a sigh, telling herself she should be glad he seemed willing to just let it slide.

She looked around at the various campsites as they went. The one thing she was aware of overall was how neat and tidy everything was. Not just the campsites but the entire grounds were spotless, trash-free, trimmed and, as her father was wont to say, shipshape. It fit right in this tidy little neighborhood.

She'd noticed tents in a couple of spots, and wondered if they were only here for the summer; it could get pretty cold here in the winter, especially at night. There were several pickup trucks with varying sorts of campers, from small shells to those with cab-over sleeping spaces. There was one bigger RV that looked older, although well-kept. The remainder were vans, like any other van she saw on the road, just being lived in.

Jordan's, parked at his site that was a bit away from the rest, was the only one she saw of its size and shape, a little longer and taller than the others. It had a canopy that unreeled from the top corner of the van and was held up by poles at each corner. There was a canvas chair beside the firepit, which showed fresh ash beneath the grill over the top.

His van was clearly dedicated to the purpose it was serving. And nicely, from what she could see through the open door. Two large seats in front, where the driver and a passenger would sit while on the road. She imagined they probably swiveled around, although he hadn't done that. She could see a small table that appeared to fold away when not in use, in front of an upholstered bench seat that could hold two if they were friendly.

She had to grab control of her thoughts before they veered off again. "This looks nice," she said. "Could I see the inside?"

He shrugged. "It's nothing much, but go ahead."

There was a drop-down step in front of the main door, making it easy to get into the main cabin of the vehicle. And when she did, her eyes widened. Along the side of the van opposite the table and seat was a counter, with a compact two-burner cooktop near the door, a small sink at the other end and a tall cabinet beyond that looked like more storage. Above the counter were more cabinets, and below a small refrigerator. A compact microwave completed the kitchen setup.

On the wall behind and above the bench seat was a panel that looked to her as complex as an airplane's controls. She saw various switches, dials and control panels and screens; she'd never realized there would be so many systems involved.

Behind that wall was a bathroom that looked as if it were all one piece, toilet and shower. It was directly opposite the outer sink, which must serve both. The bath, she noticed, was spotless and practically sparkled white.

And beyond that was a tidily made-up bed so large

it startled her. Turned sideways across the width of the van, it had to be at least four feet by over six feet long. Of course, he'd need that six plus feet, at his height.

And there were two pillows.

Unbidden her mind jumped to provide images of him sprawled in that bed. Her gaze snagged on that second pillow and her mind willingly supplied an image for that, too. Her, waking sleepily, happily, to look at him. She had to rein it in again.

She tried to focus on practicalities. There were drawers under the bed, enough to hold the limited wardrobe he'd mentioned, she guessed. And—

"Told you it wasn't much," he said from behind her. "I did it myself, so there's none of the fancy finishes or luxury materials."

She turned to stare at him. "You did this? All this?"

He shrugged. "Guy in my unit had bought the van empty to do something like this, and then ended up having twins so sold it to somebody who'd have time. I worked on it every time I was home on leave. Finished last fall."

She looked around again. That he had taken an empty shell and turned it into this was, to her, nothing short of amazing. "It's incredible, Jordan. It has everything you need, in such a small space, yet it doesn't feel cramped."

He smiled then, a true smile, although he looked a little embarrassed. "It works" was all he said.

*He can build anything, Emmie. It's incredible just to watch him look at something, with that expression that means he's figuring it all out, down to the last detail.*

"My plan was to travel, after I got out. Go anyplace I wanted, until I found a place I didn't want to leave."

She drew in a deep breath, and was unable to keep the longing out of her voice. "What a wonderful idea. That was my dream, as a kid. But I've never traveled much, and only flown here or there, so never had the chance to really see and get to know other places."

"You'd probably feel pretty cramped in one of these."

"How could you?" she asked. "When you can sit outside and look at open spaces like here, or maybe the mountains somewhere else, or a lake, or even the ocean? And everything you could ever need—" she waved her hand at the van's highly functional interior "—just goes with you."

He was staring at her now. "Eddie never said you wanted to travel."

She sighed, lowered her gaze. "He never knew. I never wanted him to think he was the reason I gave up that dream."

"To take care of him."

"It was the right choice," she said firmly. "And I'm not sorry."

"You shouldn't be. Look how Eddie turned out. A great guy."

*Just what he always said about you.*

But she didn't say it out loud. She was too busy fighting down her imagination, which had taken off on one of those trips she'd just mentioned…in this van, with Jordan at the wheel.

Grabbing for distraction, she gestured at the control panel. "What's all that?"

"It's for all the non-driving systems." He pointed at one of the small screens. "That shows the battery power left, that one shows the water level in the storage tank, that control raises and lowers the bed so I can get to the storage underneath from in here instead of outside." One corner of his mouth twisted. "Comes in handy in a snowstorm when I need something out of there."

"When were you in a snowstorm?"

"First night I left. Stopped in Rapid City, South Dakota after about fourteen hours of driving, and woke up to about six inches of it. I'd expected it, though, so I put chains on the night before so I could roll right out in the morning."

*He always plans ahead, like no one I've ever seen, except maybe Dad.*

"Planning ahead," she murmured.

He shrugged. "My mind's usually full of maybes and what-ifs and how to deal with them. Can't seem to stop it."

"Doesn't seem like something you should stop," she said. "Too many people never think that way."

Another shrug, but then he pointed at another switch on the panel, this one a bright red. "Eddie named that one."

She blinked. "He did?"

"We were talking about it, when it was the next project on my next leave. It's the switch I get to flip when hooked up to shore power, like now. All the batteries get to recharge and rest, and I can use things like the microwave. So he called it the happy switch."

She found herself smiling. "That sounds like him."

He nodded. She saw him swallow, then, as if it were an effort, he met her gaze. "I miss him. A lot."

Emotion rocketed through her, that fierce pounding of pain, sadness and emptiness that was grief, all tangled up with gladness she'd had her brother in her life at all and…that someone else also mourned him.

She couldn't think of any words and doubted she could have spoken them anyway. She knew she was on the verge of yet more tears. So she did the only thing she could think of.

She threw her arms around him in a fierce hug.

# *Chapter 10*

Just as he had the first time she'd done it, Jordan felt as if he'd been hit by a small, heat-seeking missile. Only this time, besides being rocked back on his heels, he found himself wanting more, so much more.

It was a moment before he dared lift his arms to encircle her. A moment he used to sternly remind himself she was grieving and this was comfort to someone in horrible pain. He knew the pain himself, because he hadn't lied. He missed Eddie, a lot. They'd joked about that brother from another mother thing, but it truly had felt that way. Not that he'd know anything about how having a brother felt, but if he'd tried to imagine it, it would have been exactly how he felt when the two of them got up to something, or had one of those long discussions over a beer about...almost anything. And the pain of losing that connection he'd never had in his life before was real and sharp and painful.

But on top of that, he'd spent many a night haunted by the memory that seemed to play in an endless loop, of those last seconds, the image of Eddie's life fading out of his eyes, eyes so like his sister's. It was a memory he knew would never completely go away. It was a memory only he would carry. One that Emily would never know.

But he realized now, with her pressed against him, that he would gladly carry it rather than wish it onto her.

When she finally started to pull back, it was an effort—in fact it required a firm command to himself— to let her go.

*I know this hug is for Eddie's friend, who misses him, too. I know it doesn't mean anything more than that.*

Too bad he couldn't seem to stop himself from wishing it meant more.

She seemed a little embarrassed, which only pounded home that he was right. Maybe she was even worried he'd misinterpret it. Hell, any guy who held her, who felt the silk of that blond hair against his skin, who saw those wide blue eyes looking up at him, would surely want to believe there was more to that hug than a sharing of grief. But right now it seemed wrong to even think that. She was Eddie's sister, and he shouldn't be thinking that way about her anyway, let alone now, with Eddie's death just months ago.

He leaned back against the counter and tried for a casual tone. "So, you said this was on your way home?"

*Well, that was brilliant, Crockett.*

But she seemed relieved that he'd brought up something so mundane. Just as he had been when she'd let his smart-ass remark about his underwear pass. Not that it had helped him shove the thought out of his head, because the vision of her touching him in the way that would require, maybe peeling those knit boxers off of him—

*Stop it!*

"Yes," she answered, thankfully unaware of the chaos in his head. "I have a little place closer to the cove. I bought it with the money from my mother's insurance that was in trust until I was twenty-one."

He thought of what she'd said, about having always wanted to travel. Wondered why she hadn't done that instead, once Eddie was out and on his own. Hoped it wasn't because of more sadness. Their father, maybe?

"What about your dad? Is he still in the area?" he asked carefully.

"Of course. Running the business," she said.

"Bishop Tool."

She nodded. "I work there, too. He's still in the house we grew up in." Her expression shifted, that look of sorrow taking over again. "I think he kept it so Eddie would have a place to come home to when he got out, until he got settled in his own place."

He should have known. "He used to talk about that, too. About coming home and working the family business."

She'd been looking at the control board again, but at his words she turned. "Did he? I wasn't sure he really would. He was always kind of iffy about it."

"Because he wasn't sure he could measure up. He said your father set the bar pretty high for business savvy."

She smiled briefly at that. "He did. And does. But he also knows...knew his son." The sadness flashed again, but she kept on. "And he would never force him. He had a spot in mind for him, if he was willing."

"And Eddie said he was going to try."

This time the smile lasted longer. "He said that?"

Jordan nodded. "Last time we talked about it."

"May I tell Dad? That would make him feel better, I think."

"Of course," he said. Then, again trying for a neutral tone, he asked, "Are you going to tell him? What really happened?"

Her answer came quickly enough that he knew she'd thought about it. "I think that depends on where things stand when he gets home. If Foxworth thinks there's hope for justice, then…yes. If not, I think it would only hurt him more."

"Like it did you?"

He couldn't stop the regret that echoed in his voice then. But Emily met his gaze, her chin up. "It did," she admitted. "But it also gave me something to fight. Some way to channel all the awfulness."

He studied her for a moment. "And even if Foxworth says it's hopeless, you'll keep fighting, won't you?"

"Yes."

"Eddie always said if you believed in something strongly enough, you never gave up."

Her smile then was a wistful thing, which no doubt echoed what she was feeling inside. He was usually much better at figuring out machines and mechanical problems than people, but he somehow felt as if he knew her. Probably from all of Eddie's talking about her.

The smile changed to something stronger, and she gave an odd little nod of her head, as if she'd decided something.

"I was going to cash in my frequent buyer points at the pizza place in town. Feel hungry for some really good cheese and sausage pizza?"

As if on cue, his stomach growled. Loudly.

Emily laughed. "I'm going to take that as a yes. Let's go. If we get the biggest one, I'll even split the leftovers with you."

"Assuming there are any," he muttered as his suddenly awakened stomach growled again.

"There is that," she said cheerfully.

The growling of his stomach got louder the moment they walked into the small pizza place and the luscious aromas hit. The place was Saturday-night busy, the picnic-style tables crowded. He grabbed a just vacated small table in the corner while she made the order.

He said no to her offer of a beer and went for a soda instead. There was going to be a wait for their pizza, and she sipped at her own soda as he looked around at the room, which had a couple of old-style arcade games in the back corner, where several kids were playing and laughing.

"Is that—" she nodded toward his glass "—because you don't, or because you're not in the mood?"

His head snapped back around. "Asking if I'm a drunk?"

She drew back, startled. "Funny, I didn't hear even a suggestion of that in what I asked. I just thought since you weren't driving and with everything that's happened, you might want something stronger."

"Would you?"

"If I wasn't driving? Maybe. They have a great local brew here."

"Oh." He looked a little abashed. Then, with that very male shrug he said, "Wine sometimes. The occasional beer. My bio mom was an alcoholic, so I keep it to a minimum."

She tilted her head slightly. "Is that how you think of her?"

"How else should I?" That quickly the edge was back. He was obviously touchy on the subject of his mother. But then he let out a breath. "Look, she didn't want me, so why should I obsess about her? I know she was a drunk and later a drug addict, so I steer clear of both. Beyond that, don't know, don't care."

Their pizza was ready before she could think of a response to that. And she found she, too, was hungry enough that she couldn't wait to dig in. He ate faster, and she was glad she'd suggested this.

She waited until he had two slices down before she asked, as casually as she could manage, "What was your grandmother like?"

He stopped mid-bite. "What?"

"Eddie told me she pretty much raised you."

He didn't answer for a moment. She was afraid he wouldn't at all. He set the pizza slice down, stared at it for a moment, then looked up at her.

"Yeah, she did. She was tough, rules-wise, but…she was a pistol."

"Sounds like you mean that in a good way."

"I do." He was smiling, and for the first time since she'd met him she could tell the memories in his mind now were better ones. "She was funny as hell, had a way with a wisecrack, and anybody who took her on thinking she was just some slow-witted old lady learned different in a hurry."

"Including you?"

The smile became a grin. A flashing, genuine, devastating grin. "Especially me. I was such a jerk in the beginning, but she never wavered. 'I love you, Jordan, and I always will, but right now I don't like you very much' was something I heard often."

"That was good of her, to phrase it that way."

He nodded. "She knew I felt…dumped by my mother. So she always made it clear that even if I was in trouble, she still would love me. I didn't believe her at first, and later I thought it was corny. It wasn't until I was in my twenties that I realized how special it was. How special she was."

"Whose mother was she?"

"That's the most special part. She was my mother's stepmom. So we weren't actually blood at all, and my grandfather had died years ago, but when I got dumped on her doorstep she was there for me every step of the way. She was more alive than most people half her age. She taught me to sail, first on the little lake near where we lived, then we'd trek off to other places, rent a boat for the day and take off."

"She sounds amazing."

"She was." His mouth twisted slightly. "She wouldn't even talk about my bio parents. Said they didn't deserve the time or effort, not if they were stupid enough to…"

His voice trailed off as if he were embarrassed. "To what?"

He stared down at a half-eaten slice. It was a moment before he finished it, but there was a trace of a smile when he did. "Throw away a great kid like me."

"Oh, now I know I would have loved her."

He looked up then, and said, his voice steady now, "I sure did. She died three years ago and I still miss her."

She studied him for a moment before saying quietly, "I'm a little surprised you answered me."

"She deserves it," he said simply.

And that, she thought, told her what she most needed to know about Jordan Crockett.

# Chapter 11

Jordan had thought he'd be glad when Emily left. He had
a lot to think about, most importantly if he was going to
be an active part of this Foxworth effort to bring justice
to the man who was responsible for Eddie's death. Because he had no doubt they were going to try, for Emily
if nothing else. Something about Quinn Foxworth's steely
resolve told him they wouldn't give up any more than
she would. But he just wasn't sure he wanted to be in the
middle of it. Wanted to draw any more Lyden attention
than he already had.

After their pizza dinner she'd driven him back to the
camp again, and again he'd thought she would just drop
him off. But it didn't quite work out that way. After the
marine push from the Pacific had nudged out the August
heat and brought in some evening chill, he'd built a fire
in the pit. Then she'd commented on how nice it was to
be able to smell the chill in the air but still be warm, and

crazily he'd asked if she wanted to stay and sit by the
fire for a while. And more crazily, he'd been happy when
she'd said yes, even though he was wary of the way he
seemed to vomit out answers to any question she asked.
That was not his usual way with people he'd only just
met, but then this was Eddie's sister, and he'd known
about her for years. Felt as if he'd known her personally.

He'd had to borrow a second chair from Marcus, who
had waggled his shaggy brows at him when he saw her
but loaned the chair immediately. And somewhat to his
relief, she seemed content to just sit and enjoy the fire;
he'd been afraid she'd launch into more questions.

Sarge, making his nightly camp checks, paused beside
the fire. "Got that extinguisher handy, son?"

"Right there," Jordan answered, gesturing toward the
open storage compartment on the van where he kept the
fire extinguisher along with the chair Emily was sitting
in and the ice chest that was serving as a table at the moment.

Sarge nodded in approval. "You clear tomorrow?"

"Yeah. What's up?"

"Tree went down at Mr. Lancaster's, blocking his driveway. Can you and Marcus handle it?"

"Sure. When?"

"Ten or so. It's going to take a chain saw, so don't want
to make too much noise too early on a Sunday morning."

Jordan nodded. "Okay."

"Good." Sarge smiled at her then. "Have to keep the
neighborhood shipshape."

After he'd gone Emily asked, "Who's Mr. Lancaster?
A friend?"

"A neighbor. Well, and a friend, too. He's a vet himself,
and stood up for Sarge when he was trying to get this place

going and some of the other neighbors were wary. So now, if we can help him out, we do."

She looked thoughtful for a moment before saying, "When I first came here I noticed how tidy everything was, how all the campsites were neat and the whole place felt ordered, cared for. And I thought how well it fit into this neighborhood that looks the same way."

He didn't say anything, because he suspected he didn't have to. And he didn't; she had gotten there on her own.

"It's you, isn't it?" she asked. "You guys see to it that it all stays that way. Not just here, but the neighborhood."

"Sarge calls it part of the rent. Since he charges us the absolute minimum, nobody complains about helping keep the whole area shipshape. And the neighbors appreciate it, and so no more complaints about us being here. Except when some overambitious politician got their head too far up into a dark place and tried to interfere."

"Up into a dark place?" She laughed at the metaphor.

He smiled at her. "That was from my grandmother."

"I think I would have liked her."

"And she you," he said, certain of it as he was certain of little these days. Memories welled up, trying to hammer their way in, and he fought to keep the door closed. Grabbed at the first thought that floated free. "Anyway, I didn't know this until now, but that's why Sarge knew of Foxworth. They helped out when that happened."

"Good for them."

He blinked in sudden realization. "Maybe that politician just didn't want to go up against their lawyer. Especially when their lawyer is Gavin de Marco. I didn't know that before, but it makes sense now she'd run like hell, just hearing the name."

"Especially after what happened to the governor."

"From what Sarge said she's about the same ilk, minus the murder. I think," he amended wryly.

She laughed at that, although she said in almost the same tone he'd used, "I wish that were funnier."

"Me, too."

Silence descended for a while, and to his surprise it wasn't in the least uncomfortable. Maybe because she seemed totally relaxed, leaning back in the chair with her toes outstretched toward the fire.

"This is lovely," she murmured. "I can just imagine doing this in all sorts of beautiful places. Having familiar things around you but in unfamiliar, wondrous places…"

She sighed as if that idea was the most wonderful thing she'd ever contemplated. And he suddenly wanted more than anything to pull up stakes and do just that, take off for those wondrous places…if she'd come with him. The possibilities rolled out in his mind like a video—the coast here, the mountains there, maybe a few national parks, and then some off the beaten path places. And he came darn close to suggesting it, and only imagining what her expression would be if he asked her to take off with him stopped him.

Well, that and the voice in the back of his head saying, *Running again, Crockett?*

At least he wasn't dreaming about running alone this time. But that just made it a more impossible dream. And sillier. She had a life here, her father, a job with the family business and no doubt friends who would talk her out of anything so insane as to take off on the road with some itinerant vet she barely knew, no matter that he'd been Eddie's friend.

And they'd be right.

\* \* \*

When she had to smother a yawn a second time, Emily knew it was time for her to leave. She'd probably long overstayed her welcome anyway, but Jordan was too polite to kick her out.

She got to her feet, looking down at the firepit. "I should bring you some firewood I have. I'm sure you wouldn't have used up this much on your own."

"It's okay. We have a lot here, from downed trees we've helped move."

"Like the one tomorrow morning?"

He nodded. "Since we don't take payment, most people at least offer us some of the wood. We've got stacks from the last three years curing up behind Sarge's house."

"In that case," she said, looking at the grill atop the last embers of the fire she'd so enjoyed, "why don't I bring steaks tomorrow evening? Least I can do after this lovely evening by the fire. And you'll probably be tired after a day of playing logger."

He was looking at her, brow furrowed. "You don't need to do that."

"But I want to. It's really nice out here." She lowered her gaze as the obvious belatedly hit her. "Of course, if you'd rather be alone, I understand."

"No!" It came out sharply enough she felt a little less embarrassed. "I just meant, you bought the pizza."

"It was a freebie," she pointed out.

"On your frequent buyer card."

"Still, I didn't pay for it." She tried for the best smile she could manage, given she was doing something she'd never done in her life—essentially inviting herself to a guy's house for dinner. "So if I bring the steaks, you're responsible for veggies and drinks."

"I... Okay."

"And think about it, okay? Never mind me, think about what Eddie would want you to do."

"Emily—"

"I know what I'm asking. In essence I'm asking you to paint a target on your back for my brother's sake. But from what Sloan said, Foxworth is quite capable of keeping you safe. And now that I've met the rest of them, I believe it."

"I think I would have believed it even if it was just Quinn."

He said it with the slightest of laughs, and it gave her hope.

As she was driving home she could think of nothing else. Until she'd actually put it into words, she hadn't quite realized the truth of what she was asking him to do. That standing up to the Lydens truly could put a target on him. He'd survived years in the military, much of it in combat zones if not actual combat, yet this could be a bigger threat to him than anything he'd encountered there. After all, it hadn't been the enemy who had killed her brother.

It had been the man she was asking Jordan to stand and face.

# *Chapter 12*

As restless nights went, last night had been a prize winner.

Jordan figured he was lucky he hadn't cut a hand off working on that big tree this morning, his focus was so scattered. But the job was done, thanks to some experienced advice from Marcus, who apparently had done some tree work at some point. And in gratitude Mr. Lancaster had given them all the wood they could lug back to the camp, and cutting and stacking that had eaten up the rest of the morning and into the afternoon.

He'd grabbed a shower as soon as he could after they were done. They drew straws for the one in the outbuilding, and he came in second. The shower in his camper worked fine, especially hooked up to the camp's water system, but he wanted to save as much wear and tear on it as he could. And if that meant living in his seriously sweaty clothes for an hour or so, so be it.

Once he was clean, he put on the jeans he'd washed

yesterday and his least worn T-shirt. Which was about the best he could do when it came to dressing up for... whatever this was. Certainly not a date. Emily could do a lot better than him and she had to know that. So more like a sales meeting, probably.

He wanted to say yes. Wanted to tell her he'd fight to take down the man who'd killed her brother. The man who'd killed his best friend. What the hell kind of man wouldn't want to do that?

*A coward, that's who.*

Like the coward who, every time a combat platoon went out in a vehicle he'd kept running, felt relief that he was staying back in the relative safety of the forward base. The coward who, every time one of those vehicles came back with bullet holes or shrapnel damage in it, felt relief he hadn't been in it at the time. The coward who listened to the stories they told, the soldiers who had been in the middle of it, and marveled at their courage while acknowledging his own lack of it. The worst he'd ever had to do was retrieval runs, or a perimeter check when they were shorthanded, which never amounted to anything.

*Except for the time it did. The time Eddie died.*

He was pacing now. Nothing else to do. Mrs. Sarge had picked up some potato salad, asparagus and a six-pack of the soda he'd noticed Emily drinking on her grocery run, and had had the grace not to ask why he was suddenly interested in a balanced sort of menu.

When he realized the pacing was only winding him up more, he made himself sit down at the small table. And that made him suddenly realize that this was the only logical place here to eat a meal such as this one. It was hard to cut a steak with the plate in your lap. Which meant they'd be sitting here together. At least he could sit in the driver's seat, spun around to face the table. Otherwise they'd be jammed up together on that small bench seat, unable to move without touching. While that had a certain—okay, great—appeal to him, he was certain Emily would prefer the table between them.

When he caught himself trying to think of ways to make it necessary to sit together, he swore under his breath. Ordering himself to stop obsessing, he went to the drawer beneath the upholstered bench and pulled out the design he'd been working on. It was something he'd thought about often, when he'd been handling something so routine he could do it in his sleep. He'd always wondered how he could rig a satellite dish for internet on the camper and make it retractable, so he didn't have to climb up and take it down and stow it every time he moved from one place to another.

He'd worked out a way to automate it from a switch on the control panel, but given the necessary size of the dish he wasn't sure there was any place on the van, even on the roof, where it would fit. He could build something on top to house it, of course, but he didn't want the van any taller than it already was. But he couldn't drop it into the interior without having a spot he'd be banging his head on. The only option he could think of was dropping it into one of the cabinets, but that would eat up a huge chunk of his already limited kitchen storage.

As with many things he tackled, it was as much an exercise in figuring something out as reaching an actual, working plan. It was the way his mind worked, and most times he enjoyed it, did it for fun.

Today it was pure distraction.

But it worked, because when he heard a car approaching and looked up, an hour and a half had passed and it was nearly 6:00 p.m.

He could see from the table that it was Emily's car. She parked it neatly, away from the fire and out of the way of anyone else. For a moment he just sat there, watching as she got out. He thought he could watch her simply move for hours and never get bored. That was some excellent construction there, and the snug, tan jeans she wore emphasized it. The silky-looking blue blouse that skimmed her lovely upper curves didn't hurt any, either.

She had her not-small purse slung over her shoulder and was carrying a grocery bag in one hand and her phone in the other. Then she slid the phone into the back pocket of those jeans that hugged her sweet backside, and he found himself envying the stupid device.

She looked over then, and smiled when she saw him. That smile was like a gut punch, and he sucked in a breath. She started walking toward him, no doubt wondering what he was doing sitting there just staring at her. He got up, finally, went to the door and jumped to the ground, not wanting to look down—as in away from her—to be sure where the step was.

"They had some lovely steaks," she said as she came up to him.

"Nice," he said, without even looking in the bag.

"Hope you're starved. I got big ones."

*I'm starved, all right.* "Good."

"How'd the tree thing go?"

"Fine."

"No problems?"

"None."

She tilted her head, giving him a quizzical look. "I

won't ask for more than one-word answers, but maybe more than four letters?"

"Sorry," he muttered. "I was…distracted."

"Not surprising. You have a lot to think about."

And there it was, the big reason he had no business thinking about her in the way he had been. Because he had no doubt that if he decided he wanted nothing to do with this futile idea of taking down the likes of Hartwell Lyden, she'd never want to see him again.

And he couldn't blame her.

Emily looked at the papers spread out on the table. They looked as complex as anything she'd seen at work, and Bishop Tool had some sophisticated products, from power hand tools to complete automated systems.

"What's this going to be?"

"Nothing," he said. "Just something I was messing with. An idea that won't work."

"Why won't it work?" She listened as he explained the problem to her, then looked at the minimal clearance between his head and the roof of the van. "Ouch," she said. "Guess it doesn't always pay to be tall."

That got her a smile at least. So she was glad she hadn't said what she'd been thinking. Hunkily tall. Very male tall. Sexy tall.

She busied herself getting the steaks ready to grill with her favorite seasonings. As she did, she found herself wondering yet again why she was reacting to him this way. A way she hadn't reacted to any man in a long time. If she ever had at all.

It had to be his connection to Eddie. It must be all tied up with her love for her brother and her grief at losing him. Other than Dad, who was mourning as deeply as she was, there was no one else who'd been so connected to him other than Jordan. That's why she was so tangled up about him. It had to be, because she simply didn't normally react this way. And there was nothing normal in her life right now.

She looked again at the neat little holder he'd put the asparagus in to grill, a hinged grid that would keep it flat and organized, yet open to the flames below. "You design that?"

He gave her a startled look. "I…made it. It didn't really require a design."

*Sure. Just anybody could put that together without any real thought.* "You should market it."

He laughed. "I'm sure there are better things out there to do it. How do you like your steak?"

"Warm." This time he blinked. Then he grinned. "You and Eddie. He used to say he liked his beef still mooing."

She was caught between tears and a laugh. "Yes, he did. It always made me cringe a little."

And she knew now that she'd been right—it was this man's connection to her brother that had her so tangled up. It had to be. Because she was in no way ready for what she was feeling toward him, if it had been on its own.

# Chapter 13

It was like a rerun of last night. Jordan leaned back in the borrowed chair—he'd had to endure Marcus's teasing when he'd asked to hang on to it another evening—and soaked it in. The fire, the fresh air and the full stomach were lulling him, but Emily's presence prevented him from relaxing completely.

"Thanks," he said. "That was some really good meat."

"Wasn't it? And the asparagus came out perfectly, and that potato salad was great."

After that she didn't seem to feel the need to fill the silence with chatter, and he appreciated that. He especially appreciated that since her comment about him having a lot to think about, she hadn't said a word about the situation he knew she cared most about. She was giving him space to think about it, no doubt hoping he'd reach the decision she wanted.

The brave decision. The not-cowardly decision.

The right decision.

He heard the sound of a vehicle approaching, which surprised him since all the residents appeared to be here. But then he saw a dark-colored SUV approaching, one he thought he recognized.

"Is that the Foxworths?" Emily asked.

"I think so."

"I think I hear Cutter barking, even from here," she said with a smile.

All doubt was removed when, the vehicle still some distance away, the back hatch opened and an instant later a dog leaped out and headed for them at a run.

"Has he been here to your spot before?" she asked.

"No. But it's sure not stopping him, is it?" The dog arrived, eyes bright in the firelight, tail wagging happily. "Hey, Cutter," he said, not sure what it meant that the Foxworths were here.

Emily gave the dog a more effusive greeting, scratching him behind both ears and cooing at him. "Hello, you sweet boy. Have you come for a visit? How'd you find us here so fast? Are you just that clever?"

The yip the dog let out as she said that sounded for all the world more like "Yep!"

He was followed a minute later by both the Foxworths.

"Bit of an update," Quinn explained as they joined them.

"Plus," Hayley added cheerfully, declining Jordan's offer of his chair and taking a seat next to her husband on one of the stones beside the pit, "adding a bit more pressure, Jordan."

"I kind of guessed that," he said with a grimace. "Otherwise you could have just called."

Hayley laughed and nodded toward her dog. "You

haven't tried to say no to this guy. He's the one who decided we needed to come here."

Jordan blinked. "The dog decided?"

"He did," Quinn said. "He can make a heck of a racket until you figure out what he wants. And once you're in the car, heaven help your ears if you make a wrong turn."

Jordan stared at the couple who otherwise seemed completely sane. People and their dogs…

"So what's the update?" Emily asked.

"First, we've confirmed what you heard, that Lyden Junior will be running in the next senatorial election. An exploratory committee's been working for the past six months, and a PAC is already set up."

"Great," he muttered. "I gather there's a second?"

"Yes, and it's actually more important. We weren't the only ones interested in that storage place video."

He went very still. "Lyden?"

Quinn nodded. "His father. Our source said he's got a business connection to the current mayor of your town, and told him he was trying to find someone who served with his son. To thank him."

Jordan snorted. "I'll bet. I can guess what kind of thanks."

"Did they give it to him?" Emily asked, sounding anxious now.

"Afraid so," Quinn answered. "And from what we saw, the license on this—" he nodded toward the camper van "—was pretty visible."

"So they know what to look for."

"Yes."

"Maybe I should pull the plates off," he said.

"Couldn't hurt."

"Or you could re-register it here," Emily suggested.

As if she were convinced that now that he was here, he was going to stay. He wasn't sure how that made him feel.

"I wouldn't suggest that just yet," Hayley said. "Not as deeply embedded as Lyden influence is in this state."

Emily's eyes widened. "Oh, of course. I didn't think of that. He doesn't need his name in any system here."

Jordan wasn't sure if he'd dodged a bullet with Hayley's logical answer, or if he'd missed a chance to...actually commit to something.

Maybe he should never have left the Army. Maybe he needed the regimentation, maybe he wasn't going to be any good at living outside that controlled world. Maybe he wasn't any good at—

Cutter nudged him with a cold nose. He automatically moved to stroke the dog's head without thinking about it, but turned to look at the animal when that sense of ease flowed into him again. He looked into those dark eyes, noted again the goldish flecks that seemed to somehow amplify the intensity of the dog's gaze. When a pink tongue slipped out and swiped a doggy kiss across his wrist, he had no words for the feeling that filled him.

He looked up at Hayley, because it seemed easier to face her. "Your dog always so friendly to strangers?"

Her smile was kind. "You're not a stranger to him. He recognizes you as connected to the tags he found. He also recognizes you as someone with a problem we can fix. Most of all, he recognizes you as a hero."

A snort of laughter he couldn't stop escaped him. "I'm no hero." He nodded toward Quinn. "Guys like him are the heroes."

"Oh, he is," Hayley said proudly. "But as he's said, he couldn't have done what he did without guys like you doing what you did."

"What I did? I'm the guy who ran the first chance I got, remember?"

"Only after trying to tell the truth and hitting the brick wall that is Lyden influence," Quinn said.

"Not to mention the genuine threat to your life he could pose," Hayley put in.

Jordan slid a sideways glance at Emily to see how she was taking this. She caught his eye, but looked back at the Foxworths. "I've been trying to tell him that," she said. "But he's kind of stubborn."

"Good," Quinn said. "Sometimes that's all that gets you through." His mouth twisted. "Ask Rafe about that. He's probably the stubbornest guy you'll ever meet."

"And another hero," Hayley said solemnly. "The name engraved on trophies kind."

"Rafer Crawford!" Jordan suddenly yelped as it hit him why the name had seemed familiar. "He's that guy? The sniper? The multiple Hathcock Trophy guy?"

"That," Quinn said with undisguised satisfaction, "would be him."

"I heard some guys coming through camp talking about him once. They were in total awe."

"Rightfully so. The man's supernaturally good at what he does." Quinn looked at Jordan consideringly, then said, "You should talk to him sometime. When he's not busy making mile-and-a-half or better bullseyes, he's a heck of a mechanic. Deals with most of our gear, from generators to aircraft."

Jordan blinked. Of all the things he would have expected, that wasn't on the list.

"And," Hayley added, smiling again, "he even talks now."

"He didn't?" Emily asked.

"I think he got so used to being alone he kind of forgot how for a while."

"Or maybe he just saw too much," Jordan said. "Sometimes it's hard to get words out past all the…memories." He could only imagine what a Marine sniper on that level must have in his memory banks.

"That, too," Hayley agreed. "But we've been working on him—well, hammering at him, to be honest—and he's a lot better than he used to be."

"Meaning," Quinn said dryly, "you can sometimes get entire sentences out of him."

The conversation continued, and Jordan couldn't help but wonder if this was all part of a plan. If they were acting as if they were all just friends gathered around a campfire talking, in the hope it would convince him to do what they wanted.

After a while Sarge joined them, welcomed enthusiastically by Quinn and Hayley and greeted with wagging tail by Cutter. Then a couple of the other guys—Marcus, who had loaned him the chair, and Tyrus Jones, who had been passing by on his way back from the showers—joined in. And pretty soon there were at least a dozen people gathered, with, he noticed in amusement, the attentive dog greeting each one. He guessed by the way they reacted that most of them had interacted with military K9s at some point and saw the resemblance.

Jordan heard topics anywhere from the expected military references to their campers and supplies, to gardening, to jobs they had upcoming—Sarge was building an efficient handyman operation here—and even cooking. At which point both Emily and Hayley laughingly begged off, saying they weren't about to get pigeonholed as proficient at that just because they were female.

"Besides," Hayley said, "Quinn's a better cook than I'll ever be."

And as he watched Quinn, the former Ranger, chat amiably with all of them, clearly not caring that in the ranking structure he was far above a few of them, and Hayley going out of her way to make sure all were included, he began to believe that maybe, just maybe, Foxworth was who and what it was cracked up to be.

Even as he thought it, Cutter, who'd finished his self-appointed rounds, appeared at his side and gave him that look again, that steady stare that, at this moment, seemed somehow supportive. He reached out to pet the dog, just to see if it happened again, that feeling of reassurance. It did.

When things began to wind down, those who had jobs to go to in the morning said good-night, and Quinn and Hayley stood up to go. After a moment he stood up as well. He glanced at Emily, who had gotten to her feet the moment he had. As if they were a unit, like Quinn and Hayley obviously were. He gave himself another silent lecture on foolishness.

But she gave him a warm smile, and it made him feel stronger somehow. He sucked in a breath, turned to Quinn and spoke.

"What happens if...we start this?"

He thought he heard Emily make a sound, but he kept his gaze fastened on Quinn. The man studied him for a moment before saying, "We build an offense. Enough information to bury them. That will take a little time. But as soon as we've got it, we strike first. Defending yourself once they've made their move is a losing strategy."

"What if... I change my mind?"

"Then the goal changes, and so would the tactics."

He took in a deep breath. He had to at least try, didn't he? "All right."

"You're sure? We can't guarantee our turning over rocks won't alert them, even early on."

"I'm sure. I owe that much at least to Eddie." And the woman beside him, but he didn't say that part.

"All right," Quinn said. "First things first, and that's protect the asset."

His brow furrowed, and Hayley said with a smile, "That's you."

"Oh." He grimaced; being called an asset hadn't happened that often in his life.

"We'd prefer," Quinn said, "that you relocate to our headquarters."

He blinked then. "Relocate? I can't leave here, leave these guys. I…fit here. Besides, I told Sarge I'd help him with a few projects, and I have a couple of jobs coming up next week." Not to mention he liked it here. He'd found a peace here he hadn't felt since before Eddie had died. He wondered how much of that had to do with Emily, who spoke at last.

"They just want to keep you safe, Jordy."

It took everything he had not to buckle just at the sweet, gentle entreaty in her voice. As if keeping him safe was the most important thing to her. But then, it probably was, since he was the one with the truth about what had happened. But he'd also made some promises he didn't want to break.

"But they don't know where I am, do they? Not yet, anyway?"

"We don't think so," Hayley said. "But it's only a matter of time."

He looked around, listened to the bustle of activity as

the people who had welcomed the Foxworths and been welcomed by them went about the preparations for another night in this safe haven Sarge had provided.

"I don't want to leave," he said quietly. "But I don't want any of these guys endangered, either. They could probably handle the Lydens or whoever they send, but they shouldn't have to." He let out a weary breath. "Not because of me."

Quinn nodded, his expression approving. And in that moment Jordan was certain this was a man who, when in uniform, had always seen to the safety of those who served with and around him.

"How much do they know?" he asked.

"Just that I saw something over there that could bring some power brokers here down on my head."

"And how'd they react to that?" Hayley asked.

He half smiled at that. "They pretty much said 'bring it.'"

Hayley grinned. "Thought it would be something like that."

"How about a deal?" Quinn said. "You stay here for now, while we start digging, and we'll see to some extra security, especially at night. But the moment we suspect the Lydens know you're in the area, you move. We can secure your van in our outbuilding, out of sight, and the main building has living quarters and a solid alarm system."

Cutter yipped, startling Jordan. The dog had been so quiet during this discussion, just standing watching them, he'd almost forgotten he was there.

"Yes, you're part of that alarm system," Hayley said with a laugh.

As if he'd been waiting to be sure he had her attention, the dog walked over and sat at Jordan's feet, but facing his owners. Owners who exchanged a raised eyebrow look, then looked back at Cutter.

"You sure?" Quinn asked, for all the world looking as if he were asking the dog. Jordan glanced at Emily, but she looked as puzzled as he felt.

Cutter yipped again. And didn't budge.

"Well," Hayley said, "looks like you've acquired a bodyguard."

Jordan blinked and drew back. "What?"

She nodded at the dog. "He's decided you need him here. And when that dog has decided, arguing with him is pointless."

"I'll get his go bag," Quinn said, sounding amusedly resigned.

"He has a go bag?" Jordan asked, too bemused to think of anything else to say.

"He does," Hayley said. "With food, bowls, all the necessities. Because he does this rather often."

"You're saying…what, you're leaving your dog here?"

"Don't worry about dog sitting," she said. "He's very low maintenance when he's working."

"Working?" Emily asked, sounding as befuddled as he felt.

"He's the best early warning system you could have," Quinn said as he came back from their vehicle holding a dark blue backpack. "Not to mention having excellent judgment about who's an enemy and no hesitation at taking them on. Between him and Rafe on overwatch at night, you should be good."

Jordan blinked, starting to feel a little off balance. Having the obviously well-trained dog with him eased his worry. The thought of one of the most famous snipers in all branches of the military essentially standing guard for him was almost too much to believe.

He'd gone from feeling utterly alone with the Lydens hunting him, to having a small army at his back.

## Chapter 14

"What made you decide to trust them?" Emily asked as she stroked Cutter's dark head—so strange how soothing that simple action was—as they sat beside the waning fire.

She'd considered leaving when the Foxworths had, but she thought it might seem too much like now that she'd gotten what she'd wanted—him agreeing to help—she wasn't interested in staying around. And that, she admitted to herself, was far, far from the truth.

So she'd stayed. And she hadn't missed the instant of surprise that flashed across his face, as if he'd expected her to leave when everyone else did. Or maybe… wanted her to leave? She hadn't really considered that until she'd already sat back down by the fire.

"Seeing them with all the people from here," he said after a moment. "I thought a guy who'd been special ops would have been…"

"Snootier?" she asked when he trailed off.

"Yeah," he admitted, sounding a little sheepish.

"But instead he hung out with a mechanic and a mere sergeant and a few others of lower rank as if they were equals," she said, grinning at him. "Not to mention leaving his dog as a bodyguard."

"Yeah," he repeated in the same tone as he reached over to pat Cutter himself. "Made me believe he meant what he said."

"I'm sure when he was on active duty he was as commanding as he needed to be. And maybe even sometimes now, when necessary. But it's obvious he doesn't think he's better than anyone else who served."

"No, he doesn't." Jordan's voice held a touch of wonder, maybe even amazement. Whatever it was, if it had convinced him, she was glad of it.

But her voice hardened as she hit the crux of what she'd wanted to say. "Unlike Hartwell Lyden. Who thinks he's so much better than all of you put together."

"Yes, he does. He made it clear he was no mere grunt like us."

"A supposed soldier who can't tell the difference between a gunshot and a backfire."

"Pretty much."

"Thank you for deciding this has to be done."

"I meant what I said. I owe it to Eddie." He paused and looked away from her to the fire before he added, "And now to you."

"You don't owe me anything. All I want is right done for my brother."

He stared into the last remaining flames for a moment before he spoke again. "Eddie told me a little about the

Lydens when Hart arrived. Said he'd grown up seeing and hearing the name all the time."

"They are definitely movers and shakers around here and beyond," she agreed. "Our father had plenty to say about them, and not much of it good. He said they always talked a good game about supporting the little guy, and assuring the safety of citizens. And then promoted legislation and candidates who would do the exact opposite."

"Pretty much what Eddie told me," he said.

"And it seems Foxworth agrees."

Cutter let out a little woof, and she assumed it was at the mention of his people's name, and not the assent it had funnily sounded like. Still, it made her laugh.

"I can't believe they just left him here," Jordan said, reaching out to stroke the soft fur.

"Do you mind?"

"No, it's just…they just met me, barely know me, and they trust me with their dog?"

"You trusted them with your life," she pointed out.

He blinked, turning his head to stare at her for a moment before saying slowly, "I didn't think of it like that."

"Hayley told me he has a very strong mind of his own. And that he's as much a member of their team as any of them. In fact, she said he brings them a lot of their cases, in one way or another."

She'd expected him to laugh that off, since he hadn't heard the tales Hayley had told her. But instead he looked very thoughtful before saying quietly, "He brought them my dog tags."

"Yes. Which is why they called Sloan, to see if maybe you were a poster in the *Accountability Counts* forums."

"Sloan Burke," he said slowly. "We all watched those hearings, even over there. Watched her fight them, for her husband. She's got more guts than a lot of the guys I know."

"She fought people just like the Lydens," she said. "So it can be done."

He didn't say anything to that, and she wondered what he was thinking. Knowing what she knew so far, she guessed he was wondering if he had the same kind of guts as Sloan had shown when she'd taken on those be-medaled stuffed shirts in the capital who had gotten her SEAL husband killed.

"Sloan Burke and Rafer Crawford," he muttered with a shake of his head. "Who would have ever thought…?"

"They'd be on your side? I would have. Eddie would have."

She didn't think her voice had changed, but he turned his head to look at her. "It hurts to even say his name, doesn't it?"

She didn't even try to lie. "Yes. And it probably will for a long time." She hesitated, then said what had been on her mind for a while, beneath all the stir about the Lydens. "Dad will want to meet you, right away, when he gets home."

He looked startled, and very wary. "You're going to tell him?"

"Now that…things are in motion? Of course. I couldn't withhold this, or lie to him about it."

"What if I chicken out? Run?"

A dozen things came into her mind to say. That she understood how hard this would be. That he should still meet her father, because he was Eddie's best friend. That they would forgive him if he felt he had to back out, al-though that might take some time.

But in the end she went with what was, for her, the bottom line truth.

"I don't believe you will."

*I don't believe you will.*

The phrase rang in Jordan's head long after she'd gone. Not so much the words but the way she'd said them. Not thoughtfully. Not hopefully. Not even encouragingly.

No, she'd said it as if she were certain.

"I wish I had your faith in me, Emmie," he murmured to the air.

The Foxworth dog gave a low, soft whine, as if he sensed Jordan's mood. As he probably did, judging by what he'd seen of the animal so far.

"It's okay, dog. I'm down, but I'm not out. Yet, any-way." Cutter nudged his hand. Jordan stroked the dog's head. "I don't know which is weirder, mutt, that you know when to push someone to pet you, or that it helps so much when they do."

He filled one of the bowls they'd left him with water and the other with kibble from the go bag, as Hayley had explained. The dog ate some, drank a little more, then walked away. She'd said he self-regulated, which he found interesting, wondering what dogs like this had that chowhounds did not. Maybe it was the same thing in people, some trigger in their head or metabolism.

The dog seemed perfectly happy to curl up in the small amount of floor space next to the bunk. Never having had one, he worried about whether he'd need to go out during the night, but Hayley had also assured him he'd know.

"He's remarkably clear about what needs to be done," she'd said.

And it wasn't until after they'd gone that it occurred

to him to wonder if she'd meant what the dog needed to do, or him.

He shifted in the bed. The temperature had dropped after sunset, but it was still warm enough inside the camper that he'd popped open one of the windows here in the back of the van. He needed to get to sleep. He had a 6:00 a.m. call in the morning. He and two other guys— led by Sarge himself, since the customer was another long-time neighbor—were scheduled to do some major brush cleanup on a half-acre lot.

But sleep didn't seem inclined to visit. He propped himself up on the pillows and looked out at the night. Thought of all the times he and Eddie had sat outside looking at a different section of sky, talking about the worst mechanical disaster they'd ever dealt with, baseball—hard though it was to converse with a Mariners fan when obviously the Cardinals rule—and Jordan's impending departure for home. Which had brought them to the topic of being homesick, something Jordan had never really felt. He'd wanted out of where they were, but had felt no pull to a particular place. He'd loved the Mississippi River, been fascinated by the history of it and how it had helped build the country, but it was more of an intellectual interest. It didn't tug at his heart, his gut.

But home did just that for Eddie. Of course he'd missed his dad…and his sister. But it was more than that. He missed everything about his home in the Pacific Northwest, except, he'd added with a grimace, some of the people. He even, he'd said with a laugh at his own glumness, missed the rain.

And now that he was here, Jordan understood. Although what he would have missed was the kind of green that rain produced. The towering evergreen trees, the cedars, the spruce and the redwoods that had given the neighboring village its name. And the lack of the humidity he'd grown up with was a welcome change.

Above all, there was the presence of Puget Sound, glimpsed here and there through those tall trees, and in spots a wide vista that made him want to stop and just stare, it was so beautiful.

*I can just imagine doing this in all sorts of beautiful places. Having familiar things around you but in unfamiliar, wondrous places...*

Emily's words about the van, and traveling in it, snuck past the barriers he'd mentally put up. And his mind immediately seized upon them, picturing her here beside him, looking out at someplace neither of them had ever seen before. A feeling it took him a moment to identify as longing, a deep yearning, took hold so fiercely he forgot to breathe for a moment.

*Yeah, picture her here in bed with you, Crockett. That'll help.*

He yanked one pillow out from behind him, and punched the other—rather forcefully—into shape. Leaving the window open he laid down, listening to the night noises as he tried again for sleep.

It was a long time coming.

# Chapter 15

Jordan yawned widely. It had not been a restful night, to say the least. In fact, the only sleep he'd gotten had been after Cutter, seeming to sense his restlessness, had hopped up on the bunk and settled down beside him. It had been comforting, somehow, and let him finally drift off. But that had been after midnight, so he was still running short.

He understood the necessity for the early rollout, even though they had a strict rule of no power tools before 8:00 a.m. on weekdays, 10:00 a.m. on weekends—more of that neighborliness Sarge was so adamant about. But he also wanted to assess the location, work out a plan of attack and decide where they were going to stack the brush for later removal.

He yawned again, rubbing at his eyes as he walked up to the house. Mrs. Sarge, bless her, always had coffee on for the guys who had to roll out early for jobs, and she made it strong. Sarge had truly lucked out in that depart-ment, Jordan thought. They'd been married almost fifty years, been together since they were sixteen, and no one who looked at them together could doubt the love they had for each other. And more than once Jordan had seen some of the residents of the camp watching them in a sort of wonder.

"They kinda give you hope, y'know?" Marcus had once said.

After they'd downed enough coffee to wake up, and Mrs. Sarge had slipped Cutter a small piece of toast, they piled into Sarge's big truck. Sarge never turned a hair when it became clear that the dog had every intention of sticking to Jordan's side.

"He knows his job," the man said approvingly.

Jordan decided not to explain how it had apparently been the dog's own decision; explaining that the animal had appointed himself as bodyguard was a little beyond believability. If it hadn't happened before his own eyes, he'd have laughed off the idea.

Once out the gate, Sarge made a right turn, heading to-ward the small enclave of houses on the first street south, where the last house at the dead end was their destination. They'd only gone about a quarter of the distance when Cutter, looking out the side window of the back seat, gave a quiet little woof that made Jordan look. He saw a car pulled into a spot off the road that was half-hidden by trees and shrubbery like the stuff they were heading out to remove. The silver coupe looked like a million others on the road, but the ding in the left rear fender made his brow furrow. It seemed familiar, like he'd seen the same model car, same color, same ding somewhere before.

They were past it and turning onto the neighboring

street when it hit him. He'd seen that car, all right. Parked at the far end of the gravel entry to the Foxworth headquarters. Near the outbuilding that served as home to their helicopter, generator and… Rafe Crawford.

He looked at Cutter. Had that little woof been recognition? Dogs could recognize cars?

He gave a shake of his head and made himself focus on the day ahead. It would be good to get out and do some hard, physical work. Maybe if he exhausted himself he'd sleep tonight. Not need a dog beside him to do it.

And maybe not spend so much time wishing it was Emily.

In the end it turned out to be a good day. Everybody worked hard, including Cutter. Jordan marveled at the dog's quick understanding of the task at hand, and laughed when he started dragging some of the smaller cut branches over to the pile they were building. Even Tyrus, who almost never laughed, did so at the dog's actions.

And Jordan didn't miss how the animal paused every now and then, head up, gazing into the distance as his nose worked rapidly. The action made his own muscles tighten, and he wondered what he would do if the dog took off after something.

Or someone.

Fortunately, each time the dog assessed and dismissed whatever had caught his attention and gone back to the task he'd set himself. Leaving Jordan wondering how he had so quickly come to trust the instincts of a dog. An admittedly clever one, but still a dog.

Sarge called a halt to the work a little past five, and pronounced it a good start. Once they were back home at the camp and Jordan had cleaned up from the long day's work, he was pondering what to eat from his dwindling supplies—he was obviously going to have to make a run for food—when Cutter repeated the action that had put Jordan on edge several times today. He'd gone from lolling on the ground outside the door of the van to his feet in an instant, his nose pointed downhill toward the gate.

But after a few seconds Jordan saw the tip of his tail begin to wag, signaling a friend, or at least someone known not to be a threat. He figured it must be one of the Foxworth crew, probably coming to see if their dog was okay, and if he himself had managed to survive. But instead of the dark blue SUV he expected, he saw Emily's smaller, bright blue one approaching, and he felt the jolt of his pulse kicking into a higher gear.

Cutter let out a little yip, and Jordan found himself answering aloud, "Yeah." Which in turn made him shake his head.

In truth, he'd been talking to the dog off and on ever since Foxworth had left him here, and he wondered if it was a sign he'd been a little too isolated. Or maybe it was just the way the dog reacted, as if he understood perfectly, that encouraged the conversation that didn't seem at all one-sided.

The moment her vehicle pulled to a stop at his site, Cutter trotted over to greet her. He felt like hurrying a bit himself, but managed to keep it to a walk.

"Hey," she said cheerfully as she reached down to stroke the dog's head. "How'd it go today?"

"We got a lot of it done, but it's going to take another day or two to finish it to Sarge's standards."

She smiled at that. "I quite like your Sarge. He reminds me of my dad."

*Dad's...exacting. But he's fair, and if you're honest with him, he respects you. But the bottom line is that*

*Emmie and I have always known he loves us and that he'd die to protect us.*

Eddie's words, prompted by his own rare question about what it was like to grow up with a father, rang in his head now.

"I think," he said, "they're probably a lot alike."

She smiled at that. Then, with a glance toward the open door of the camper, she asked, "You haven't eaten dinner yet, have you?"

"No," he said. "I was just trying to figure that out."

"Good. Come on, we're going to Foxworth."

He blinked. "We are?"

She nodded. "Hayley called and said to bring you for dinner." She said it as if it were routine, as if it were assumed the two of them were…together. He fought down the feeling that gave him as she bent to give Cutter a scratch behind the ears. "And you, too, of course," she added.

"They have news?" he asked, belatedly realizing that was probably the reason behind the invitation.

She straightened up. "No big developments. More in the way of a progress report. And something about communications."

His brow furrowed at that. Communications? Had he been supposed to call them? About what? Had they asked for a check-in about their dog and he'd missed it?

"Do you need to lock up?"

He shook his head. "We don't worry much about that here. Somebody's always here and watching." His mouth quirked. "I don't have much worth stealing anyway."

She looked at him for a long moment before she said, in a soft, quiet voice, "No, the things you have that are worth the most can't be stolen. Ready?" she asked, before he had a chance to ask what she'd meant. "Come along, Cutter, we're going to see your family."

The dog hopped into the vehicle willingly—the back seat this time, Jordan noted—and then Emily turned to look at him. Part of him wanted to mention that he'd never actually been asked if he wanted to go, but considering what they all were doing for him, it seemed ungrateful. So he got in the passenger seat, to a mild, approving bark from the back seat.

He gave a wry shake of his head. *Applying human emotions to a dog now? You're really on a downhill slide, Crockett.*

"You don't want to go?" Emily asked.

The worried question snapped him out of his musings. "No," he said quickly. "I mean, that's not what I was—" He stopped, then tried again, wondering why he became so befuddled around her. He tried again. "I was just thinking about how that dog gets me to thinking he's half human half the time."

Emily laughed, and he felt a sense of relief. "Quinn says he's smarter than they are a lot of the time. Especially about people. Which is why they trust his judgment."

He glanced back at the dog again. "Are you that smart, dog?"

He'd swear the dog gave him an "Of course" kind of eye roll.

"Hayley told me the only time he's ever been flummoxed was a couple of months ago, when a woman arrived looking for someone. He—" she nodded at the dog "—started to greet her like any stranger, but then suddenly sat down and just stared at her, confused. Turned out she was Teague's long-lost sister."

"And they think he somehow…knew that?"

"They think he sensed something. That she was connected to someone he knew and trusted."

That launched a discussion of dogs and their capabilities—and the ones they kept wanting to attribute to the one in the back seat—that lasted until they turned onto the drive through the trees to the Foxworth headquarters. And in the same place as before, he spotted the silver sedan.

"He was out there, last night. I saw the car early this morning."

"You sound surprised. They promised extra security."

"Yeah, I know, but this guy is…legendary."

Again she gave him that smile that had tangled him up before. "Obviously they know you're worth it."

And with that she slid out of the car and opened the back door for Cutter, who trotted off toward the front door of the house, no doubt to cleverly open it again all on his own.

For a moment Jordan just sat there, wondering how on earth he had ended up with people—and a dog—like this looking out for him.

And a woman like Emily thinking he was worth it.

# Chapter 16

"Told you Quinn was a good cook."

"That," Emily said with a grin at the man sitting across from them, "I would not argue."

"I'm too busy eating to argue," Jordan said.

Quinn merely smiled, like a man who knew his own worth. The kind of smile she would give anything to see from Jordan.

When she had nothing but a plate of bones from the delicious ribs Quinn had grilled, she spoke again.

"Too bad Rafe's not here," she said. "I know Jordan would like to thank him. And so would I."

"We don't mind so much that he's not joining us, because he's following up a lead, not just avoiding socializing."

Jordan looked up at that. "A lead?"

"One of his local military contacts," Quinn said. "Don't know what it was, he just texted that it could be something. Or nothing."

"After he spent all night being my guardian angel?" Jordan asked quietly.

Quinn raised a brow. "I know Rafe well enough to know you didn't spot him."

"Saw his car, down the road aways. I wasn't sure it was his, but—" he glanced over at Cutter "—he let me know it was."

Quinn smiled. "So, you're starting to accept he's useful."

"I never doubted he was useful. I wasn't convinced he was..." He trailed off as if words had failed him.

"Uncanny? Exceptional? Inspired? Supernatural?" Hayley suggested, laughter in her tone. "Believe me, we've been there. We finally had to just accept that he's a different kind of dog."

"Or a very smart human in a dog suit?" Emily suggested.

"Maybe an alien," Jordan muttered as he wiped his fingers on a napkin.

"I've thought that, too," Hayley said.

Because she needed something to do, and it seemed right, Emily began to clean up after the meal. Jordan joined her immediately, saying it was only right after the Foxworths had hosted them and cooked. She liked that they were in sync about it, then almost laughed at herself for taking pleasure in such a small thing.

The kitchen was efficient but compact, and they bumped into each other more than once. Each time Jordan murmured a quiet apology. Finally, the next time he said, "Sorry," she stopped and turned to face him.

"I'm not," she said.

He blinked. She saw the corners of his mouth twitch, and she was certain he was fighting a smile. Maybe one day soon she could get him to stop fighting.

When they adjourned to the great room, Quinn didn't waste any time getting down to business. "We're monitoring the Lydens as closely as we can without tipping them off. So far there's no sign of unexpected activity, but we're going to assume they're still looking for you, Jordan."

Emily felt her stomach knot. He was in danger, and the possibility of something happening to him had become something she didn't think she could bear. And she was no longer certain it was simply because he'd been Eddie's best friend.

Quinn picked up what looked like a couple of cell phones from the coffee table. He handed one to each of them. She only had time to notice the red button on the top edge before he explained. "These are connected to our own private network. The red button is a live contact function. Someone from Foxworth will be reachable 24-7 using that button. Don't hesitate to use it if necessary."

Emily doubted she would ever need to, but she was glad Jordan would have it.

"Emily," Hayley said quietly, as if she'd read her thought, "don't think they aren't monitoring you."

"Me?" she said, startled.

"Just because they're heartless themselves doesn't mean they don't know other people, real people, are different," Hayley said.

"That's how they maneuver and manipulate," Quinn put in. "They use people's feelings and emotions against them." He shifted his gaze to Jordan. "Old man Lyden is many things, but not stupid. I can promise that the idea you would eventually come to see Emily and visit Eddie's grave has occurred to them."

Emily felt a sudden chill sweep her, while at the same

time her skin felt clammy. She guessed this was what they called a cold sweat, although she'd never experienced one before.

"What if I've led them to him?" she asked, horrified at the thought. She darted a glance at Jordan, to find him staring at her as if stunned. When he spoke, he sounded as incredulous as he looked.

"He tells you they're watching you, and that's what you're worried about?"

"Of course," she exclaimed. "You're the one in danger—"

"Do you really think they wouldn't take you out, too, if they thought I'd told you the truth of what happened?"

She hadn't really thought about that at all. The idea of something happening to him because of her had blasted everything else out of her mind.

Jordan was now on the edge of the couch, staring at Quinn. "You've got to—"

Quinn lifted a hand. "Yes. We will keep her safe."

"Assign Rafe to her," Jordan said, his tone urgent. "Keep her here, where she'll be protected."

"May I remind you *she* is right here," Emily said, coming out of her shock now.

Jordan shifted his gaze to her. "And you should stay here."

"You're the one in real danger. You need Rafe's protection more than I. And I can't stay here. I have a job to do, especially while my dad's out of town."

"But they probably know you work there—"

"Exactly. They probably already know where I am. My father's had to deal with one of their minions on the city council." Her voice nearly broke as the horror rose in her again. "But they wouldn't know where you are, unless I led them straight to you."

"There's no reason to think that, but—"

He broke off as Cutter let out a sharp bark. They both turned to look at the dog, who was—she couldn't think of another word for it—glaring at them. As if he didn't like that they were disagreeing.

"I think we can resolve this," Hayley said, and Emily wondered if it was part of her job to be the peacemaker. "Emily, I think you need to have a friend stay with you, visiting from out of town. One you want to show around at work, too."

"I do?" she asked. Clearly Hayley meant someone from Foxworth, and Emily was more than a little bit nervous as she thought of the intimidating Rafe.

"Yes," Hayley said with a grin. "Meaning me."

"Oh!" she exclaimed, relaxing a little.

"Are you—" Jordan broke off, gave a wary glance at Quinn, then looked back at Hayley. "All due respect, are you…"

"Trained to be a bodyguard?" Hayley asked cheerfully. "I am. Quinn saw to that."

"No choice," her husband muttered.

"Since I refused to leave all the fieldwork to the boys?"

"Yeah, yeah," Quinn said, but the look he gave his wife was proud. "And I have to say, you get the job done. The bad guys never expect a gorgeous woman like you to explode and take them down."

"There are all kinds of disguises," Hayley said, looking back at her husband with the purest kind of love Emily had ever seen. She suspected Mrs. Foxworth was implying that Mr. Foxworth's tough, uncompromising exterior hid a heart that was putty in her hands. And more, she suspected it was true. "So," Hayley said, briskly now, "now that I've invited myself to move in with you—"

She broke off when Cutter let out an odd string of short barks and longer sounds, something Emily thought she'd heard before. The dog scrambled to his feet and trotted toward the front door.

"If he's coming here, he's got something," Quinn said, getting to his feet.

"I'll get some coffee poured," Hayley said, following suit.

"Rafe?" Jordan asked.

Hayley nodded as she headed for the kitchen. "That was his bark."

Emily's first instinct was to laugh, but with this dog they could very possibly be serious. Maybe everybody in the clever animal's life had a different bark.

Cutter pushed the door control and it started to swing open. A bare moment later the tall, rangy man stepped inside. He bent to ruffle the dog's ears and said something to him Emily couldn't hear but that made the dog's tail wag enthusiastically. Then he straightened and strode into the great room. His gaze flicked to where she and Jordan had also gotten up, then to his boss.

"Go," Quinn commanded. "They're current."

Emily realized he'd been waiting to see if he should reveal what he'd learned in front of them. When he spoke it was short and to the point.

"My contact works for the state VA and has a friend who works at the Tahoma National Cemetery over in Kent. That friend told him somebody from the Lyden camp called not long ago asking if an Edward Bishop was buried there."

Emily's breath caught. It was true. It was real.

# Chapter 17

A chill went down Jordan's spine. He'd known it, in an abstract sort of way, but this pounded home the reality. The Lydens were hunting him.

Hayley came back with fresh coffee, and they all sat down again. Jordan ignored the coffee for the moment. He was getting much more warmth and comfort from the fact that Emily had, after dodging Cutter, not only sat down right next to him, she'd grabbed his hand with hers. He tightened his fingers in response, rather dazedly amazed at how much that simple touch meant, coming from her.

"Did he know what reason Lyden's flunky gave?" Quinn asked Rafe.

The man's mouth curved in a dismissive twist. "She told them Mr. Lyden's military hero son wanted to visit the grave, to honor his fallen comrade."

Those words seared away every emotion except anger,

and Jordan snorted derisively. "Hartwell Lyden never wanted to honor anyone except himself."

"I'm surprised his daddy didn't buy him a generalship," Emily said, her voice holding the same scathing tone his had. But then her eyes widened as she stared at Quinn. "I'm sorry, I didn't mean to insult—"

She stopped when Quinn shook his head. "Can't say it hasn't happened. That's pretty obvious these days. But indirectly, you bring up a good point. It takes a certain lack of effort to be a West Point graduate and leave the Army after your five years is up still a second lieutenant."

"Especially coming from that family," Rafe said. "You'd have to righteously screw up."

"I heard some rumors," Jordan said, "that when he was assigned in DC he got caught offering some kind of drug to the daughter of one of the joint chiefs and that's how he ended up downrange. I blew it off at the time because I didn't think even he would be that stupid, but…"

Quinn appeared to consider that for a moment, then nodded. "Could be. The Lydens are huge here, but haven't quite become full power players nationally."

"I'd guess that's what Lyden Junior was supposed to do for them," Hayley said.

Quinn nodded, then shifted his gaze to Jordan. "And you're the one who could destroy that plan."

"Well, then it's a good thing that call didn't help them," Emily said. Jordan turned his head to look at her. "He's not buried in a military cemetery. Dad and I thought about it, but…he's next to Mom." She looked at Quinn as she explained. "In the little cemetery up the hill from the high school. There's a section for our family, because we've been here for generations."

Quinn grabbed his phone, typed out a text, then looked

at her and asked, "Have you entered anything on any of the online grave searching sites?"

She blinked and drew back. "No. I wouldn't. Nor would Dad."

Quinn nodded, added a line to his text and sent it. "I'll have Ty—our IT guy in St. Louis, who's doing what Liam would do for us if he wasn't on his honeymoon—find out if anyone has uploaded anything, and, if so if it's been searched for."

"You mean people can just…do that?" Emily asked, looking both disconcerted and upset. "To somebody's who's not even famous or anything?"

"They can and they do," Hayley said. "We found that out on a case a while back. They search obituaries and post the information. It's like a competition with some of them, how many they can get listed."

"What about the families, the people grieving?" Emily sounded a bit angry now. He didn't blame her.

"Apparently they don't care." Hayley didn't sound much happier.

"That's…"

"Weird? Sick? Twisted?" Jordan suggested.

"I'd say all of those might apply, depending," Quinn said. "But for now, unless Ty turns up something, I'd say it's unlikely the Lydens have figured it out yet."

"Does that mean Jordan can still…visit his grave?" Emily gave him a hasty glance. "I mean, if you still want to."

"Of course I do."

"Then I suggest as soon as possible," Quinn said. "Because eventually, somebody who knows where he's buried will hear that Lyden load of garbage about honoring his comrade and believe it. Or if that fails, they'll simply buy it, one way or another."

Emily looked at the Foxworth phone, then back at Jordan. "How about now? It will be light for another couple of hours."

He could no more have resisted her look of entreaty than he could have flown back to Missouri without a plane. "All right."

Rafe was on his feet without a word, and at a nod from Quinn said only, "Give me twenty," and left out the back door.

"What was that about?" Emily asked.

"He's going to pick his spot," Quinn said. "You won't see him, but he'll be there until you leave."

She frowned. "He's going to the cemetery?"

"Just in case."

Quinn's voice had taken on a comforting tone. Jordan wondered if it was something he'd learned from his observant, intuitive wife. Emily made a little sound, as if she had only just realized what "pick his spot" had meant.

For Jordan, he'd just wondered again how on earth he'd ended up with people like this covering his back.

It was closer to thirty-five minutes before they actually reached the small cemetery on the hill. But he knew that snipers were among the most patient of the human species and an extra fifteen minutes would mean nothing. And Quinn had been right—there was no sign of the man anywhere. Yet Jordan knew he was there, and was glad of it, if only for Emily's sake. Between knowing Rafe Crawford was watching over them, and Cutter by their side, he wasn't worried about the Lydens at the moment.

Cutter wasn't happy about staying in Emily's car, but dogs weren't allowed on the grounds. It was still warm out, so they left all the windows plus the sunroof wide open for him.

Given the relatively small size of the place, it didn't take them long to reach their destination. He spotted the grave site from several feet away. Grass had begun to take root, but it had a different color and wasn't quite as thick as that in the surrounding area. Including that over the grave next to it, which he guessed was their mother's. Nearly fresh flowers were at each grave, and he wondered when Emily had been here. Maybe she came every weekend.

He took a step closer, close enough to read the headstone that said Tricia Bishop, Beloved Wife and Mother, Gone Far Too Soon. He hesitated there. Didn't look at the next marker.

As if not looking at it could make Eddie's grave not real.

He closed his eyes for a long moment, searching inwardly for at least some little bit of courage. Then he felt a touch, Emily's fingers brushing against his. She said nothing, but somehow the touch was enough. He opened his eyes and looked. His gaze zeroed in on the dates, and he was grateful it was only the years of birth and death, although that was bad enough. That the final date was this year still knotted up his gut.

Edward Steven Bishop
Beloved son and brother
With Mom at last.

He was barely aware of going to his knees.

"It should have been me," he said hoarsely, staring at the metal plaque.

But instead, here he was, and there Eddie was, his life ended in that faraway place. But oddly, it wasn't those last moments that ran through his mind again, but rather the first time he'd met Eddie. They'd sent Jordan to get the new guy when he'd gotten off the helicopter that had dropped him off at the camp as a replacement for Kevin Lund. Kev had wrapped his service and was headed home. He'd been a bit of a pain, and Jordan wasn't going to miss him much. He'd just been hoping the new guy wouldn't be worse.

Then he'd seen Eddie wave the pilot goodbye and look around at the camp, then at the barren hills beyond.

"Shoulda joined the Navy I guess," he'd said, "because I'd a hell of a lot rather be on a boat."

Jordan had laughed, because he'd had a very similar thought himself the first time he saw the place. That had been the beginning of what became the best friendship of his life. It had been Eddie who, after he'd been there a couple of months, had made the "brother from another mother" joke. And at first Jordan laughed. But he'd gotten rather solemn after that.

*I don't know. I never had a brother.*

*You do now. If you want.*

*Yeah. Yeah, I want.*

They'd scrambled for an escape from the unexpectedly intense moment, and ended up tossing a football around until a delivery brought them the part they'd been waiting on to get the captain's Hummer going again.

Later that night, after a video call from his sister—who apparently didn't care what hour she had to be up and ready to match the time her brother had free here—Eddie had looked over to where Jordan was sitting on his bunk.

*I only wish you could have had a sister like Emmie.*

That memory made him turn to look at her now. But she wasn't where she'd been. She'd backed off to several feet away. And he instinctively knew it was to give him room to be with his thoughts and memories as he knelt at the graveside.

*Your sister's a class act, Eddie.*

But then, he already knew that. Knew from Eddie how, when the woman he now lay buried beside had died, his barely twelve-year-old sister had stepped in.

*She was just a kid herself. But she was always there for me. Not sayin' we didn't fight now and then, we did. But let somebody come at me from the outside and she was there. She was always there for me.*

Jordan hadn't doubted it then, but he was utterly certain of it now. This was a woman who would stand her ground, and if you were lucky enough to be someone she loved, she would stand beside you to the end, if necessary.

*Someone she loved...*

He felt a nudge, the poke of a cold, canine nose. Cutter obviously hadn't read the No Dogs sign. Or had, and didn't care. Jordan reflexively stroked the soft, dark fur, but all it did this time was make him think of Emily again, and how she cooed to the clever animal.

He scrambled to his feet, knowing he had to get out of here. It was bad enough he was having crazy thoughts about her, but to do it here, at Eddie's grave, seemed wrong somehow.

Even if Eddie had once joked that if he ever met her and they fell in love, then they could really be brothers.

## Chapter 18

Was it twisted of her, the fact that seeing someone else missing Eddie as she did eased her own pain?

Emily wasn't sure, she only knew it was true. She could almost feel the pain radiating off of him, and while it reminded her of those first days and brought back the harsh agony, it also, on another level, made it easier to bear. As if knowing it was shared had truly lightened her burden.

She should have tried harder to reach Jordan after Eddie had been killed. She'd written him to thank him for risking his own life to try and save her brother, but she wasn't sure he'd ever gotten the email since he'd never answered and her next one bounced back, saying the address no longer existed.

She thought about her father, and how he would feel when he found out that not only had she connected with Eddie's friend, but that he was here. He'd be delighted, and anxious to meet him. But that happy thought was

immediately wiped away by the image of having to tell
Dad what had really happened, that Eddie hadn't died
from an insurgent attack but rather the cowardly panic
of an entitled idiot.

Not to mention the fact that the family of "self-
appointed elites," as he'd called the Lydens, was hunting for that friend. It was hard for her, having grown up
in peace and surrounded by normal life, to picture that
truly happening here and now. It wasn't that she didn't
know there were evil people here at home, and that far
too many of them had far too much power—she did.
She'd just never had it essentially on her doorstep before.

When Jordan abruptly stood up, he glanced at her.
She crossed the space she'd given him, although it hadn't
been far enough that she hadn't heard the quiet words
he'd said. That it should have been him. She never would
have guessed he would feel that way, and wondered why
he did.

But now she noticed the sheen in his eyes, seeing it
past the stinging in her own. She wasn't certain what his
expression meant, but took a guess.

"Seeing it makes it real. Makes it hurt all over again."

She saw him suck in a deep breath, and he blinked
rapidly for a moment. His jaw tightened, as if he were
clenching his teeth. Against crying? Or speaking? Or
showing anything at all?

The rule-breaking Cutter moved then, stepping behind her and leaning against the backs of her legs. As
if he wanted her to take that last step between her and
Jordan. The dog leaned harder, and suddenly it was the
only thing to do. She took that step to Jordan and hugged
him again, as if together they could stave off the pain she
knew deep down would never really leave her.

He stiffened, and she felt him start to pull away. In the instant before she would have—reluctantly—let him go, he stopped. And then, hesitantly at first and then more decidedly, his arms came around her. His embrace was warm and strong, and it comforted her more than she ever would have thought possible. Odd, since she had meant to comfort him.

It was then, with her cheek pressed against his chest, that she asked what had bothered her since she'd heard it.

"Why did you say it should have been you?"

He went very still again. She feared she'd pushed too hard, that he wasn't going to answer. Then, his voice a low rumble she felt almost as much as she heard, he did.

"Eddie had you and your father to come home to. He had a family business to help run. I... I had nothing but the camper van and a crazy idea of seeing the country I'd signed up to defend."

What he said about Eddie threatened to overwhelm her already wobbly emotions, so she made herself focus on the rest. She remembered the talk they'd had when she'd first seen his mobile living quarters. That seemed safe enough.

"I still think that's a wonderful idea," she said, looking up at him. "Touring the country you spent years serving."

He didn't meet her gaze. She wondered if he was avoiding looking at her, but decided to take advantage of the chance to really look at him up close. His jaw really was that broad and strong, his nose that straight and well shaped, and his eyelashes really were that long and thick. And that mouth, that tempting mouth...

She yanked her gaze away, half-afraid she'd say something utterly stupid. And after a moment he spoke, hesitantly.

"So…you meant it, when you said you'd always wanted to travel?"

The rather ordinary question abruptly made her focus on the fact that he was still holding her. She was careful not to make any move he might interpret as wanting him to let go. Because she very much did not want him to. And she kept her voice even when she answered, fighting to sound normal despite feeling a bit breathless.

"I did. I still want to, someday."

"You should, someday." His voice had taken on an edge now. "In something better than a camper van."

She noticed he didn't say *my* camper van.

"Under the right circumstances," she said carefully, "I'm not sure there could be anything better than a nice camper van."

Again he went still. And this time he let go of her. She told herself she couldn't possibly feel as chilled as she did simply because he'd taken a step back. It was a warm, summer day, there was no excuse for wanting to go back to him, to huddle in his arms as if she needed him to keep her from freezing.

No excuse except the obvious.

She looked at him, standing between two stripes of shade from the towering trees that grew around the area cleared for the cemetery. The afternoon sun arrowing through the break in the evergreens seemed to paint him with light, but at an angle that cast his eyes into shadow even as it gilded the rest of his face.

Something about it made her remember the picture Eddie had sent her, of the two of them in helmets and camo gear, their faces coated in sand to the point of being unrecognizable, but laughing as they posed in front of an army vehicle someone had rolled on a desert road and they were now expected to fix. Quickly.

A sudden thought hit her. Silly, she supposed, but she spoke anyway. "That picture Eddie sent to me, of the two of you in front of a crashed Jeep or whatever it was…"

"Yeah?"

"Who crashed it?"

His brows shot up, and a split second later one corner of his mouth twitched. "Not Lyden, if that's what you're asking."

She was startled he'd read her thoughts. "I was just wondering."

"Nah, it was some visiting major who insisted on driving. He lost it barely a mile out of the gate." He grimaced then. "Of course, Eddie and I had to go retrieve the thing, and limp it back to camp."

"Should have made him sit and wait."

"A mere 91B make a major wait?"

She knew that was the number for the occupational specialty of Wheeled Vehicle Mechanic. She'd done a lot of research after Eddie had enlisted. And she used some of it now. "Could've been worse. You could have been a 91A."

The brows rose again. Then he chuckled and said, "Tanks, but no thanks."

Her throat tightened anew almost unbearably, as he used the joke Eddie often had.

"Sorry," he muttered, looking away. "Didn't mean to—"

"Don't. It's all right. Yes, it hurts, but… I treasure those little flashes of my brother."

Emily's churning thoughts kept her awake much of that night after she'd dropped Jordan and Cutter off at the camp. From Jordan's haunted words as he knelt at the grave to the slight laugh as he used the phrase she'd heard from Eddie, it all swirled around in her brain, refusing to release her into the sleep she needed.

So now she was facing a day in her office, trying to keep up her usual pace and not succeeding very well. Of course, being interrupted for decisions on things her father would usually handle didn't help any, and more than once she caught herself wishing he was here, only to immediately retract the wish when she remembered what she would have to tell him when he was.

Thankfully Dad's assistant, Rahul, was there, and he quickly picked up that she was working at a bit of a deficit this morning. For the three things that needed decisions or approval right now, he brought the research and her father's notes and laid it all out for her.

When she was done she looked at him and said, heartfelt, "You truly are the conqueror of all miseries, Rahul."

He grinned at her. One day shortly after he'd started at Bishop, she'd complimented him on a well-done but nitpicky task. He'd only nodded, but said, "It's in my name." That had made her look up the name's meaning, which had then made her laugh and remember it.

When he reappeared in her doorway a couple of hours later, she was afraid he'd found something she'd missed or forgotten to sign. But instead he nodded back over his shoulder.

"Somebody was here looking for your dad. Nobody I know. He said it's personal, not business."

Her mind raced as she closed out the file she'd been working on, pushed the keyboard out of the way and stood up. "Was here? He's gone?" Rahul nodded. "What did you tell him?"

"That Mr. Bishop's out of town. That's all."

"Did he give you a name?"

"He gave me this," Rahul said, holding out a business card. He studied her for a second before adding, "He didn't ask and I didn't mention you, because I sense something's wrong. You were really on edge yesterday, and you still are."

"Bless your insight again," she said as she took the card.

"You've both been so good to me, and my family. Beyond good. If there's anything I can do, you have only to ask."

And that was the kind of place her father had built, she thought as he left and she stared down at the card. The name on it was not one she recognized. But she didn't know the names of all the lawyers Bishop Tool came in contact with; that was her father's bailiwick. All she knew for certain was that there was no legal action pending at the moment, either by or against them.

She went back to her computer and did a quick search of their records to make sure it wasn't someone they had other business dealings with. It came up blank. She ran the name on the card and found the man was a senior partner at a fairly large firm in the city.

She tapped the card on her keyboard for a moment, thinking. Wondering. Normally, she would just text her father and ask. Or wait and see if the lawyer came back after her father returned. Or call him herself and find out what the visit had been about.

But there was nothing normal about now. Especially since there was probably no one in the state who had more lawyers on the payroll than the Lydens.

Especially since the one most likely to pay the price for any wrong assumptions she made was Jordan.

She tapped the business card once more, then reached for her purse on the shelf behind her desk. She pulled out the Foxworth phone.

# Chapter 19

It took Jordan a moment to react when he heard and felt the unfamiliar buzz.

He'd been standing next to Sarge's truck, grabbing a bottle of water against the heat when it happened. Cutter nudged his pocket, and he suddenly realized it was the Foxworth phone Quinn had given him. His personal phone, left in Sarge's truck at the moment, was pretty much bare bones, since nobody outside the camp called or texted him except the occasional reach out from other guys he'd served with. No one else had the number.

Except Emily.

She'd asked for it yesterday when they'd been at Foxworth. "Just in case," she'd said, as if she were assuring him it wasn't for any other reason.

*Like the reason you wish it was?*

He gave a sharp shake of his head and pulled the Foxworth phone out of his jeans pocket. Quinn had told them the phones were designed in-house to have the comms app, as he'd called it, open automatically any time a message was sent. And it clearly worked, because the text that had signaled was already on screen.

From Emily.

He tried to ignore the little kick of his pulse at her name and read her message about the lawyer who'd shown up at work.

I don't know if it has anything to do with this, but there's nothing going on here that would precipitate this visit, so just throwing it out there.

Even as he read it the phone buzzed again, with an answer from Hayley.

Good call. It's best we know everything, whether related or not. We'll do some research on our end. Jordan, you copying this?

It took him a moment to call up the virtual keyboard and type out, Got it.

Will advise, Hayley sent.

Jordan waited, watching the screen. But nothing new appeared, and when he realized he'd been hoping Emily would say something else—something more personal—he shoved the phone back in his pocket in irritation at himself. As if she would use the Foxworth phone for that.

As if she had anything more personal to say to him in the first place. This was about Eddie, and it should stay that way. *Would* stay that way, he ordered himself firmly.

He was back at the camp, hungry, pondering dinner and wondering if he could get away with just a peanut butter sandwich, when the phone buzzed again. This time it was Hayley.

A small bit of news. Meet at our HQ tonight, 6ish? We'll cook.

He wondered if she meant the steak emoji she added literally. Just the thought made his stomach growl. He glanced at his battered watch. Just enough time to clean up and change shirts; they'd finished the clearing job today, thanks to an early start. And since he'd been awake before dawn anyway, he'd been glad to have had something constructive to do.

Of course, he was going to have to figure out how to get there. It would take him until after six to pull up stakes here and drive the van. He could bike it, but on this warm evening it would likely defeat the purpose of the shower—he'd be as sweaty as he was now by the time he got there. Maybe he could—

The phone buzzed again. He pulled it out.

Pick you and Cutter up in an hour?

Emily.

He had to double-check to convince himself. Realized he was smiling goofily at the screen, while she was no doubt waiting for a response.

He quickly sent back, Thanks.

*Can't wait. Looking forward to it. It'll be good to see you. I've missed you.*

He stopped himself from sending all the words, all the hackneyed phrases that were popping into his head. Barely.

See you then.

And that was it. Short and not so sweet. Businesslike.
*Grab a clue, Crockett. That's what this is to her. It's all about Eddie for her, and it should be for you, too.*

He was not at all happy with how hard it was to focus on his best friend, because of the distraction of that best friend's sister.

Emily was still bent down to pet Cutter, who had been outside the camper van and had romped over to give her a happy greeting, when Sarge walked by.

"I lock the gate at midnight," he said cheerfully.

She straightened and looked at the usually rather crusty old man she'd come to like despite his gruff demeanor. "So that's Jordan's curfew?"

The older man grinned at her, all grumpiness vanished. "Just sayin', get him back by midnight or keep him until morning."

She was very relieved that the man kept walking, because she was certain her cheeks were the color of the cherries she'd bought last week. How could they not be, at the parade of images that raced through her mind at the thought of keeping him, and how they might fill the time until morning.

She thought of last week. Last week, when she'd been keeping herself deeply focused on her work so she barely had time to think about anything else. Last week, when that concentration made her think she'd been making progress in her grieving. Last week, when she'd thought her brother had been killed by the enemy.

Last week, before she'd ever met Jordan Crockett.

Her whole life had been turned upside down yet again, but this time in a totally different way.

"Hey."

The man in question stepped down from the camper, running one hand through what appeared to be damp hair. She knew he'd been out with the crew to finish that clearing job, in the August heat, so he must have just grabbed a shower. And that realization brought back that flood of thoughts that made her flush all over again.

"Hi," she said, bending to give Cutter a final pat, but in truth to hide her face until it felt less hot. "He just stays, when you let him out?"

"Yeah. Crazy, huh? But Hayley said he knows I'm his job, so he won't go far. And if he ever does, it's for good reason."

She straightened, feeling more in control now. "He's... remarkable. Foxworth is remarkable."

"I didn't think people like them really existed anymore."

"Talk about taking tragedy and building something good out of it," she said. Then sighed. "The saddest part is that tragedy was part of the same battle that put you and Eddie in harm's way, all these years later."

"Does make you wonder if it will ever end," he said.

She had often wondered exactly that, and that he clearly had, too, made her feel...something. As if they were in sync.

She told herself she was just looking for things that made her other imaginings more reasonable, and in businesslike tones asked if he was ready to go. He only nodded, and she turned to Cutter.

"Ready, boy? Want to go see your people?"

The dog hopped eagerly into the back seat, as if he'd

understood where they were going. And when they arrived and Jordan got out and opened the back door for him, the animal raced for the front door and batted it open. Then he turned and looked back at them.

Emily laughed. "He looks as if he's wondering why we aren't running, too."

"Maybe it really is steak for dinner and he knows it," Jordan suggested, making her laugh again. In fact, she'd laughed more since he—and Cutter—had come into her life than she had since the day they'd gotten the news about Eddie.

"I'm not sure anything about that dog would surprise me," she said as they walked, not ran, toward the door the dog had now vanished through.

Jordan gave her a sideways glance, then looked away. And after a couple of silent steps he said, very quietly, "He's something, all right. He really seems to sense when…you need an anchor. When your brain's getting out of control with thoughts."

She knew what he meant, that it was him who needed that anchor, that base. And she understood; her own thoughts had careened crazily in the last week. In no small part thanks to the man beside her.

"Petting him when I'm upset or wound up is the most amazing feeling," she said as they reached the door.

His mouth twisted slightly. "Which I'm guessing is pretty much all the time since you got that letter?"

She paused in the doorway as he held it open for her. "Yes," she admitted. And then, to herself, she admitted "wound up" was definitely the term for how she'd felt since she'd met him. And seen everything her brother had seen in him.

"That letter," she began. He didn't speak, just looked

at her warily. "Or rather," she went on, "the stamp on that letter…" She didn't have to ask, the answer showed in the way he rather shyly looked away. "You picked it on purpose, didn't you. The kingfisher."

He gave a half shrug. "Eddie said it was your favorite, so when I saw it there in the post office…" He looked back at her with a wry smile. "It comes in a sheet of birds, but I only wanted that one. They don't normally do that, but the guy working the counter was a vet, so he did it for me when I told him what it was for."

A letter to the sister of a fallen brother in arms. She couldn't describe how that made her feel. All she could think of was how Eddie would feel.

*I wonder what he would say about what I'm feeling…*

Would he approve? What would Eddie think about his sister falling for his best friend?

Her breath caught. She'd never quite put it into those words before, not even in her thoughts. But now that she had, she could no long pretend she wasn't falling for him. The question was, was it because he was Eddie's best friend, and it somehow made her feel closer to the brother she'd lost, or was it his undeniably attractive, sexy self?

At this point, she wasn't sure the why mattered. Later, maybe, when she was alone and could think straight, something that seemed impossible for her when she was with him.

When she was with him, she wasn't sure she was thinking at all.

# Chapter 20

"Info first, or food?" Quinn asked.

Jordan eyed the luscious-looking steaks on the platter. "Simultaneous?" he suggested hopefully.

That got him a grin from the former Ranger, a smile from Hayley and a laugh from Emily. He sensed that laughs were rare for her these days, and so he treasured every time he managed to make it happen.

Quinn looked at Emily. "How do you like your steak?"

Jordan waited for it. She delivered. "Warm? Barely."

At Quinn's sudden grin Jordan laughed. "She's a woman after my own heart," he said.

She turned her head, and those blue eyes the color of the dawn he'd watched this morning, thinking of her the whole time, gazed back at him steadily. "You noticed, huh?"

Her voice was light, teasing, but those eyes were anything but. And for a moment he couldn't think of a single word to say. Couldn't think, period. He managed an awkward smile, then turned away. He stood watching Quinn skillfully grill the meat on the barbecue out on the patio, thankful for the fact that Emily had turned to helping Hayley organize the side dishes and condiments. Feeling the need to be useful at least, he stood by to hand Quinn whatever implement he needed, from seasoning to tongs.

When they sat down at the small patio table, he focused on the indeed delicious beef. And was relieved when, after they'd finished eating, Quinn didn't waste any time on preliminaries.

"You should all have photos now of the man who visited your offices, Emily," he said briskly. "Gavin recognized him, although he said he doesn't know him personally."

"So he really is an attorney?" she asked.

Quinn smiled approvingly. "Always good to start your questioning at the foundation. Yes, he is actually an attorney. And the firm is indeed retained by 'the Lyden machine,' as Gavin called it."

"I checked our records," Emily said, as she reached for the phone they'd given her. Jordan did the same and was soon looking at a rather ordinary-looking man in a suit that looked expensive. Not that he'd know, since suits were hardly his attire of choice. "We've never done business with or dealt with him."

"That you know of," Jordan said wryly.

"Good point," Hayley put in. "Teague's research has shown they have tentacles all over, often hidden many layers deep."

"And all with the same goal—making the Lydens richer and more powerful," Quinn said.

"And harder to beat," Jordan said.

"Hard," Quinn agreed, "but not impossible."

He studied Jordan for a moment, and it was like a flashback moment, as if some superior officer was assessing whether or not he could do the job at hand. And he figured Quinn probably had guessed the truth, that the answer was no. And he found himself having to fight the urge to say it, even though it was the last thing he wanted to do, especially in front of Emily. Eddie had been his best friend, and he'd let him—and her—down.

*Be honest, that's why even looking at her like you do, like she's an oasis when you've been lost in the desert, is so wrong. Because you betrayed her when you betrayed him.*

He had to say it. Even though it would make her hate him. Which might be the best thing that could happen; if she hated him, she wouldn't give him those looks anymore, those looks that had him thinking things he had no business thinking.

He braced himself, then met Quinn's steady gaze and did it.

"I didn't stand up for Eddie when I should have. I told them the truth, and when it was clear they either didn't believe me or didn't care, I didn't fight them. I just wanted out of there. I was on my way home and that's all I could think about, not spending another day in that hellhole where he'd died."

"Understandable," Quinn said, surprising him. It must have shown, because the man smiled. "That's the kind of focus that earned you just about every honor and award a 91B can get."

He thought he was probably gaping but couldn't help it. He should have realized that an operation as big and successful as Foxworth apparently was didn't get there by not being thorough. And obviously that thoroughness had included a background check on him.

"It's not like they're combat medals," he said uncomfortably.

"But how many combat medals would have never been won if you hadn't been good enough to win those?" Quinn asked. "They make it pretty clear. If something needed to be fixed, they came to you. If something needed to be adapted to a new purpose, they came to you. And I gather if a piece of ruined equipment could be cannibalized to fix another piece of equipment, you were the one who could do it."

"That kind of record could get you just about any job in your field that you want," Hayley said.

"If you're asking why I'm not working—"

"I wasn't," Hayley said quickly. "After what happened you've got every reason—and right—to take some time to regain your balance. Besides, you are working. We know how highly thought of Mr. Rockford and his people are by their neighbors. We learned when we were helping him deal with his land use situation how the entire neighborhood appreciates all the work you do to keep things in shape."

"That's Sarge," Jordan said. "It's all his doing."

"A good staff sergeant is worth his weight in the gold of efficiency and jobs well done," Quinn said.

Jordan gave him a sideways look. "Who said that? General Washington?"

Quinn grinned. "Actually, I did. But thanks for the compliment."

"It's true," Jordan said. "Sarge is…the best."

"So you'd say he has good judgment?" Hayley asked. "That he isn't easily fooled?"

His brow furrowed. "Yeah, he does, he can see through bull—" He broke off, seeing what she'd done.

Hayley smiled back at him. "Yes, he can. And you've got his full-on seal of approval, Jordan."

He didn't know what to say, so instead sat staring down at his now empty plate.

"You two," Emily, who had been quiet throughout that last exchange, said, "are something else."

Jordan stole a glance at her. She was smiling widely at the Foxworths, and not for the first time he had the feeling he was missing something. How could she be smiling when he'd finally told the truth, that he hadn't stood up for Eddie when he could have? That he'd let Hart Lyden's lie stand, that he'd let the truth of how Eddie had died be buried along with him?

But then, she was smiling at the Foxworths, not at him. Because he didn't deserve anything more than her scorn, and now she knew it.

A buzz he now recognized sounded from Quinn's phone. He watched as Quinn picked it up, read a text and answered it. Then he set the phone down and looked across the table at Emily.

"That was Ty. He was able to backtrack and find that the Lyden operation has now checked with every military cemetery on record asking if your brother is buried there."

Jordan heard Emily's breath catch. He wanted to reach over and take her hand, but doubted now that she knew what he'd done—or rather, hadn't done—that she'd welcome it. Instead he picked up the glass of wine he'd only half finished; he meant it when he'd told her he didn't drink much, and when he did he went slow.

"Ty kept going—" Quinn's mouth twisted wryly for

a moment "—in ways I've learned not to question. The same IP address searched obituaries and the main on-line registry for grave sites for all the major cemeteries in this area."

"There's not much information online about the local site," Hayley said soothingly when Emily made a dis-tressed little sound. "It's administered by one of the big-ger companies, but since there are no new spaces to be sold, they don't give it much attention."

"I never thought I'd be glad funerals are a business and run that way." Emily's tone came as close to bitter-ness as he'd ever heard from her. He hated the sound of it.

"Exactly," Quinn agreed. "And there's no reason for the Lyden machine to think that a place that has no room for new burials would be something to pursue, at least not now. Eventually they may figure out how deep your family's connection to the area is, and then the possibil-ity may occur to them, but I think that will take a while."

"We didn't put any details of the burial in the obitu-ary," she said, sounding more thoughtful than pained at having to remember. "Eddie always said he never wanted a big funeral. I think because our mom's was so hard for him. So we kept it small and private."

"Then that's another layer for them to have to dig through," Quinn said with a nod.

Emily was silent for a moment, then asked tentatively, "What are the chances this is…innocent? That Lyden might actually just be looking for Eddie's grave to pay his respects? Or maybe even apologize to ease his con-science?"

Jordan nearly choked on the wine he'd been in the pro-cess of swallowing. He put his glass down so sharply the remaining wine sloshed almost to the rim.

"I'm guessing," Quinn said blandly, not quite smiling as he looked at him, "you're questioning the existence of Hartwell Lyden's conscience?"

Jordan cleared his throat, then said, "I don't think that guy's ever felt guilty about anything in his life."

"Why would he," Hayley said dryly, "when anything bad that happens is always someone else's fault?"

Emily let out an audible sigh. "That was silly of me, wasn't it." It wasn't really a question, and she just went on. "I should have realized he wouldn't feel badly about anything except potentially damaging his future prospects."

"It wasn't silly," Hayley said reassuringly. "Your mind just doesn't—thankfully—work that way. You're a kind, generous soul, and Hart Lyden is…"

"A self-absorbed, arrogant, pompous jackass?" Jordan finished it for her when she paused.

"Pretty much," Hayley agreed.

He was just thinking about how accurate Hayley's assessment of Emily was when Cutter jumped to his feet, letting out a rhythmic bark that seemed to repeat as he trotted over to the door.

"Teague," Quinn said, and Jordan suddenly remembered that first day here, when the sandy-haired former Marine had come down the stairs, greeted by the dog with that exact same bark.

And now Cutter was rising up to bat at the door control with his front paws, and the door began to swing open. A moment later, Teague came through, pausing to greet the animal with an affectionate scritch behind the ears.

Jordan glanced at Emily, who was watching the action with a bemused smile. And in that moment, there was nothing of pain or sorrow or grief in her eyes.

"Maybe you should get a dog," he said impulsively.

"I think I've underestimated how much company and comfort they can be." She gave him a sideways look. "Maybe we both need one."

He blinked. Did she mean two dogs, or one for…both of them? The thought of them together enough to take on a pet threatened to send his mind down that rabbit hole again, and he was thankful when Teague neared the table.

"Plenty of food left if you're hungry," Hayley offered.

Teague shook his head, grinning. "Laney's making lasagna tonight, and I plan on eating half of the whole batch. I only stopped rather than texted because it's on the way."

"Texted what?" Quinn asked.

Teague glanced at Emily before he spoke, which made Jordan sit upright, tension spiking abruptly. And when the Foxworth man went on, he knew it was justified.

"I did that canvas you asked for. And that lawyer showed up yesterday afternoon at Emily's house."

## Chapter 21

Emily tried to calm herself. It wasn't as if her address was hidden. There had never been any reason. She'd lived happily in the little cottage she'd bought eight years ago, proud that she'd been able to buy it at a relatively young age.

But given what she now knew, the thought that someone who worked for the Lydens had been there looking for her was beyond unsettling.

"Mrs. Fielding," she said suddenly, looking at Teague, who nodded in answer.

"He talked to her."

She was able to smile then. "I'll bet he regretted that."

Teague flashed a charming grin. "She's a tough one, all right. She told me she asked him what his business was, and why he thought he could go poking around a person's home when they weren't there and bother their neighbors with nosy questions."

Even Jordan smiled at that. But after a moment he asked Teague, "But she talked to you?"

Emily laughed. She picked up the phone, showing him the photo of the lawyer. "That's because the lawyer looks like this, and he—" she nodded at Teague "—looks like that. Mrs. Fielding is always appreciative of a good-looking man."

Teague looked slightly embarrassed and quickly shifted to reporting to Quinn. "He asked if Emily lived there, and mentioned her working at Bishop Tool. Asked about her hours, said he wanted to come back when she was home, just to speak to her." He glanced at Emily with a smile. "She told him if he already knew Emily worked at Bishop, why didn't he just go see her there?"

"That sounds like her," Emily said with a smile, then her brow furrowed. "And she does have a point. Why didn't he?"

"Maybe he wanted to find out if you'd had any personal visitors lately before he confronted you at work, in front of a lot of people," Hayley said, with a quick look at Jordan, who was staring down at his plate again, his jaw tensed.

"Oh!" Emily hadn't thought of that, but it certainly made sense out of the man's visit to her home.

"That was my guess," Teague said. "But your Mrs. Fielding is quite an effective bulwark, and she didn't tell him anything useful. Oh, and warned him she was home and watching most of the time."

"I take back the times I've been annoyed at that," Emily said. "In fact I may have to bake her a cake or cookies or something."

"Thanks, Teague," Quinn said. "Get on home for that lasagna. I'll keep you posted on developments."

"And give our love to Laney," Hayley added.

"Got some of my own to deliver first," Teague said with a wide grin before he turned on his heel and left in an obvious hurry.

"You'll have to forgive him," Hayley said with a laugh as the door swung shut behind him. "He and Laney just got married three months ago."

"I don't know," Quinn drawled out. "I feel the same way about you, and it's been over a year and a half since we got married."

That seemed to ease the tension, and Emily was fairly sure that had been at least part of the intent. The other part, of which she was utterly certain, was that the words were true. She didn't think she'd ever met a couple who radiated such…permanence.

She wasn't sure it had worked on Jordan, however. He still seemed as wound up as he'd been since the moment Teague had told them what he'd found out. And when they moved back to the great room, to sit in front of the fireplace that was unlit now in the height of summer, she thought he probably would be pacing if Cutter hadn't followed and gotten tangled up with his feet, practically forcing him to sit.

Next to her, Emily thought. Again. She remembered all the teasing about the dog's many skills.

"You need to shift your focus," Jordan said abruptly to Quinn, his voice flat. "I can take care of myself. You just make sure Emily is safe."

Quinn gave him a considering look, and Emily had the feeling there was approval in it. "I think we can manage both. It seems right now they're sticking with the cover story, of Lyden wanting to pay his respects."

"It plays well, to the public," Hayley said, and her tone was more than a little sour.

"And if he comes back, either to work or my home, I'll just tell him I haven't seen or heard from Jordan, that I don't know where he is. Maybe that I don't know him at all," Emily added thoughtfully. "Since we'd never met until now, they couldn't disprove that."

From where he sat beside her she could feel the tension practically radiating from him. "I don't want you dealing with anyone connected to them." Jordan's tone was adamant.

Emily was torn. She didn't take being told what she could or couldn't do outside of work very well. Yet at the same time she couldn't deny the vehemence in his voice, the protectiveness of his words, made her feel an odd sort of pleasure, down deep.

"Right now," Quinn said, his voice even more measured than usual, "they may suspect but clearly don't know for sure where you are, or if you've connected with Eddie's family. So they're playing it cautious. And if Emily suddenly disappears, or changes her routine, it will only add to their suspicions."

"That's why we give her a reason," Hayley said, glancing at Emily but then looking steadily at Jordan. "Her friend visiting from out of town. Her female friend."

Emily remembered what Hayley had said just before Rafe had arrived with the news that the Lydens had been looking for Eddie's grave.

"That's perfect," she agreed. "No one will suspect anything if…my schedule's a bit abnormal."

"And if they do," Quinn said, his tone a little too casual, "I'll be around, out of sight. Teague and Rafe will continue at the camp."

"I'd rather they helped watch out for Emily," Jordan said. "I told you, I can take—"

"Care of yourself, yes," Quinn said. "And under normal circumstances I wouldn't dispute that. But this is the Lyden family, and all bets are off."

Jordan frowned. A moment of rather strained silence passed before he said, "This can't go on forever."

"No," Quinn agreed. "But they've come up with a good cover. We're going to need some concrete evidence that what they're after is anything more than what they say it is."

"Maybe I should go knock on *their* door."

"Jordan, no," Emily exclaimed, reaching out to grab his hand.

He looked at her then, and she saw something she'd not seen in those distinctive hazel eyes before. Something her mind told her was the heat of anger, but her heart wanted to believe was a different kind of heat altogether.

"It's me they're after. If they find me, there's no reason for them to even look at you."

Out of the corner of her eye Emily saw Quinn start to speak, but oddly, Hayley stilled him with a touch to his arm.

"So you what, paint a target on your back and walk into their reach?"

"If it will keep them off you."

For a moment, just a moment amid this mess, she let herself believe he wanted to protect her for himself, not just in memory of her brother. "Thank you for that," she whispered. "But please, don't. I don't want to lose… Eddie's best friend, too."

Her mind supplied the words she's stopped herself from saying. *I don't want to lose you, before I ever re-*

*ally know you. Before I find out if you're feeling even a
tiny bit of what I'm feeling...*

Something changed in his eyes then, something that
made the green seem to deepen. Something that made
her think—or at least hope—that he did feel…something.
And the way his fingers curled around hers for a moment
made that hope a little stronger.

Her thoughts were cut off by Cutter, suddenly on his
feet and letting out that odd, rhythmic series of barks. A
moment later Rafe walked in the back door. Quinn looked
at him, and he shook his head as if to silently signal he
wasn't here with news.

"Just checking status," he said. Quinn nodded, then
turned back to them as Rafe went to the kitchen for coffee.

Before Quinn spoke, Emily had the thought that
maybe Hayley had stopped him before to enable them
to have that moment, whatever it had been. She certainly
seemed intuitive enough.

"I understand you want to keep them on you," the head
of Foxworth said quietly. "I'd do the same."

His gaze flicked for an instant to Hayley, and Emily's
breath caught. Obviously Quinn meant he'd do it for Hayley, but was he implying she was right, that Jordan would
do it for her? Not just for Eddie? He went on before she
could tumble down that particular rabbit hole.

"But given the scope and power of the Lyden machine,
I don't think we can assume that they would quit with
you. Because even though you were smart enough to not
leave an electronic trail of communication with Emily,
they do know she exists, and they would be fools not to
at least consider the possibility you somehow contacted
her with the truth."

Jordan grimaced. "And the fact that they're looking here now, instead of back home, says that they think I'm here, or at least coming here, to do it in person."

"A reasonable assumption," Quinn agreed.

"Anything from Ty on that truck?" Rafe asked, coming out from the kitchen with a coffee mug in hand and taking a seat in one of the big armchairs. Emily assumed he meant the one that had almost hit Jordan back in Missouri.

"Last report late yesterday, he'd made out all but one digit of the license plate, so it's been process of elimination now," Quinn answered. "I'd hoped to hear from him by now."

Even as he said it Quinn's phone, on the coffee table, buzzed.

"And right on cue," Hayley said with a grin.

Quinn picked it up and looked at the screen. He flicked a glance at Rafe that was so quick it would have been easy to miss had Emily not been looking at him. Then he tapped the screen a couple of times and the big flat-screen TV above the fireplace came to life. But the image that appeared wasn't a nerdy sort she would have expected the chief Foxworth IT and research guy to be, but instead a strikingly beautiful woman with long, dark hair that fell in thick waves to her shoulders, and eyes that seemed the same color as her lovely teal blouse.

"Charlie!" Hayley exclaimed in obvious surprise.

"Hey, sis," Quinn said, his tone a little wary.

Instinctively Emily looked at Rafe, wondering what the glance from Quinn had been about. The man's expression was unreadable as usual, but she noticed the hand that held his coffee had tightened around the ceramic mug. He wasn't even looking at the screen. And she had the strangest feeling he was fighting the urge—the need?—to get up and leave. A strong feeling. Given how little the man talked in the first place, it was odd how sure she was when he hadn't said a word now.

"Not even a hello, Mr. Crawford?" The woman's voice had taken on a strange tone, half teasing, half…angry? No. Fierce, maybe. And she suddenly remembered that this was the woman who had built the obviously substantial financial framework of Foxworth, apparently single-handedly.

Rafe's head came up, and his expression betrayed nothing. But his voice did; he sounded like some upper-crust guy being introduced at a society function, something she never would have guessed at. "Good evening, Ms. Foxworth. The same pleasure it always is."

It hadn't even been aimed at her, but Emily almost winced. *Wow, that was loaded.* The woman's gaze narrowed. Yes, *fierce* was definitely the word.

Hayley stepped in quickly, as if she'd had to referee this match—whatever it was—more than once. "Where's Ty?"

"Working on something big for your brother," the woman answered, focusing on her brother and sister-in-law as Rafe went back to studying his coffee. "Apparently there's chaos in California."

"When is there not?" Quinn asked dryly.

"Point taken."

"As you've no doubt guessed, this is Quinn's sister, Charlaine," Hayley said to Emily and Jordan, then introduced them in turn.

The woman nodded, then focused on Jordan. "We've located the truck that nearly hit you."

Jordan straightened. "That was fast."

"Ty did the heavy lifting, before Walker's mess of a

case hit." Walker must be Hayley's brother, Emily thought. "I just finished it off. Turns out the truck was stored in the same facility you were in, Jordan. The driver wasn't particularly cooperative, but we got there eventually, once I confronted him."

Rafe's head came up sharply. "In person? Alone?"

Even via the screen Emily could see the tension fairly snapping between them. There was definitely some history here, and it wasn't pleasant.

"You think I need the cavalry with me?" The snap in her voice now was undeniable. "Or maybe a sniper?"

"You're sniping pretty well on your own," Quinn said, a little snap in his voice as well. "Can we cut to the chase?"

Emily recognized the look on Quinn's sister's face then, because she'd worn it herself on occasion when Eddie had called her out for not knowing when to let something go. Charlie was back to businesslike tones when she spoke again. And her words made Emily shudder.

"Bottom line, the Lydens paid him to take Jordan out."

# Chapter 22

Jordan sat staring at the screen long after it had gone black, the beautiful woman vanishing. The Foxworths had gone outside, with an apparently reluctant Cutter, saying they would give Jordan a few minutes to process. Rafe had departed altogether, immediately after the screen had blacked out.

But Emily had stayed.

He hadn't realized until now how much he had still hoped this was all the result of an overactive imagination. That he'd never had much of one before—give him reality, a machine he could make work or a design he could figure out, that was enough—was something he'd tried to ignore. But this, added to what Foxworth had already learned, shattered what little was left of that hope. And he'd brought this down on Emily, who least deserved it.

He should never have written that letter. Should have let her go on believing the official version of how her brother had died. But he had done it. And he couldn't take it back, no matter how much he might want to.

"I'm sorry," he said, unable to meet Emily's gaze.

"Sorry? What on earth for?"

She sounded so astonished he looked up. Her expression matched her voice. "For bringing this down on you."

For a moment she just stared at him. Then with a slight shake of her head, she said, "As opposed to what, not telling me the truth? Letting me believe a lie about how Eddie died?"

"You would have been safer."

"I'd prefer the truth, thank you. Besides, you still would know. They would still be after you."

"But not you."

"You can't know that. Even if you hadn't come here, they'd suspect you might have told me."

He let out a long breath. He knew she was probably right. "Maybe," he admitted.

She got to her feet as if she couldn't stand being still any longer. Her hands moved and her fingers stretched out, as if she were having to work not to clench them into fists. When she spoke her voice was sharper, angrier, but clearly it wasn't aimed at him.

"It's obvious now that's who they are, the kind of people who believe everyone should be held accountable except them."

"Pretty much," he muttered.

"Well, that will be their downfall. Because they also believe everyone else is as self-centered and venal as they are. They can't even conceive that people like us, people like the Foxworths, are for real."

That "us" warmed him. Assuming she'd meant it as he

hoped she did. And despite it all he found himself smiling at her vehemence. She was a fighter, was Emily Bishop.

And then she smiled back at him, and he had to dig his nails into his palm to stop himself from reaching out and grabbing her. She came back and sat down beside him again, calmer now. She glanced up at the now dark flat-screen TV and said, "What do you suppose is going on with Rafe and Quinn's sister? He seemed awfully tense, especially when she said she'd confronted that driver."

Jordan swallowed tightly. "He sounded like I feel, thinking about you being in danger. Only I feel worse, because it's my fault."

She reached out and grabbed his hands. Held them tightly, almost urgently. And his pulse kicked into over-drive at her touch.

"It is not your fault, any more than Eddie dying was your fault." She said it with an intensity that calmed him a little. "This is no one's fault except that buffoon Hart-well Lyden and his horrible, evil family."

He couldn't help it, the tiniest of grins broke through. "Tell me how you really feel."

And in an instant her entire demeanor changed. She let go of his hands, to his regret, and said quietly, "You don't want to know that."

"Emily, I—"

The sound of the back door opening made him stop. He heard Cutter first, racing across the floor toward them. The dog came to a sudden halt before them, looking from him to Emily and then back again. He tilted his head as if he were assessing, then sat at their feet, looking up at them with what for all the world looked like impatience.

Quinn was sliding his phone back into his pocket as

he walked in from outside. His gaze was fixed on Jordan, and he stood up. Quinn fired a question at him.

"Did you know that someone made an offer to buy the camp property last week?"

He blinked. "Yeah, Sarge told me. Said he turned it down, even though it was a lot."

"The offer was double the assessed value," Quinn confirmed. "Seven figures' worth."

Jordan's eyes widened. "I didn't realize it was that much. That could have set them up for life."

"If he was the type who cared more about that," Quinn said. "But that's not the interesting part."

*Uh-oh.* He'd already gathered that when Quinn Foxworth said something was interesting, it probably meant challenging...or dangerous.

"What is?" he asked warily.

"Ty just called. He did a lot of the groundwork on that original encampment case, so he was familiar. He found that large amount curious and did some digging. Turns out that the company that made the offer is owned by a larger company owned by a conglomerate with several investors. The controlling interest is the Lyden family."

"They tried to buy the camp?" Emily asked.

"So it seems."

"But why? Jordan only got there last week. How could they know he was there already?"

"They may not. Ty went a little deeper and found a few other veteran-related operations they were connected to, either by donations or having people get involved."

"And I'm sure," Jordan said wryly, "they play up that it's because their hero son is a vet."

"Exactly," Quinn said. "But that made Ty wonder why

they only started all this in the last two weeks, when he's been out for a couple of months. So he dug even deeper."

"Your Ty is a bulldog," Emily said.

"He is," Quinn said with a smile. "Although he prefers to think of himself as a finely tuned machine." He looked at Jordan. "Something I'm sure you can appreciate."

"I can," Jordan agreed. "So what did he find down that rabbit hole?"

"That the same conglomerate, with the majority interest held by the Lydens, is doing the same thing in your hometown."

He blinked. "St. Louis? They're getting involved in vet organizations there, too?"

"Yes," Quinn said. "And most interesting of all, as far as Ty could find—and believe me, he finds everything— they're involved in only those two places."

"They're planting people," Emily exclaimed. "And buying influence, for information on Jordan."

Quinn nodded. "That's our guess."

Jordan felt faintly nauseous at this proof of the size of the monster he'd brought down on Emily. "I never should have come here. They probably would have left you alone, they wouldn't have—"

"You can't know that," Emily said, cutting him off. "And I'm getting tired of you blaming yourself for…well, everything. So stop."

He only wished it were that easy.

"She's right," Hayley said, the first thing she'd said since coming back inside. "The Lydens are nothing if not thorough, especially in anticipating opposition of any kind. Their favored tactic is to destroy an opponent's options before the battle even begins, so they would have absolutely no qualms about going after all of Eddie's family."

"I wish them luck going up against my dad," Emily said, no small amount of pride in her voice. Jordan had heard the same thing from Eddie, often, that his old man was the toughest of tough old birds. It always made him feel a twinge, as he wondered what it must be like to have a father like that. To have had a father, period.

"Am I correct in thinking you haven't told your father about any of this yet?" Hayley asked Emily.

"You're right, I haven't," she answered. "He's out of town until a week from Friday. I wanted to wait until he was home to do it." Her brow furrowed. "You don't think he's in any danger, do you?"

"The Lydens are ruthless, but not stupid. Your family has some standing in the county."

"Unlike just another disturbed veteran," Jordan said sourly.

"Unfortunately true," Quinn said. "And the number of veteran suicides gives them a lot of cover."

"But I don't think they'd do anything rash until they're sure your family is a threat," Hayley said.

"You mean until they're sure we know the truth about their good-for-nothing coward of a son?" Emily said harshly.

"Exactly," Quinn said. "They also will have priorities. And Jordan is priority one."

"So if they're only looking here and in St. Louis, I should leave," he said, hating the thought even as he said it. "Go somewhere they'd never expect, somewhere they wouldn't look."

"It's an idea," Quinn said, his tone neutral. "Depends on what the goal is."

"Staying alive is pretty close to the top of the list," Jordan said with a grimace. Once it would have been the top of the list, but not now.

"A given," Quinn said.

"But keeping Emily safe takes the top spot, and maybe a couple more under that."

"Also a given." Quinn said it smoothly, as if he'd expected no less. "So the real question is, do you want to let the Lydens get away with it?"

He swallowed. Hard. "You really think you can take them down?"

"Not without your help. You're the key, Jordan. Sucks, but you are. So in the end it's your decision."

"But keep in mind," Hayley said, "that as long as they're hunting you, they'll also be keeping an eye on Emily and her father. Because they'll be thinking you could reach out to them with the truth at any moment."

That nausea came back, because he knew it was true.

"And before you blame this all on yourself," Quinn added, "just realize that this would likely have happened even if you hadn't written that letter. In the Lyden's world, information is ammunition, and they won't believe that anyone would have it and not use it."

"Because they would," Emily said.

"It's the nature of the beast," Quinn agreed. He looked back at Jordan. "So you have a choice to make."

He'd known this was coming since the moment he'd agreed to let them start this. Knew that sooner or later he was going to have to make a final decision. He'd been hoping it would be a little longer, but Foxworth obviously wasted no time. And now he was up against it. They'd said all along it was his call, and he didn't doubt they meant it; they'd let him walk away if he insisted. But if he did, Emily...

He couldn't even finish the thought. "A choice," he muttered.

"Yes," Quinn said. "Option one, a delaying action, trying to vanish, hoping they believe you'll never talk and hence give up."

Even as the man said it, Jordan could tell Quinn didn't believe it would happen that way. When it came down to it, neither did he. It was much more likely they'd find him and, as the saying went, suicide him.

*You say a damned word about this and I'll see you dead, Crockett. Nobody will believe you, not against me.*

Hart Lyden's words immediately after he'd shot Eddie rose up from the deep place in his mind where he'd buried them. And now that he knew more about the guy's family, he knew he'd meant them and had the tools to carry out the threat. Or rather, his very wealthy and influential family did.

"And option two?" he finally asked.

"Pick your battleground, here and now, with Foxworth at your back."

"And me beside you, every step of the way," Emily said softly.

Jordan wasn't sure which statement convinced him, but he suspected it was hers. Or simply she herself.

He studied Quinn for a moment, knowing with deep certainty what he would do were their positions reversed. Or Teague, or Rafe. He thought of Emily's father, and what Eddie had told him about the man. He thought about Sarge, and the guys at the camp, and what they'd said, even though he was a newcomer.

But most of all he thought of Emily. There was no way

he could leave her to face this alone. No way he could walk away and leave her in danger.

He pulled together every bit of nerve he had. And gave the only answer he could.

"Then bring it."

# Chapter 23

"You do what you gotta do, son," Sarge said. "We'll hold the fort here. And if you manage to take down or even damage those arrogant jerks, we'll throw the biggest celebration you've ever seen."

Jordan nodded. All it had taken was for him to explain it was all about another vet who hadn't come home, and the man was on board.

"I'll save the spot for you, in case you need it back," Sarge added as they broke down and stowed what gear was outside the camper van and loaded it up. And both of them laughed as Cutter began carrying things from the firepit to the door of the van, as if he knew.

"If someone needs the spot," he began, but Sarge shook his head.

"Got another one open, if necessary."

When they were done and the van was ready to roll, he turned to face the man who had become a great deal more than just his landlord. "Sarge," he began, but the man waved him off gruffly.

"Don't go getting all syrupy on me now. Just get it done, boy."

For a moment Jordan just looked at the older man who had done so much to make him, and others, feel almost stable again. And then he did something he hadn't done since he'd taken off the uniform for the last time. He drew himself up and snapped his right hand to his forehead in a salute.

"Yes, sir," he said crisply.

Sarge's mouth curved into the slightest of smiles. Then he nodded. "Keep me posted. And be careful. You're back in a war zone, son, and those folks are as slimy as any enemy you've ever encountered."

"I will."

As he was steering slowly down the long access road—Cutter in the passenger seat and secured with the harness Hayley had given him after her dog had announced he was staying—he looked anew at the campground. At the differing types of setups at each campsite, from RVs to tents, but all with one thing in common. They all held to Sarge's high standards. He was a good man, doing a good thing here.

About three minutes after he'd pulled out onto the road, Cutter let out that sort of singsong bark of his that Jordan had heard before. The one he used to announce the approach of Rafe Crawford. Belatedly, he took a long look in the rearview mirror and realized the vehicle approaching from some distance behind him was a now familiar silver coupe, a model that was so ubiquitous it would normally fade into the background. Which he supposed was the point.

Even as he recognized the car the Foxworth phone buzzed, and he reached up to the console where he'd placed it and tapped the flashing red button.

"Yeah, it's me."

He found himself smiling at Rafe's wording. "So Cutter told me. Hey, at least no more nights spent hiding in the woods on overwatch."

"Didn't mind."

"Tell me, were you up the hill beyond the well house?"

"Cutter again?" He sounded amused this time.

"Yeah. He kept looking that way."

"He has great situational awareness."

Jordan was still chuckling over all the amazing attributes the Foxworth people gave to this dog when the animal yipped politely and he realized he needed to slow down for the turn onto the drive that led to their headquarters.

"I should let you drive, dog," he muttered as he made the turn.

The Foxworth phone flashed red. "Head for the hangar," came Rafe's voice. "Quinn's in the office, but he's already got the door open for you."

"Copy," he said, and kept going past the headquarters building.

He went carefully, but once he got close enough he saw that the rolled-up door gave him plenty of room. He looked around at the area in front of the hangar, decided there was enough room for the maneuver and turned the van to back into the empty space. He went slowly, very aware of what was already parked next to the open space—the helicopter he'd seen the first day he'd come here. He brought his home on wheels to a stop, set the parking brake just in case and glanced over at it. It was black and sleek, gleaming and obviously in tip-top shape. Except…

His gaze fastened on something on one of the polished side panels. He slid out of the driver's seat, staring, unable to quite believe what he was seeing. But he'd seen it too often before. Hell, he'd repaired it too often before.

A bullet hole.

He stood there, in this hangar with tools and machinery he was familiar with, had worked with so often, staring at a bullet hole in a helicopter, as he had also done so many times before. And for a moment, a brief flash of time, he was back there, hearing enemy fire in the distance as he scrambled to get a piece of equipment moving again, airborne again, so they could rejoin the fray.

"Bring back memories?"

Rafe's deep, rough voice came from so close behind him he almost jumped. Cutter was beside him now, telling him how lost he'd been for that moment since Rafe had obviously unharnessed the dog and he hadn't even realized. He reached down, automatically now, and stroked the dog's head. And the calmness seemed to feed in through his fingers on the soft fur yet again.

"Yeah," he muttered. Then he remembered who he was talking to. "Nothing like yours, I'm sure."

"Different doesn't make it pleasant."

Jordan hesitated, then said, "I didn't get the idea Foxworth couldn't afford to have that fixed."

Rafe laughed. It was more rough than his voice had been, as if rustier, less used. "Quinn won't have it. We just contain it, so nothing rusts out or does further damage."

Jordan's brow furrowed. "Why?"

"It's a souvenir. For Quinn. It happened on the job where he met Hayley."

Jordan looked back at the damage, seeing now it was carefully sealed. "She was in trouble?"

"Innocent bystander. But this guy," Rafe said, nodding toward the dog, "dragged her right into the middle of it all." The tall, rangy man's mouth quirked. "We ended up sort of kidnapping her, to protect the client."

Jordan blinked. Thought of the bond between Quinn and Hayley, so obvious, so fierce even he could feel it. "And that became…"

"What they are now. Unbreakable."

As he said it, Rafe's attention shifted, looking toward the still open hangar door. Jordan turned to look and saw Quinn approaching. He didn't bother with greetings—except for Cutter, who got a scratch behind the ears—but just nodded at them both.

"Get what you want to hand and bring it inside," he said to Jordan. "We'll get you set up. And there's room in the fridge inside if you've got any perishables you need to put in there."

Jordan voiced the concern that had been hovering over all of this craziness since he'd decided to forge full speed ahead on this. "What about Emily?"

"Hayley's on that. She's already at Bishop Tool. And Teague's in the area for backup if necessary."

"But what if—"

"If it becomes necessary, we'll move her, too. We'll keep her safe, Jordan."

It was as close to a guarantee as you could get in life, and given by a man Jordan believed could back it up. He gave the bullet hole a last glance, thinking of how Quinn would feel if anything ever happened to Hayley. And he knew the man understood.

But his jaw was still tight as he went back into the van

and began to gather some belongings. It wasn't until he opened the small, under-counter refrigerator and took out the leftover pizza from the night after they'd visited Eddie's grave that it hit him that he'd just equated his feelings for Emily with Quinn's for his wife.

"You should be very proud," Hayley said.

"We are," Emily answered. She'd just given Hayley the grand tour of Bishop Tool, from the production building to the offices to the workshop where they—including her—tested the tools before they were marketed. "It's been a little tough lately, keeping up with demand. A lot of people seemed to have suddenly discovered the concept of do-it-yourself."

Hayley laughed. "So, your father's the head of the company?"

She nodded. "His grandfather founded it, seventy-five years ago. It's been Bishop run ever since." She sighed. "Eddie was supposed to take over that aspect in ten years or so, when Dad retired. I'd be awful at it, all the sales stuff he has to do. I'm great at tracking stuff, doing the numbers, the development plans and balance sheets, but I hate selling."

She shook off the too-familiar mood that threatened and continued the tour of the workshop—quiet at the moment—and the various projects that were underway. Each was used to demonstrate the efficiency and effectiveness of everything from sanders to drills, nail guns to saws, and shop vacs to clean up the mess afterward, including one her father—who had never left his design instincts behind—was working on to separate out any metals that might be picked up from the rest of the shop debris.

Hayley looked around the shop, at the things in different stages of completion, at the tools hanging neatly on racks or sitting on shelves built by them, then looked at Emily. "I'd think Jordan would feel quite at home here."

Emily stared at the table they'd been using to fine-tune their new, lightweight sander. Had the woman guessed? Was she giving off some kind of lovesick vibe or something? Or had she truly been that obvious?

"Eddie used to say that," she said, without looking at her. "That the smartest thing Dad could do was hire Jordan when he got out."

"Sounds like a solution that would work on more than one level, once we get this all sorted out."

She did look at Hayley then. "I have to believe that will happen."

"It will. Quinn's got his teeth into this now. This is exactly the kind of case he built Foxworth to take on. Failure is not in his lexicon."

Emily felt a tug of longing deep inside, a longing to have what this woman had, the kind of love that fairly radiated from her, and equally from the tough, capable man she'd married. What it must feel like, to have a man like that so obviously adore you...

The thought that she might never know was painful.

The thought that she might never know because the only man she'd ever wanted it with might be killed before this was over was unbearable.

# Chapter 24

Emily had introduced Hayley to the staff as they'd agreed, as a visiting friend, not mentioning that she lived less than ten miles away. All of the Bishop people had welcomed her kindly, with the good cheer that her father worked so hard to maintain.

"You've built a good thing here," Hayley said as they entered Emily's office. "That's a happy and fulfilled bunch out there."

"My father has made sure all our people know how valued they are." Emily closed the door behind them, and for the moment the façade dropped. "We have a good, solid team here now, and they go the extra mile for us because they know we will for them, too."

"That's the foundation of Foxworth as well," Hayley said approvingly. "Quinn made sure of that from the beginning."

After Hayley had taken the seat in front of the clut-

tered—she had been a bit distracted of late, after all—
desk, Emily chose to sit in the chair opposite her rather
than her work chair. She saw Hayley's gaze fasten on the
photograph on the wall behind her. She didn't have to look
herself. The image lived in her mind daily. Dad, her and
Eddie, when she'd been fifteen and her brother twelve. It
had been taken out in front of this building, when Dad had
brought them in for a visit. Mom had been gone three years
by then, and they'd finally reached some sort of balance.

Emily saw the genuine sadness in Hayley's expression. Knew she understood, in the way someone who
had never suffered true loss could not. Then she looked
back at Emily and said softly, "Do you want to talk about
Jordan? Your feelings for him?"

Caught off guard, she didn't try to deny it. "Is it that
obvious?"

"Only because I've had a lot of practice recognizing
it, thanks to Cutter."

She blinked. "Cutter?"

"Teague wasn't really joking when he called him our
resident matchmaker. He has an uncanny instinct about
people who belong together."

She didn't know what to say to that. The dog was
clearly very, very clever, and obviously had been well
trained somewhere along the line. He also had a knack
for understanding what was going on around him, so who
was she to say he couldn't do this as well?

*Of course it's probably easy for him when someone's
bleeding it all over, like you are.*

She remembered Hayley's look of sadness, and her
thought that this woman understood. She might never
have known Eddie, or the closeness of their relationship—both as brother and sister and with Emily acting

as his surrogate mother—but she understood. Understood like any of her friends wouldn't.

It was then that Emily decided to take the chance.

"I do…have feelings for Jordan. But how do I know if it's real? Maybe it's just that he was close to my brother, and now that he's gone…"

"So you think it's your grief coloring your emotions?"

"Exactly." Emily felt a rush of relief. She did understand, she really did. And that certainty opened up the floodgates. "I'm afraid it's all crazy, that I'm just not thinking straight, because of losing Eddie. That it's all tangled up with that. That it's not really real, it's just…reaction."

"I understand that. Because I've been there. Thinking what I was feeling was just a need to get out from under the grief."

Emily's eyes widened slightly. "Yes. Yes, that's exactly how I feel."

Hayley smiled, in that way she had that was almost as soothing as petting Cutter. "Let me tell you a bit of Quinn's and my history. He landed—literally—in my life shortly after my mother died. We'd lost my father years before, so she was…the last of my little family. I was awash in grief, drowning in it, when two things happened. One, Cutter showed up on my doorstep, needing a new home. And not long after that, he led—or make that *dragged*—me to Quinn."

"That matchmaker thing?"

Hayley's smile widened as she nodded. "My first experience with it. Anyway, when things began between Quinn and me, I felt the same way you do, half-certain my feelings were just a desperate effort to cast aside that grief, to feel good, hopeful, for the first time since she'd died."

"But they obviously weren't."

This time Hayley gave her a smile so wide some of the pressure she was feeling lifted. "No, they weren't. And it was Cutter who helped me believe that. He was the one who trusted Quinn first, the one who kept trying to push us together."

"Like he…" She stopped, afraid she was being silly.

But Hayley nodded. "Just like he's doing with you and Jordan."

Emily shook her head slowly. "It's just… I'm so surprised. I expected to feel…"

"Sisterly?" Hayley suggested.

"Yes, since I knew Eddie thought of him as a brother."

"So Eddie would approve."

For a moment Emily just stared at her. She hadn't thought of it like that. All this had happened so quickly, over just a few days, and her reaction to her brother's best friend had been so unexpected, she hadn't really processed it all.

Now, as if triggered by Hayley's words, a memory shot through her mind. Of her brother saying, with emphasis, "Emmie, you're going to love him when you meet him."

She'd assumed he'd meant it in the same way she did, that she'd like the man in that sisterly way. But now… had Eddie somehow known? Had he known her so well he could anticipate how she would react to Jordan?

Had he, in advance, given Jordan his stamp of approval?

"Emily?"

Hayley's soft voice nudged her out of her shock. "I was just remembering something Eddie said to me during a phone call. About Jordan. Then, I just thought he was saying I'd love his friend, in that casual way people talk, but now…"

"I'd say your brother knew you well. Well enough to predict."

Something about the way Hayley was looking at her, with that steady gaze, as if she were seeing the big picture in a way few did, made her believe the words she spoke. And she couldn't deny that Eddie had known her well. Better than anyone, even their father. Sometimes especially their father, she added silently, remembering some of the crazier things they'd gotten up to in their youth that to this day Dad didn't know about.

*You always did get me, Eddie.*

The rest of the day was at least a distraction, as she had some things she'd neglected since this had begun. To her surprise Hayley was a great help, and was not above doing some of the grunt work that enabled her to catch up. Who'd have ever thought someone assigned as a bodyguard would offer to tackle boring inventory work? But then, the Foxworths were clearly very special people.

She felt a kick of pride, a welcome change amid the chaos of late, when she later welcomed Hayley to her little cottage. It was picturesque, surrounded on three sides by tall trees, and closed in by a garden full of summer flowers that bounded a curving stone walkway to a covered front porch. Hayley complimented all the things she loved most, which made Emily feel even better.

"I noticed your magnolia tree by the patio," she said as they stood beside her own, more established edition of the small, shapely tree.

"Yes, I just love the scent of the flowers and hoped it would do just what it has—make it even nicer out there. One of our clients planted it for us when he was staying there." She gave Emily a considering look. "He was in a situation not unlike Jordan's, as far as being hunted."

"And where is he now?"

Hayley smiled, as if she'd hoped Emily would ask. "Actually, he's running an outreach program for us, and doing a great job."

"And the threat?"

"Eliminated. And we'll do the same for Jordan, Emily. Quinn, Rafe and Teague are all former military, and they feel strongly about this case. They'll go to the wall and beyond for him."

The phone Foxworth had given her buzzed, although it sounded different this time. She realized as she pulled it out it was because Hayley's had buzzed at the same time. She assumed they were getting the same message.

Still clear. An idea to discuss. Meet at HQ in an hour.

She saw Hayley tapping out an answer, and a moment later she read, We'll bring food.

The emoji of a slice of pizza that appeared in response almost made Emily laugh out loud. Foxworth was so impressive, so powerful, able to deal with things as big as taking out a sitting governor, but seeing that everyday symbol reminded her they were still people. But people with heart and determination, and a need to do good that made her gladder than ever that they were on their side.

*Their* side. Her and Jordan's side.

She did like the sound of that.

And after her talk with Hayley, after the other woman's sweet, calming story of her own journey through grief to love, for the first time she thought it might be possible.

She just had to convince Jordan to give them a chance.

# Chapter 25

"No!" Emily almost yelped. "Are you crazy?"

"It's been said," Quinn answered, completely unruffled.

Jordan admired the man's cool. If she'd said that to him that way, he'd have winced. Of course, Quinn wasn't half in love with her.

*You sure it's only half?*

"He's already got a target on his back," she protested. "Now you want to put a spotlight on it?"

He didn't know what to call what he was feeling, hearing her in essence fighting for him so vociferously. All he knew for sure was that it made him feel things he never had. Which seemed to be a regular thing since she'd strode into his life.

"What we want," Hayley said, her tone soothing, "is to end this as soon as possible."

"So you're going to lay out a trail for them to find him?" Cutter clearly noticed the anxiety in her tone, because the dog walked over to her, sat and rested his chin on her knee.

"That," Quinn said gently, "is up to Jordan."

All three sets of eyes turned to him then, and the next revelation hit him. It really was up to him. The novelty of being out of the Army, of being able to decide where he went and when, what he did each day, of owning his own life again had not yet worn off. But this was a different kind of decision, one that might end that life sooner rather than later. And as he sat there, hearing Emily protest even the possibility of that so strongly, it hit him that he had more reason to live now than ever before. Because he wanted this woman in his life, for a very long time.

But he couldn't have that, couldn't even ask if she wanted it, too, with this hanging over his head.

He took a couple of deep breaths to steady himself. The meticulous side of his brain finally kicked in. "Tell me how it would work."

Quinn smiled. "There's the question I expected." Then he leaned forward, focused on Jordan. "It was Teague's idea. We would put Ty to work on it, because that man can find things that barely exist online. Plus he's familiar with your old stomping grounds, being in St. Louis."

Jordan listened as Quinn laid out the plan. After the first minute he made himself stop questioning whether they could do it—the man's quietly confident tone declared they could. When he'd finished, Jordan took a moment to process it all before speaking.

"So, this is based on the assumption they're doing regular online searches for me? Even though I have almost no presence there?"

Hayley nodded. "You may not have a presence as far as, say, social media, but there's more out there than you probably realize. For instance, we know you spent a night in Omaha. That you stopped at both Mount Rushmore and Deadwood, South Dakota. Then up to Glacier National Park. There are a couple more, but you get the idea."

He knew he was gaping at her, but... *How the hell?*

"Only one place had a record of your name," Quinn said. "The campground in Omaha. The others had your license plate—or at least partials—from various records and park video sources. And a couple of photos posted online from other people, where your van was visible in the background. It's all a few layers down, as information goes, but it's out there."

"And you...found all this?"

"Ty's the best," Quinn said. "Which means he found it and put it all together more quickly than they'll be able to, although I'm sure they're working on it. And no doubt they got your license plate from the guy in the truck who tried to take you out."

"And your guy is going to...what?"

"Move it all up to the top," Hayley said simply.

"And plant more for them to find." Quinn was smiling at his wife, as he so often did, but then looked at Jordan as he went on outlining the plan. "Add your name here and there, in reviews, blog posts and the like. In a chronological order, and proceeding westward. If they have, as we believe they probably do, a regular search running for any instance of your name, they'll see the pattern and suspect you're headed this way. Ty can Photoshop your van and the license plate in here and there. It will take a while for him to organize it all, but then we'd pick the time to plant the first seed, as it were, for the Lyden machine to find. Then the next, and so on."

"You mean lead them right to him?" Emily asked, still sounding upset, but not angry. Cutter had done his work there.

"Eventually," Quinn said, in a tone that said he understood her worry.

Jordan looked at her then, wishing they were alone so he could thank her for being so worried about him.

So he could hug her for it.

So he could hold her.

Kiss her. That was what he really wanted.

But they weren't alone, and it wasn't going to happen.

It would never happen, unless this ended. It might not even then, but there was no chance with this hanging over his head. And he would never have this kind of support again. The Foxworth Foundation. Sarge. In his own unique way, Cutter.

Most of all, Emily.

He felt as if he were teetering on the edge of a cliff. He sat there, eyes unfocused, trying to summon the will not to be his parents' son. Not to be the coward they both had been, running from their responsibilities and the child they had created.

He hadn't even been aware of Cutter moving, but then the dog was there, nudging at the hand he hadn't even realized was clenched into a fist. He uncurled his fingers, and Cutter shoved his head under them. He couldn't not stroke the persistent dog, and it was there again, that sense of calm, of serenity, as if his uncertainty was unfounded, and all would turn out okay. It was absurd, but there it was and he couldn't deny it.

He looked up from the dog and saw Emily watching him.

Emily. If he went along with this, if he agreed to letting the Lydens find him, it would take her out of the line of fire, wouldn't it? Since they couldn't know about the letter, they were only interested in her as a means to find him. Even if they did know, if he was out of the picture it would only be her secondhand information, not his eyewitness statement they had to deal with. If they found this trail Quinn was talking about, then they'd leave her alone.

With the feeling that this was the biggest decision he would make since he'd decided to join the Army, he shifted his gaze to the dog's owners. Both Foxworths waited patiently.

"I want this over," he finally said, glad that his voice was steady. *And I want Emily safe. For so many reasons.* "I have things I want to focus on—" he glanced back at Emily, whose eyes widened "—and a life outside the military to build."

"All righty, then," Hayley said cheerfully, as if she'd expected no other answer.

Quinn nodded, and Jordan couldn't deny the approval in those steady eyes warmed him. "Then we'll get started. I'll give Ty the go-ahead, and he should have a full plan worked out by our lunchtime tomorrow. Then we'll go over it and decide when to launch."

And that quickly it was settled. Jordan gave an amazed shake of his head; he'd seen highly praised field commanders who couldn't move as fast and decisively as these people did.

"Why didn't you end up a general?" he asked Quinn wryly.

"They don't seem to want my kind any longer," Quinn answered, his tone just as wry.

"Can't argue that," Jordan agreed, thinking of the last couple he'd seen go through camp.

A little while later, as he helped Quinn gather up the debris from the pizza dinner the women had brought, he registered he still felt remarkably calm, considering what he'd agreed to. That alone told him it had been the right call. He glanced over to where Emily and Hayley were sitting beside each other on the couch, in apparently deep conversation.

"You agreed to this more for her than yourself, didn't you."

Quinn's words weren't really a question; he'd sounded certain. With good reason, since he was right.

"I just want her safe."

"I get that," Quinn said, shifting his gaze to his wife, then back. "So Cutter was right. Again."

Cutter. Their matchmaking dog. Whose head had come up at the mention of his name, even from his bed out in the great room. A moment later he was on his feet and headed for the kitchen. He sat down in front of the refrigerator expectantly but politely.

"Ah," Quinn said. "Now that you're on his home turf, he'll expect this, so you might as well start now."

Jordan blinked. "You mean I still have my bodyguard?"

"Until it's no longer necessary, he'll be on you like Velcro-dog."

He gave a wondering shake of his head, which shifted to surprise when Quinn opened the fridge door and pulled out a bag of baby carrots. Cutter's ears came up. Quinn handed the bag to Jordan, and the dog's gaze shifted with the bag.

He'd never heard of a carrot-eating dog before, but this animal was different in so many ways he didn't question it, just pulled out one of the small vegetables and handed it over. Cutter chomped it with gusto and waited politely for a refill.

"How many?" he asked Quinn as he handed it over.

"He'll let you know, but he usually stops at three."

Jordan dispensed the third carrot, and as predicted the dog gobbled it up, nudged his hand as if in thanks, then trotted back to his bed near the fireplace. And the ladies, Jordan thought.

"Smart dog," he said.

"He is."

Jordan looked over at the dog, who looked back at him with an expression that looked oddly smug. As if he'd understood what they were saying about him. At this point not much would surprise him about that dog. About any of this. And just five days ago he would have laughed at the idea of any of this happening. Five days ago, he'd never heard of Foxworth. Five days ago, he'd never met their astonishingly clever dog.

Five days ago, Emily had been only a pretty, remembered image from a video call.

Now protecting her was the most important thing in his life.

# *Chapter 26*

"It's up to you," Hayley said.

Emily cast a wary glance at the two men in the kitchen. "What if he doesn't want me to stay?"

Hayley let out a tiny laugh as she smiled. "Emily, there isn't a doubt in my mind he wants you to." Then, more seriously, she added, "Just be sure you're both honest. You're in a tricky place right now, with outside pressures. That can affect perception, so just be clear that you both know that."

"Voice of experience?"

"Repeated experience," Hayley said, the smile wider now. "Don't forget, I've witnessed this a few times."

"Your dog," Emily said. "Is there anyone he hasn't matched up?"

The smile faded. Her voice took on a sad undertone. "Only one." Then, briskly, she asked, "So, are we off to your place, or shall I come back and pick you up in the morning? With, of course," she added quickly, making Emily think her expression must have shown the jab of apprehension she felt, "the proviso that if you need to leave, you just call and I'll be here in less than ten minutes." The smile came back as she glanced toward Jordan and then back. "But somehow I don't think that'll happen. And by the way, check the nightstand drawer, if you get there."

*I wish I had your confidence.*

But then Jordan turned his head and looked at her, and the smile he gave her held the same kind of longing she was feeling, and this time the jolt she felt was hope.

When Hayley and Quinn left—after assuring them Rafe and Teague were on duty tonight, along with Cutter, and he and Hayley would be back bright and early—Jordan didn't even ask why she was staying. Nor did he even give Cutter a sideways look when the dog nudged him to sit beside her on the couch.

They spent a quiet few minutes she found unexpectedly stress-free. Gradually she relaxed, enough to ask, "Would you tell me…about when you first met my brother? Do you remember?"

Jordan hesitated, but only for a moment. "Perfectly," he answered. "He came in to replace a guy who had mustered out, and they sent me to pick him up from the heliport. His first words after he got off and looked around were that he should have joined the Navy, because he'd rather be on a boat."

She laughed. That was so like Eddie.

"I'd pretty much thought the same thing when I first got there, so I figured we'd get along okay." He took a deep breath. "A couple of months later he made the old 'brother from another mother' joke. I laughed, but told him I didn't know, because I'd never had a brother."

When he didn't go on she asked quietly, "Then what?"

She saw him swallow, as if he were having trouble getting words out. "He said... I did now, if I wanted one."

"Oh, Jordy..." Her breath caught, and tears stung her eyes.

She heard him let out a compressed breath that sounded disgusted before he said, "I'm sorry, I didn't mean to... hurt you."

"No!" she exclaimed. "I mean yes, it hurts, but...it hurts more, a lot more, when nobody will talk about him. My friends barely acknowledge I ever had a brother."

"They probably just don't know what to say." His mouth twisted wryly. "Or in my case, what not to say."

"Say anything. Everything. Just remember that if I seem upset it's because I miss him, not because I'm angry with you."

He didn't say anything, but instead reached out and put his arm around her. It felt so good she didn't dare speak for a moment, afraid all her longing, all the need she'd suppressed, would trumpet in her voice. Instead she simply leaned against him, reveling in his heat and strength—and the fact that he didn't pull away.

"Tell me more. Please."

He did. He told her of camp, the food, the annoying brass and the good guys, the baseball and touch football games the mechanics had played while waiting on a part to arrive, all the things he and Eddie had shared. He told her of wisecracks her brother had made, of the time he'd snuck a dead jerboa—a strange local rodent that looked like a cross between a rabbit and a mouse—that had al-

ready started to smell under the driver's seat of a particularly obnoxious major's vehicle.

"He watched them pull out, and the major was already
wrinkling his nose. By the time they reached their destination in the heat, the thing had to have been pretty rank."

This made her laugh, and she snuggled closer. "Did
he get in trouble?"

"Nah. I doubt they ever even suspected us. We were
just fobbits, after all."

She tilted her head to look up at him. It was a little
awkward, pressed against him as she was, but she wasn't
about to give that up. "Fobbits?"

"It's what some called those of us who were noncom-
batants, the people who almost never leave the Forward
Operating Base. The FOB. Hence Fobbits."

She wanted to smile at that, but was uncertain how
to react. "Were they nasty about it? Was it an insult?"

"Depends on who said it. Some, yes. But those guys
could say mechanic and make it an insult, even as they
drove off in the vehicle we'd just fixed for them. But
there was also one major who pointed out that the hob-
bits saved the world in the story." He smiled then. "Quinn
reminds me of him."

"Now that doesn't surprise me."

"He's the kind of guy we'd go the extra mile for. Or
two or three extra miles."

"As he's doing now, for us." He went quiet, and very
still. "Jordan? What's wrong?"

"Nothing. Nothing at all. I liked the sound of that."

"Which part?" she asked, hoping she knew the answer, but needing to hear it.

"The 'us' part."

The tension that had been building inside her broke,

and she put everything she was feeling into her smile. "So do I."

"You're amazing, Emmie. Just as Eddie told me." He said it with a touch of…almost awe in his voice, a tone that did crazy things to her pulse. But then, as if he regretted saying it—or saying it like that—he quickly added, "Don't worry. I get it, Emily. You loved your brother, and those feelings are tangled up with this, with now, with… us. I know it's not more than that."

"How?"

He blinked. "What?"

"How do you know that?"

He looked away, staring into a distance that wasn't even there in the room. She wondered what he was seeing. Then he closed his eyes and finally answered. "Because…why would you?"

"Why wouldn't I?"

"Because you could do so much better."

That sparked her. "Better? Better than a man willing to give up everything, even to risk his own life, to keep me safe? I don't think so. That's as alpha male as it gets, Jordan Crockett."

His gaze snapped back to her face. She realized he was startled at her words. And suddenly something else occurred to her.

"You believed them. The ones who thought you were cowards, because your job wasn't to fight."

"I…" He gave a shake of his head. Looked away again as he said, slowly, "I used to watch them head out, knowing some of them might not come back. Wondered how they did it, knowing that themselves. Knowing… I didn't have that in me."

Something else Eddie had once said came back to her.

*He's pretty hard on himself. I think it's all connected to being abandoned as a kid.* Another thought hit her.

"Your parents," she said. "The bio ones, I mean. They ran. Is that it? You think you're like them?"

He looked back, staring at her now. He started to speak, then stopped, as if he were searching for words. Or the nerve to say them. "My grandmother… When I was a kid, she once called them cowards. Afraid to face the responsibility."

"Sounds like she had their number." She reached up, unable to stop herself from touching his cheek. "But it's not yours. I don't have to know them to know you're nothing like them."

He pulled her closer, as if trying to put into his embrace what he couldn't find words for. She understood, realizing he was still processing, so she said nothing and merely savored the feel of his arms around her. It felt so perfect, so right…

She awoke with a little start. She didn't know how long she'd been asleep, but Jordan hadn't moved at all. She looked up at him.

"I'm sorry. I didn't mean to fall asleep on you. Why didn't you wake me up?"

The smile he gave her then was different somehow, and she wasn't quite sure why. The way he was looking at her had changed, too, and it matched his voice when he said, "I didn't have the heart to disturb you. You looked so peaceful. And…" He hesitated, then added, "So beautiful."

Her pulse kicked up. So did hope, her hope that she wasn't misreading the change in him. She gave him the best smile she could manage.

"Speaking of that, Eddie never bothered to mention how gorgeous you are."

He snorted audibly, looking away and sounding embarrassed. "For good reason. I'm not."

"You are to me." His gaze shot back to her face, and she saw his lips part, as if he needed more air. She knew the feeling. "But do you know what Eddie did tell me about you?" He tilted his head, now looking at her almost warily. "He told me that I'd love you when I met you."

He went very still.

"Eddie knew me very well," she added, silently thanking Hayley for her observation.

"Emmie," he whispered.

She started to speak, then stopped herself, sensing that anything else she said might dampen that heat that had kindled in his voice, in his eyes. And she didn't want that. She wanted it to grow, to blaze, until he wanted her as much as she wanted him. So, silently, she reached up and cupped his cheek. Ran her thumb over his lips as she parted her own.

At last he moved, swiftly, fiercely, lowering his mouth to hers and kissing her as if he'd been lost forever until this moment. It felt so perfect, so right, yet she wanted more, wanted to taste more, to feel more, wanted to absorb everything he was into her heart and hold it there forever.

It didn't matter that she'd only met him a few days ago—she knew him. Her brother had made sure of that.

*You were right, Eddie. I love him.*

# Chapter 27

*He told me that I'd love you when I met you.*

Her words rang in Jordan's ears until he could have sworn he felt the echo in his chest. He'd tried to hold back, tried to tell himself it was too soon, too fast, but his heart—and his body—weren't listening.

The moment he'd tasted her, his pulse took off like a rocket. Now, he couldn't just feel it, he could hear it hammering in his ears. He heard a low groan, but it took him a moment to realize it had come from him.

What she'd said rang in his mind again. It was…almost a go-ahead, wasn't it? Like Eddie had given his approval, to them? Or was he just reaching, because he wanted this so badly? He didn't know, wasn't sure he cared. He was barely thinking anyway.

His tongue swept over her lips, those sweet lips that so often smiled at him, and when she parted them for him he groaned again before he probed deeper. She was sweeter than he'd ever imagined, and since he'd met her he'd been imagining quite a bit.

When her tongue met his, swiped, teased, as if she wanted to taste him as much as he had her, he thought he was going to lose it. His entire body tensed as a wave of need unlike anything he'd ever felt before swept over him. And it didn't ebb, just continued to build, until the pressure was almost unbearable. If she called a halt now he didn't know how he'd stop. But the tiny, still functioning part of his brain acknowledged that he would, that this was Emmie, Eddie's sister, so he would.

She never called that halt. Instead she urged him on, her mouth hungry, her hands busy and her body pressing against him. She was burning him alive, and he didn't care. He was so ready it was painful, but he didn't care about that, either. He just wanted more, and more. He wanted it all. And he wanted it for as long as she would give it to him.

It took every bit of will he had to break their passionate kiss long enough to say, "Emmie, I'm not…prepared for this."

He was surprised to hear her giggle. "That's okay," she whispered, and even the feel of that little breath against his ear sent another ripple of cramping need through him. "Foxworth is prepared on all fronts, it seems. We just need to check the nightstand drawer."

Foxworth was indeed prepared, it seemed, although he wasn't sure a single box of condoms was going to be enough. Not the way he was feeling, especially when she tugged off his shirt and started to unzip his jeans. When he stroked his hands up under her sweater and she didn't stop him, in fact urged him on, he was almost certain of it.

Her breasts rounded so perfectly into his hands, and the way she gasped with pleasure when he ran his thumbs over the peaks sent another jolt of white-hot fire through him.

"Emmie," he groaned out. "I can't go slow. I want you too much."

"I don't want slow." Certainty rang in her voice. "Slow can be for next time."

Next time. And the next. And the next. He didn't think there would ever be an end to him wanting the next.

He fumbled with the condom—it had been a while— then almost made it pointless when she touched him to help roll it on.

"Next time," he echoed through clenched teeth as he took them both down to the bed.

In the moment before he slid into her, her body already slick and welcoming, what she'd said flashed through his mind again.

*He told me that I'd love you when I met you. Eddie knew me very well.*

He could only hope it was true. Because he didn't just want this for as long as she would give it to him.

Forever. He wanted this forever.

Then there was no room for thoughts, no room for anything except the fierce, consuming sensations she sent through him, the tight, hot feel of her around his aching flesh. He drove into her, hard and deep, because he had to. And she welcomed that, too, with a breathy exclamation of "Yes!" over and over with every thrust.

And in the moment when he knew he couldn't hold back any longer, she convulsed around him, holding on to him as if he were her last anchor to life. He gave it up then and let himself go, barely aware of saying her name over and over again as they shuddered together.

* * *

"Morning."

Jordan nearly jumped as Rafe's voice came from directly behind him. He spun around on the patio to see the man standing there in a shaft of morning light. "Damn. Stealth attack."

The slightest of smiles flickered across the man's face. "It's a habit."

Cutter, the reason he was out here in the first place, away from Emmie, trotted in from the meadow and greeted Rafe happily.

Rafe straightened. "So…you and Emily."

"Oh." If he was the blushing sort, he would be now. "Yeah."

"Second thoughts?"

He shook his head instantly, sharply. How could he possibly have second thoughts about the most amazing night of his life? "Hell no. I just hope she doesn't have any."

"Doubt it." Rafe rubbed at his unshaven jaw. "She decided yesterday."

"What?"

Rafe nodded toward the parking area. "No car. She came with Hayley. And when Hayley left…she didn't."

Jordan turned to stare in that direction. He couldn't see all of the gravel space from here behind the building, but he had no doubt what Rafe said was true. The man never missed a thing. There was no car. Hayley had gone, she had stayed.

With him.

*She decided yesterday.*

She'd intended last night to happen since before the Foxworths had left yesterday. Images of her and Hayley on the couch, deep in conversation, shot through his

mind. Had they been talking about it? About her decision? Women did that, didn't they? Talked about things
like that? All that...emotional stuff?

Hayley had known, and had what, approved? Or simply acknowledged it was Emily's decision to make?

"Just as well," Rafe said, his voice lighter than anything he'd heard from the man before. "She's safer here
anyway."

Jordan felt as if he'd been sucker punched despite the
untroubled tone. He'd been so tangled up in what he was
feeling he'd almost forgotten the reason behind it all.
How did women do it, dealing with this emotional crap
all the time?

*That's messed up, man.*

*Yeah.*

*Screw 'em. Want a beer?*

*Yeah. Thanks.*

He was hit with the memory of that conversation with
Eddie, after Jordan had gotten chewed out for not reading some Zoomie's mind—what the ground guys called
the flyers—about where to stack his gear, something that
wasn't really his job in the first place.

For him and Eddie, that exchange was about the extent of their dealing with emotions. Acknowledge, com-
miserate, move on.

"Maybe she should stay for the duration," Rafe said,
almost blithely. "Just as easy to watch two as one, here."

"You partnering with the dog, now?" Jordan asked
dryly.

That got him a flash of a surprised grin, which he
guessed didn't happen very often with this guy. "Keeps
him off me."

Before he could come up with a retort to that, the sound

of a vehicle approaching drew his attention. The Foxworths, signaling the start of another day of hiding. He'd managed to put that out of his mind last night, lying with Emmie in his arms, telling himself if this was hiding out, bring it. And then she'd started to touch him, stroke him again, and he'd forgotten about the hovering threat altogether.

He watched Rafe—and Cutter, letting out a joyous warble of welcome—head off to greet the arrivals, grimacing inwardly at the unwelcome return of having to deal with his situation.

*But if not for this, last night might not have happened.*

He hadn't thought about it quite that way until this moment, and it kind of put everything in a different light.

"Hey."

He didn't jump this time. Instead, Emily's soft, warm voice made him spin around eagerly, and the matching smile, with a touch of shyness, almost made him melt right there on the spot.

"Hey," he said as he pulled her into his arms.

"Looks like another day begins."

"Yeah."

"I wish I didn't have to go to work today, but Dad's due back a week from tomorrow, and there are a few things I need to finish up."

A week. Dad. Her father. Eddie's father. He felt sucker punched again. Which pretty much made him a class A sucker.

He could only imagine how Ben Bishop was going to feel about all this. About what Jordan had brought down on his daughter. And despite all the assurances, from both Emily and the Foxworths, he couldn't quite quash that twinge of guilt.

## Chapter 28

Emily sat in her office, pondering the fact that usually the first time she would look at a clock during her workday—especially on a Monday like today—was when her stomach would growl its announcement that she hadn't eaten all day. The second time was usually about an hour or two after what would be quitting time for anybody on a normal job.

But today she'd been glued to the time passing all day long. All the while thinking of Jordan holed up at Foxworth headquarters. All the while remembering the glorious weekend they'd had.

She was certain the Foxworth people had tactfully left them alone together for most of it. The only one of them who was always around was Cutter, who seemed quite pleased with himself as he plopped on his dog bed and watched them in between what she'd come to think of as making his rounds, checking all the doors and windows periodically.

But despite all the work she'd come back to after that luscious weekend, all she could think of was getting back to Jordan. She'd found she could talk to him like she'd only ever been able to do with her brother. And once he was certain she'd meant what she'd said, he freely reminisced with her about Eddie, which meant more to her than she could ever say. They even had progressed to being able to laugh at some of the sillier things that had happened, or her brother's quirky sense of humor that had driven him to the occasional prank that ended up either in disaster or the funniest thing ever.

From there they'd grown into talking about anything and everything. She told him about Bishop Tool and how it worked, its successes and thankfully rare failures. Dad had been in love with that small-space sander idea, but it just hadn't been ready for prime time. That had sparked Jordan's thought process, and as he worked through the idea she had the chance to see how his mind worked, how smart he was in his chosen field. A field that kept the rest of the world running, whether some of those others liked to admit it or not.

She treasured those hours, all of them.

But most of all she treasured the nights, and the wonder she found in his arms. She'd always thought of herself as career driven, had never expected to be consumed by such passion, had even, in her more cynical moments, doubted it was even real, or possible, especially for her.

She knew better now. Because just thinking about him, about that taut, muscled body naked beside her, on top of her, beneath her, about hearing him groan out her name as he throbbed within her, was enough to set her pulse racing and have her reaching for the air conditioning controls.

"Yep," she said aloud to the empty office, "you're a goner all right. Five nights in his bed and you're ready for forever."

She was smiling when she said it. It wasn't a solid smile, though, because she didn't know for sure that Jordan felt the same way about that forever.

Mere seconds later, Hayley arrived back at the office. It had taken Emily most of that first day she'd come to Bishop with her to realize that the alert, capable woman was doing much as her alert, capable dog did—making rounds, doing a security check, whatever they called it.

Emily felt her cheeks heat as Hayley came in. If she'd been five seconds earlier, she'd have heard that silly declaration. Then again, if anyone would understand, it would be Hayley. Hadn't she been the one who'd encouraged her to stay that first night? Hadn't she been the one who had realized right off where things were headed?

*I've witnessed this a few times.*

"Hayley? May I ask you something?"

"Of course," Hayley answered, sounding surprised.

"About all those times you've witnessed Cutter's matchmaking," she began, thinking it sounded so silly when you said it aloud but unable to deny it just might be true.

Hayley smiled. "Sounds crazy, doesn't it? I didn't believe it until about the fourth time, and Quinn took even longer."

She smiled back before she went on with her question. "How many of those are...still together?"

"Ah," Hayley said, understanding now evident on her

face. And her smile was even wider when she said clearly, "All of them. He doesn't make mistakes."

And at that, Emily found herself smiling back just as widely.

Mondays had never meant anything in particular to Jordan, since the military didn't run on a Monday to Friday schedule, and now they didn't matter at all. Or they hadn't, until now. Now Monday meant Emily had to go to work, and he didn't like that.

He spent most of the day thinking about Emily at work. Thankfully she had Hayley at her side, which eased his stress a bit. But he was still twitching a little at the realization that her father would be back in mere days. How would he feel about walking into the middle of this mess?

*And how about that she'd slept with the guy who had brought it all to them?*

A flood of heated memories rushed through him. He'd had some good sex in his life, now and then, but nothing came even close to what he'd found in her arms. He hadn't known it could be like that. And even if he had, he doubted he would have believed himself capable of it. He would carry the sound of Emily crying out her need for him, his name escaping her as her body tightened around him, to his grave.

*Which you may be in sooner than you thought.*

He was back pacing the floor for at least the third time when Cutter trotted over to him and blocked his path. He looked down and saw the dog held a tennis ball in his mouth. Jordan immediately perked up. The Foxworths had told him to treat the dog as if he were his own, and while he'd never had one, he knew enough to recognize the request when he saw it.

"Now *that* I can handle," he told the dog, and they went out the back door.

The dog seemed tireless. At least, he was more tireless than Jordan's arm, which after an hour of the same throwing motion began to signal it was time to stop.

"Too bad I'm not ambidextrous, dog," he told Cutter as he romped back with the now grubby yellow ball once more. "Then we could keep this up for another hour."

"He'll quit when you're ready."

He managed not to jump this time when Rafe spoke from just a yard or so away. "He will, huh?"

"I'm guessing he started it?"

Jordan's brow furrowed. "Well, yeah, he walked up to me with the ball."

"He knew you needed to do something. A distraction."

Jordan looked back at the dog who had now dropped the ball at his feet and, after a hello to Rafe, walked over to the bowl of water on the patio and began to lap furiously. He supposed he could buy that the dog had sensed he was a bit wound up. It was obvious the animal was very tuned in.

"So did I," Rafe said, "and I'm one of the least emotionally observant guys you'll find, I'm told." His mouth quirked wryly on the last words, but he went on without further explanation. "I was going to suggest you might want to do some work on your van while it's parked, but looking at it I can't see a thing that needs doing. You keep it shipshape."

Jordan nodded. "It's the only thing I own."

"And it's second nature to you to keep something mechanical working smoothly."

"Yeah," he agreed with a half shrug. "That, too." He

studied the other man for a moment, remembering what Quinn had told him. "I hear you do the same."

Rafe nodded. "Maybe for different reasons."

"I do it because it's the way my brain sees things, how they work, connect, patterns."

"I do it to keep my brain from working on other things I can't do anything about."

Jordan considered that. "Sort of like why I was just throwing that ball endlessly?"

"More exactly like," Rafe answered.

He let out a long, weary breath. "I just can't stop feeling like this is all my fault, that I've brought this down on Emmie."

"And the fact that they would have been watching her anyway, as the sister of one of their victims, doesn't ease that up much, does it."

It wasn't really a question, so Jordan only shook his head. It did make him think of what the man had said a moment ago, though, about being emotionally unobservant. It didn't seem that way to him. In fact, he seemed to sense mood almost as well as the darned dog did.

He resisted looking at his watch yet again. He never would have thought it possible to miss somebody he'd only met in the flesh—in all senses—just days ago, so very much. But he did. He felt as if his life was on hold until she came back in the evening. As if it wouldn't start up again until she was back, within reach.

Thankfully she seemed to take it for granted she would come back here after work; he was sure he would have badly mangled asking her to do it. He'd even hesitated when she and Hayley had arrived that first day, not sure how she wanted to handle this—them—in front of witnesses. She quickly made that clear by throwing her arms around him and planting a big kiss on him.

And she repeated it today, after Cutter had raced off to meet them and guide them around to the back patio of the Foxworth headquarters.

"Today," she said in a heartfelt tone after that luscious kiss, "was the longest Monday in the history of long Mondays. I missed you."

He grinned, wondering if he looked as dopily happy as he felt, and then decided he didn't care. Especially when Hayley was smiling at them both. When Cutter was practically grinning at them, at least as much as a dog could grin. Even the usually taciturn Rafe was barely stifling a lopsided smile at them.

They were still outside on the patio, enjoying the late afternoon sun and watching Cutter trying to lure Rafe into a romp in the meadow, when the dog suddenly halted his coaxing and let out a trumpeting, welcoming bark that Jordan knew by now meant Quinn had arrived.

The cheery mood faded when Quinn came around the corner and they saw his serious expression.

"Come inside."

Once in, Quinn immediately started up the stairs, which alone told Jordan this was about to turn intense; no casual gathering around the fireplace for this. He looked at Emily, who now appeared worried. Even Cutter had changed, the playful mood vanished, as if the dog somehow sensed the shift in the atmosphere.

"What is it?" Emily asked without preamble the moment they were all seated around the big meeting table.

"I think we're going to have to step things up a bit." Jordan went very still. Quinn continued. "Remember that offer the Lyden-backed company made to Sarge, for the camp property?"

"Yeah?" Jordan said warily. If this was going to drag Sarge and the other guys deeper into this, then he'd have no choice. He'd have to leave, and obviously, visibly. No way would he bring this down on Sarge, or the other guys who had already been through so much.

"An agent from that same company showed up at the camp today. Putting pressure on Sarge to sell. Threatening to have the county overrule the city, come after the camp and clear it out."

"I'll bet that went well," Rafe observed, his tone dry; clearly he knew how amenable Sarge would be to being pushed.

"Exactly," Quinn said. His gaze fastened on Jordan. "But a more interesting part was, after the failed coercion, the agent basically told Sarge that the pressure would stop, that all this trouble could go away. All he had to do was give them a call if or when you showed up."

"So if Sarge rats me out, all his troubles go away?"

"Pretty much." Quinn looked at him consideringly for a silent moment. As if there were more to it, and he was judging whether Jordan could take it, whatever it was.

"Hit me," he said sourly. "Might as well get it over with."

Quinn nodded. "The guy told Sarge the people behind the offer—not mentioning the name Lyden of course— were simply trying to do the right thing. And that their concern was for you."

Jordan barely managed to stifle a snort. "As if Hart Lyden gives a damn about anyone but himself."

"Why would he say that?" Emily asked.

"I suspect," Quinn said, "that they're building a story."

Jordan knew immediately what Quinn was getting at. "They're claiming to be worried I'll commit suicide," he said, unable to keep the bitterness out of his voice.

He heard Emily's gasp but kept his gaze fastened on Quinn, who nodded. Ironic that he was in more danger here than he'd ever been working in an actual combat zone.

"But why—" Emily began.

"That way," he began, unable to keep the bitterness out of his voice, "when I turn up dead, they're covered."

# Chapter 28

Jordan swore under his breath. He really was going to have to leave. Run. Just like his parents had.

*I don't have to know them to know you're nothing like them.*

Emily's words rang in his head. He didn't want to run, not now, not when he'd just found everything he'd never dared hope to have in his life. But he couldn't, wouldn't risk her. And there were others to worry about now. Sarge, the guys—he'd brought this down on them, and—

He suddenly tuned back in to what Quinn was saying. "—on his way over there now to talk to Sarge. Then he'll head to their city hall and we'll see if they really want to go up against Gavin de Marco, even for the Lydens."

"Can Bishop Tool help?" Emily's quiet question startled him. "We're a big part of the town's tax base, and Dad has some—well, a lot—of pull with the mayor. And the county, too, for that matter. He doesn't like to use it, it's not his way, but he supports vets more."

Quinn smiled at her. "Well, that's a nice arrow to have in the quiver. We'll see if we need to shoot it."

Jordan felt a little off balance. He hadn't realized her family company was quite that big a deal. He was having enough trouble with the Gavin de Marco part.

"But we can use this," Hayley said. "Anything involving Gavin is news, so there'll be coverage. And when Gavin gets through with the media, he'll approach the Lyden's representative and point out how the dissonance between them playing up Hart's 'military service'—" she threw up some air quotes "—and them trying to clear out a camp that serves only to help veterans is going to look. The Lydens may be big locally, but Gavin's a name known around the world."

Jordan stared at her as he shook his head slowly. "Someday I'd like to hear how he walked away from all that and ended up working with you."

"It's a story," Hayley said with a smile.

"And so will this be," Quinn added. "And probably by this afternoon."

"I don't want Sarge or any of the guys hurt by this," Jordan said.

Hayley's smile widened. "Hurt? By the time Gavin gets done they'll have people lined up to help. They'll be as untouchable as anyone can be."

Jordan thought they might be a little overoptimistic. And hoped he was wrong.

"And once we have Sarge and his group protected from their business and political machinations," Quinn said, "that will leave only one path open for the Lydens."

His gaze shifted to Jordan, and it was more than just

intent. He felt the assessment in it. He'd seen that look before, in the eyes of officers about to send men into combat. And suddenly he realized what that path was. He didn't know the details of the Foxworth plan, but he knew what the crux of it was.

"We give them what they want," he said, holding Quinn's gaze. "Me."

"What?" Emily yelped. "No!"

He couldn't deny her sharp, instant protest warmed him. He drew in a deep breath and looked at her. And despite the danger of Quinn's proposal, he knew it was the right thing. For the first time in his life he had something worth risking everything for…and he was looking at her right now.

"It's the only way to put an end to this," he said softly. "And it has to end, Emmie. It has to end, so we can move on."

At that "we," something flashed in her eyes, those beautiful blue eyes that not so long ago had been hot with need and desire, for him. Something he never would have dreamed possible, also not so long ago. But the worry was still there as well, and after a long, intense moment she turned her gaze to Quinn.

"What is this plan?"

Quinn spoke calmly, as if this were nothing more than directions to a destination. "They already have the camp on their target list, so they won't be surprised when Jordan shows up. And Gavin will have shut down their initial plan to pressure Sarge, by assuring them he will go public with the fact that it's them behind the move to clear out the camp. Very hard to reconcile with all their proclaimed support for vets."

"So they'll have to come at me directly," Jordan said.

"And we'll be ready." Quinn laid out the rest of the plan, and Jordan saw immediately how it would work, almost in the way he could look at an engine or machine and see how it functioned. Before Quinn was even finished, he was nodding.

"But what if…" Emily began, but her voice trailed away, as if she could not even bear to say the words.

"He'll be safe," Quinn assured her. "Once the ball is rolling it's all hands on deck. He'll have all of Foxworth with him. Teague and I will be close by. Rafe farther out, but deadlier than any ten men put together. And he'll have Cutter stuck to him like glue. When that dog's in protect mode, he makes better men than Hart Lyden think twice."

"Which means most of the male population," Hayley said, her words and dry tone breaking the tension. Then she looked at Jordan and said, in an entirely different, solemn tone, "This still all comes down to you, Jordan. You're sure?"

*I don't have to know them to know you're nothing like them.*

"I'm sure," he said. "I'm not going to run. Not now."

Hayley smiled, as if she'd expected nothing less. "You have a lot to stay and fight for, now."

Jordan shifted his gaze to Emily as he spoke, just as solemnly as Hayley had. "Yes, I do. And I will."

The look on Emily's face then made it all worth it. And Jordan realized there was no limit to what he would do for her, and to have her in his life.

Hayley hadn't understated, Emily thought as they sat watching the news that night. In the space of a day, Gavin de Marco had set the narrative, and his name had assured it hit every outlet, broadcast and online, in the Pacific

Northwest and probably beyond. Video of the spit-and-polish camp, a recounting of the military service of its tenants and testimony from the neighbors they so often helped—about them being hardworking, sober and orderly, while helping to keep the surrounding area the same way—established the camp in the public eye as one of the best possible solutions to veterans who hadn't quite reestablished themselves in civilian life yet.

Sarge himself had been interviewed in a couple of the pieces, and he'd practically declared war on anyone who might try to interfere or damage his mission. And Gavin de Marco showed why he'd become one of the most famous attorneys in the world. Not only was his sheer presence overwhelming, he managed to imply without saying so that he knew exactly what was going on, who was behind it and most importantly why, and that he wouldn't hesitate to use that information if necessary.

By the time it was done, it was clear that anyone who tried to go up against them would be facing resistance from not only a stubborn Sarge and his temporary troop, but most of the civilian population as well. And that resistance would be organized by a man who had enough skill, charisma and influence to put the Lydens in the shade.

"And if it got out that the Lydens were involved," Hayley said with satisfaction as the last video report they'd compiled faded to black, "it would be a PR nightmare for them."

"So that's what will keep them in check?" Emily asked. "The fear that the public will find out that all their support for veterans is fake, just like their son is a fake hero?"

"It will at least make them hesitate, regroup," Quinn said.

As impressive as the result had been, Emily thought

she still saw a touch of doubt in Jordan's expression. He confirmed it a moment later. "That's great. For now," he said. "But do you really think they'll give up?"

"No. This is just a holding action, something to occupy them while we set up the final move. Which you and Rafe will start on as soon as some gear arrives from Ty, probably tomorrow." Quinn leaned back on the couch, looking at Jordan, who seemed to be studying his hands. When he didn't speak, Quinn asked, "Unless you've changed your mind? This is all dependent on you, Jordan. And therefore up to you."

Jordan's head came up. "You mean you'd call this all off?"

"I mean your heart, mind and soul have to be in this for it to work. We can set it up, we can have your back, but in the end, as we said in the beginning, it's your call."

"I'm not quitting. I want this over," he said firmly. "But I'm not much good at subterfuge."

*Thank goodness for that.* Emily almost smiled at her own thought as she remembered a couple of times last night when he'd told her exactly what he wanted and she'd been happy to oblige.

"That's okay. We've got an expert on all kinds of maneuvering and luring people into saying things they never meant to. Gavin will be here to give you a crash course tomorrow morning, and he'll be on the network live to coach as it goes down. Assuming we've planted the right seeds."

Emily had little doubt that they had; she had the feeling Foxworth knew a great deal about the kind of people the Lydens were.

And took great satisfaction in bringing them down.

# Chapter 30

Jordan was feeling an odd sense of déjà vu as he went about setting up the campsite again. Not just that he was back here, in the same site, but that there was a snowball rolling downhill, picking up speed and mass. Kind of like he'd felt in the service sometimes, when a platoon came back from a fight with vehicles shot full of holes, or wrecked, or worse, dripping blood.

He was just finishing hooking up to the utilities when Sarge arrived. Cutter greeted him respectfully. The dog clearly sensed this was a man worthy of it. Jordan no longer doubted the animal was capable of that. Sarge greeted the dog in the same way, and Jordan remembered when he'd asked Sarge about Cutter being here, and the man told him about a dog very much like this one saving his life back in the day. "They're better than we humans deserve," he'd said. "Of course he can stay."

Now, knowing what was coming, he made sure the dog was in the van; they didn't want anyone watching—as in the Lydens—knowing about him ahead of time. Then he turned and just looked at the older man, not sure what to say. "Sarge," he began, but stopped when the man held up a hand.

"You need to know everyone here is with you. They don't know the details, just what to watch for, but they're with you. It's making them feel good to be doing something."

"Thanks," he said. "They know to stay back, though, right?"

"They do. They'll follow orders, especially given by the likes of Quinn Foxworth."

"You mean you," Jordan corrected, making Sarge smile. "You sure you want to be the face of this?"

Sarge grinned at him then. "And have a part in taking down the Lydens? Wouldn't trade it for anything. And it looks like they're ready, so just keep talking."

With an effort Jordan kept his gaze on Sarge, instead of looking over to where the attorney he'd heard of so often but had only met yesterday stood talking to a reporter accompanied by a video cameraman, who had clearly now begun to record.

Gavin de Marco was standing in a carefully chosen spot, where the backdrop of the shot would be Jordan's van—and him and Sarge. After having spent a couple of hours with the dynamic, charismatic man who had more than once held a nation rapt in a big name trial, he had no doubts he would get exactly what he wanted out of this session. And even as he thought it, out of the corner of his eye he saw the camera shift, zeroing in on him and Sarge.

It held there for a moment, and as planned, Jordan

shifted slightly, casually, until he was facing the camera but still looking at Sarge. Then, at the discreet hand signal from the lawyer, Sarge gave Jordan a wink and turned to walk over to the reporter. Jordan turned away, gratefully, and went back to work, making adjustments on some of the new equipment. He was still very conscious of the reporter's presence, but trying to look like he wasn't.

He'd done it now, there was no turning back. With Foxworth and de Marco's influence attached, that video—with his face shown clearly—would probably be widespread before he even finished setting up here. And fortuitously, his choice of this particular site would hopefully pay off now. He'd picked it originally because he was wary, and it was a bit apart and masked slightly by the surrounding trees. Now he hoped that slight seclusion would encourage the Lyden machine to make a move on him, and leave Sarge and the others alone.

When the reporter and cameraman had departed, Jordan let Cutter out of the van, which earned him a swipe of the tongue before the dog headed for de Marco at a trot. He thought of this morning, when the famous attorney had arrived at Foxworth headquarters, and Jordan had heard him say to the dog, after a hello and an ear scratch, "And thank you again, my furry friend. Get that bow tie of yours out for the wedding."

Jordan had felt a stab of longing, a fierce wish that he would someday be in that same position, thanking Cutter for bringing him and Emily together.

Now the dark-haired, dark-eyed man with the amazing presence, who had been much kinder than Jordan had expected when he'd given him that crash course in getting people to say what you needed them to say, looked around at the site and his van.

"Nice," he said. "Not a bad way to live at all. I seriously considered doing the same for a while."

Jordan almost laughed aloud; this guy had to be able to afford houses—hell, probably mansions—in every garden spot in the world. But he couldn't doubt the sincerity in his voice. Or maybe being able to project that was what had made him one of the most successful in the world at his job.

"I mean it," de Marco said, clearly having read Jordan's reaction perfectly. Also unsurprising, considering.

"What made you walk away?" Jordan asked, then winced inwardly at his own temerity.

"Lies," de Marco answered simply. "The case I built my life and career on turned out to be one big lie, and it made the rest unbearable."

*And you had the courage to quit.* "I...can't imagine walking away from everything you had."

"I had to, or I'd loathe myself. Just like," de Marco added quietly, "you had to stop running."

Okay, the guy really was too damned perceptive.

*Which you should have known. He didn't get to where he was without being able to read people.*

Cutter cut off his thoughts with a clear, sharp series of barks he'd heard before. Teague, he thought. No sooner had he recognized the dog's signal than the man appeared, walking down the drive from the house.

"It went well?" he asked after greeting the dog.

"I think so," de Marco—Jordan doubted he'd ever be able to call him Gavin as suggested; he had enough trouble dropping the "mister" even in his thoughts—said. "I'll be monitoring, and if and when I'll be live with you, Jordan, so be sure you have that earpiece on and in."

"Yes, sir," Jordan responded automatically.

The other man's mouth twitched at one corner, and Teague laughed as he said, "You can take the boy out of the Army, but…"

"Yeah, yeah, Marine." Jordan was grinning himself now. And some of the pressure that had been building in him since he'd made the move back here eased. He had good people at his back here, the best he could ask for.

And he had Emily who, after he and Quinn had both insisted she stay clear for now, had announced she would be at Foxworth until this was over. The discussion was still vivid in his mind.

*What about your work, and your dad coming back?*

*When I tell him why, he'll understand.*

*Because of Eddie.*

*And because of you. What Eddie said goes for him, too.*

*What?*

*You're going to love him when you meet him.*

He hadn't dared to ask if she'd meant he'd love her dad, or vice versa. Because how could the man love the guy who hadn't been able to save his son?

After Gavin—he'd insisted again—had gone, Teague checked the campsite, van and other equipment, pronounced all systems go and got ready to leave. But not until he told Jordan with a wink that the Foxworth phones handled video calls quite well.

"You and that dog," Jordan muttered, glancing over to where Cutter had stationed himself in the doorway to the van.

"Hard to argue with his success rate," Teague said.

"Including you?"

"With some help. He and Hayley conspired. My wife's an animal groomer, and he kept getting filthy, and Hayley kept being too busy to go pick him up."

"He's a dog. Don't they normally get dirty?"

"Not every day for days on end. And he's never rolled in mud like that before or since."

Jordan let out a bemused chuckle. "Does he read and write, too?"

Teague smiled, but answered as if he'd been serious. "In his own way. He reads people and situations, and manages to convey what needs to be done. He shoved you onto the couch with Emily yet?"

Jordan blinked. "Uh…yeah."

"There you go," Teague said cheerfully.

Jordan was still smiling after the Foxworth man had gone. It seemed inordinately quiet. He went over and sat on the step of the van next to Cutter, who leaned into him. He put an arm around the dog, and that now familiar sense of ease crept into him. He sat enjoying the peace, not really thinking about the time passing, only thinking of wanting this over so he and Emily could decide what they actually had without the Lyden threat hanging over them. Assuming he survived said threat, of course.

The sun was finally sinking in this season of long days in the Pacific Northwest when the Foxworth phone buzzed. He started to reach for it in his back pocket when he remember the earpiece and tapped it instead.

"On plan so far," Quinn's voice said. "That film clip was on every news outlet and local website, with a close-up of you and Sarge and mentioning you were a new arrival. Ty did a little discreet monitoring, and several Lyden related phones and ISPs have been lit up ever since. Can't be sure it's related, but seems likely."

"So now it's a matter of figuring out how quick they'll move?"

"And hoping we're right about who does the moving.

Now somebody wants to say hello. I'll switch it to video for her, since she's a lot nicer to look at."

Jordan grinned. "I would not argue that, sir."

Emily looked great, as usual, but sounded a little fretful. "I should be there with you."

"I wish you were, but no. Lyden needs to think you know nothing, that we've never even met."

"But—"

"Emmie, please, if you were here you'd be the only thing that mattered to me, and I'd probably blow this."

She looked both worried and pleased to him, and he thought he was finally learning to read her. Maybe it was hanging out with Cutter. He gave the dog another one-armed squeeze. Cutter reached up and swiped his tongue over Jordan's cheek. And Emily laughed.

"Give him a hug for me. He's so amazing."

"I will, and he is."

"We're going to need a dog."

A dozen answers to that tumbled through his mind, but he settled on the truest one. "I'd like that. Especially the 'we' part."

He sat for a long time after the call was over, watching the sky gradually fade to black on this moonless night. It was such a beautiful place, yet it attracted destructive locusts, it seemed. But it also had people like Emmie, and her father. And the Foxworths, and an apparently transformed Gavin de Marco.

So how unassailable were the Lydens? Enough to stand against the likes of Foxworth? Rumor had it, Quinn had mentioned, that they'd been connected to the infamous Governor Ogilvie, whom Foxworth had been instrumental in taking down. So that had to mean Foxworth could handle this, didn't it?

And sitting there in the darkness he could almost feel the certainty settle in. Like it was an undiagnosed problem with an engine, he mentally went through the steps.

The Lydens had the plan all mapped out.

They'd built their local empire first, then expanded it.

Anyone who tried to interfere or got in their way tended to vanish or turn up mysteriously dead.

The White House was the glistening goal at the end of the road.

Hart Lyden was destined for that goal, and he'd let nothing get in his way.

Only one person stood as a roadblock on that road to Washington DC, as far as the Lydens knew.

Him.

And he knew what the Lydens tended to do with roadblocks.

# Chapter 31

Once again, Emily watched the news program they'd recorded. She couldn't seem to stop watching it, even though it made her afraid. The piece played up everything necessary for anyone looking for clues to be able to find the place. Then it had blatantly zoomed in on Jordan, touting him as a new arrival to the camp run by another veteran of an older war.

Despite her nerves, that close-up on Jordan still took her breath away. He was as beautiful on screen as he was in person.

*Although maybe not quite as beautiful as he is in bed, hmm?*

The remembered heat collided with the chill of her fear for him, and the clash gave her a slight case of the shakes. She wrapped her arms around herself, wishing it was Jordan.

*What would you say, Eddie? That I'm falling too fast, we're moving too fast?*

Her breath caught as a vivid memory surfaced, of her brother the day she'd been about to go in for her driver's test for her license. She'd had qualms at the last moment, thinking she wasn't ready, that she'd screw up either the written or driving part of the test, that maybe she should wait. It had been Eddie who had laughed at her and said, "You're ready, Emmie. Quit thinking about it and just go for it."

And suddenly the shaking stopped, because she knew Eddie would say exactly the same thing now. With even more enthusiasm, because Jordan was his best friend and he'd known and trusted him.

*He's not like some friends, guys you like but know do some scummy things. He's straight-arrow. When the chips are down, he's the guy you want at your side.*

And the chips were down for Jordan now, and she was determined she would be the same for him, the one he wanted at his side.

"Amazing what the name Gavin de Marco gets done," Hayley said as she joined Emily in front of the flat-screen TV.

"You mean closing off any avenue for the Lydens to pursue except to come after Jordan?" Emily's tone was grim.

"Exactly," Hayley said, but there was a gentle understanding in her voice. "Emily, he's got the three best, most efficient protectors I know close by in Quinn, Teague and Rafe. Sarge and the other vets at the camp are all on guard for any danger. Plus, he's got the best early warning and protection system possible glued to his side."

"You mean Cutter." Hayley nodded. Glad of the distraction Emily asked, "Has he ever gotten hurt, doing… what he does?"

A fleeting shadow darkened the other woman's eyes, but for barely an instant. "Only once." Then she smiled. "The very first time. On the mission when Quinn and I met. And Quinn risked his life, in fact got shot, to get him out of there. Said he'd been as much a part of the mission as anyone."

Emily studied the other woman for a moment before asking softly, "Is that when you fell for him?"

Hayley smiled. "Oh, I'd done that well before then, but it surely wiped out any lingering doubts I had."

"You had doubts about him? About the Foxworth Foundation?"

"Oh, I didn't know about the Foundation at that point. Everything was top secret, a witness protection operation, and Quinn wouldn't tell me a thing until it was all over and the witness was safe."

"Witness protection?" Emily asked.

Hayley's smile widened, and Emily knew she'd given her those details on purpose. "Yes."

"Protection from who?"

"The biggest, most murderous drug cartel on the Mexican border," Hayley said, then, with a grin Emily could only describe as proud, added, "Or rather, it was."

Emily stared at the cheerful woman. And thought what she guessed had been Hayley's exact intent. That if Foxworth could protect a witness from something as evil as that, they could surely protect Jordan from the Lydens.

And it worked, to a point. She pulled back from the edge of panic, but she was still solidly in the realm of fear and anxiety.

"How do you not go crazy, waiting?" she asked. "Or let me guess, you're usually in the thick of things."

"There are a lot of levels to an operation like this," Hayley answered. "One of them is eliminating at least one source of worry for the people in the eye of the storm, as it were."

"So me being there would only give Foxworth one more thing to worry about." She could organize a set of accounting books, she could lay out a project plan and schedule, and she could build a piece of furniture from the ground up, but she was not trained in this kind of thing.

"And Jordan," Hayley said softly. "Because you know he'd do anything, even risk his own life, to keep you safe. I think you're the real reason he agreed to this at all."

Emily smiled, but couldn't help wondering how the woman stayed so calm when her husband, dog and friends were…well, readying for a possible battle.

"Don't worry quite so much, Emily. Don't forget the measure—or rather the lack—of the man we're waiting for."

"Lyden?" She let out a derisive huff of breath. "Good point."

"Just think about when it's over," Hayley suggested, with that knowing smile. "You've got some planning to do. A new life to build, with Jordan."

"Yes. Yes, I do." And she firmly told herself she would not accept that it could be stolen from her as her brother had been.

She settled in to wait.

Jordan hadn't meant to get up at the crack of dawn, especially since dawn was practically in the middle of the night in this area in summer, but he wasn't sleeping anyway so just lying in bed seemed useless. He sat up, rubbing at eyes that were weary after a night spent dozing in half-hour spurts.

Cutter, who had been lying beside him instead of in his usual spot on the floor of the van, lifted his head and looked at him.

"Y'know, mutt," he said, reaching out to do the ear scratch he'd learned the dog liked, "you're a great dog, but you aren't really the one I wanted to wake up next to."

A sudden memory hit him, of the day he'd first shown Emily the van.

*You'd probably feel pretty cramped in one of these.*

*How could you when you can sit outside and look at open spaces like here, or maybe the mountains somewhere else, or a lake, or even the ocean?*

His Emily-starved brain provided an imagined picture of them indeed waking up here in his bed together, and throwing the back doors open to a sunrise view of some amazing place. Some place they'd never been, with her getting to at last fulfill her dream of traveling.

And him getting to fulfill a dream he'd never really dared have, of having a woman he loved beside him.

"You've got to get through this first," he muttered to himself, and swung his legs over the side.

He let Cutter outside and watched for a moment as the dog sniffed the air seemingly from all directions. Looking for his people? Jordan didn't know, but at this point nothing much would surprise him about this dog. Then the animal trotted off to the designated spot to do his business.

Barely a moment later, the earbud he'd never taken out came to life, and Teague's voice came through.

"All good?"

He tapped it as they'd shown him to activate the mic. "As can be expected," he said. "Quiet anyway."

"Copy. Rafe's officially relieved. I'm settling in."

"He always work nights?"

"When a job needs it, yeah. He likes it. I think he was a bat in another life."

"I heard that." Rafe's voice, sounding amused, came through clearly.

Jordan chuckled, a little amazed that he could, all things considered. Then Rafe's voice came through again.

"When I get to Foxworth I'll let Emily know you're up and about, in case she wants to call."

"Thanks," Jordan said, before he thought about what Rafe had said. "Wait, she's there?"

"She didn't tell you she was staying?" Teague asked.

"Uh...no."

"Too worried about you to leave. Good woman you got there, Crockett," Rafe said.

"I know," Jordan said. "Believe me, I know."

They signed off and left Jordan sitting there thinking about Emily sleeping in the bed where they'd made love, and his crazy imagination wanted to make it because that's where she wanted to be instead of home in her own bed. The bed in the house he'd never even seen.

How could something that had happened so fast feel so right?

The doubt nagged at him, until he remembered something he himself had written, in that long letter to her.

*He talked about you so much I almost feel like I know you.*

Maybe that was it. Emily had said her brother had talked about him to her, too, so maybe they knew each other better than they thought. Maybe that was why he'd felt that instant connection.

Cutter came trotting back, ears and tail up, and Jordan was amazed at how he relaxed at this indication there was no threat in the vicinity. Amazed at how much he trusted the dog and his instincts.

He busied himself fixing Cutter's dinner, then ate a quickly thrown together sandwich himself. When they were done he took his second cup of coffee and went to sit in the folding canvas chair he'd set up, this time farther back from the firepit, purposefully. As he sipped at the brew he watched Cutter, who was making yet another circuit along an unmarked perimeter he seemed to have set in his mind, since he stuck to it every time. The animal seemed to realize things were different now, that he wasn't here "just in case," but that the threat could be imminent.

*Okay, now you're believing in Superdog here.*

In that moment Cutter looked back over his shoulder at Jordan, who almost laughed aloud at the dog's uncanny timing.

"Reading my mind again, dog?"

The plumy tail wagged, and the dog went back to what he obviously considered his business.

Jordan went through what Quinn had told him about how the command "Easy" would have the dog acting like an ordinary pet, but "Guard" would have him on full alert. And a shouted "Now!" would turn him into a machine no one would want headed at them.

"And he'll take those commands from me?" he'd asked.

"He's the one who appointed himself for the job, so yes, he will. You're his focus until this is over."

Over. Just the word snapped him back to the present.

Funny, he'd always thought of it as kind of an extreme word, and when he'd been in uniform it had too often been linked to deaths, and of people he'd known and liked. But as he'd gotten closer to getting out, to his service being finished, it had shifted to something to look forward to.

And now it was something he wanted more than anything in his life. For this to be over.

Cutter came back, sat down beside the chair and pushed his nose under Jordan's elbow so that he had no choice but to pet him. And he couldn't deny how soothing it was, somehow, as if that soft fur had some sort of magical quality.

"Maybe you really are Superdog," he murmured.

Cutter made a low sound that could have been "Mmm-hmm."

He nearly laughed. Yes, he wanted this over. Not so much for himself, or even for taking down the man who'd killed Eddie and not only gotten away with it but painted himself as a hero. No, he wanted this over so he and Emily could explore what had leaped to life between them. Explore it, expand it, build on it.

Cutter nudged him.

"Oh, yeah," he said aloud, "and get a dog."

Emily sat on the couch in the Foxworth great room, rubbing at her temples. She hadn't felt like this since the days immediately after Eddie's death—so restless, so antsy, so lost.

So afraid.

Back then it had been because of the huge, gaping hole that had been blasted into her life. She simply couldn't imagine life without her brother, without that wry grin, that silly sense of humor, the pranks, that big, wonderful laugh.

She still couldn't, but now there was something that mattered even more. Now she knew the truth of how he had died. Now she knew that the person responsible had gotten away with it, in fact had come merrily back to the life he'd known before, undamaged, untouched even by his cowardly act.

Now there was Jordan. Jordan, who had reached parts of her that had never been stirred before. Jordan, who had made her feel hope for the future for the first time since it had happened. Jordan, who had kept her awake last night even though he wasn't here, simply with the memories entangled with the scent of him—of them—on the sheets of the bed they'd shared.

And he was risking his life to get justice for Eddie.

*Are you sure about this, Jordy?*

*It will give you peace.*

He'd answered it, that last night in the darkness as he held her close, as if that was the only reason he needed. As if her peace of mind were all that mattered to him, over and above his own safety, his own life.

"You all right?"

She looked up to see Hayley holding out a steaming mug. She took it thankfully, needing the wake-up kick.

"I don't know," she said frankly.

"We'll keep him safe," Hayley promised again. "And we'll make sure Lyden pays for what he did to your brother."

"In that order?"

"I think that's your order of priority now," Hayley said gently.

Emily sucked in a quick breath. "Yes. Yes, it is. And no one's more surprised than me to realize it."

"It's hard, especially when you're in the middle of grief. But sometimes the scale balances, Emily. Sometimes, when you're feeling the worst, you find the best."

She sat there for a long, silent moment, looking at this woman who knew what she was talking about. Who understood. And said what had been bothering her all morning, since she'd awakened from the worst nightmare she'd had since the ones after Eddie had been killed. A nightmare about the same thing happening to Jordan.

"I…haven't told him," she said, her voice shaky.

"Told him?"

"The actual words, I mean. We've…danced around it, but…"

Understanding dawned in Hayley's eyes. "You mean you haven't told him you love him."

"It just seemed too soon, it happened so fast."

"But it didn't, really, did it? You knew a lot about him before you ever met in person." Hayley's smile was gentle, yet encouraging. "Besides, he was vetted by someone you trusted completely."

"Eddie."

Hayley nodded. And Emily felt something release inside her, as if all the tension that had built since they'd hatched this plan had released. She simply had to believe that it was true. That Jordan would be okay, and that when this was over they could put this behind them and move on.

Together.

# Chapter 32

It had been one of the longer days of Jordan's life. It reminded him of days spent waiting for patrols to return, for the teams of men who had left in vehicles he kept running to come back, knowing that there was no guarantee they all would. At least, not alive; rarely was anyone left behind, even dead.

*Lyden would have left Eddie.*

He knew it was true, that if it had just been the two of them, Lyden would have run. He would have run, leaving Eddie there to die alone, from the wound he had caused. But they hadn't been alone. Jordan had been there, he'd seen what happened, and that had been both blessing and curse.

He was still a little amazed that the man hadn't killed him, too. But then, ol' Hart had never been quick on the spot. He'd been guided by his powerful family his entire life, done nothing but follow their orders, and without them there to tell him what to do, he'd panicked.

*And they want this guy running the country?*

He wished that sounded more impossible than it did. But Foxworth had done a ton of research, come up with dozens of articles, speeches and videos, and Jordan had read and watched them all. And so he'd learned now about the Lyden family and the extent of their power—and their dreams for future power—and they were clearly in it for the long game.

And he was in their way.

If this worked, he wondered who they'd send. If old man Lyden had any stones, he'd make his little boy handle his own mess. So was the old man all talk? Or, when it came to blood, were all bets off?

Another thought hit him. Were there any other Lyden kids? Another offspring with maybe a little more brainpower, a little more nerve? Maybe they'd dump Hart and go with that one for the future plans.

*Or maybe send that one after you.*

Now that was a possibility that hadn't occurred to him before. He'd always kind of assumed a family like the Lydens had people on staff to handle the little annoyances.

But maybe, as a potential roadblock to all their big plans, he was more than that. Maybe the problem he presented was worth a little personal attention. Maybe he—

*Maybe, maybe, maybe... That all you got, Crockett?*

Eddie's voice rang in his ears. He supposed that it was a tribute to their friendship—or his own weird mood today—that he was able to laugh at the oft repeated teasing mockery.

*He's going to pay, Eddie. I swear to you, and your sister, he's going to pay.*

He'd kept himself as busy as possible all day, from doing every task he could think of on the van, to handling a couple of the tasks Sarge had posted on the maintenance board outside the laundry/shower building, all interspersed between sessions of throwing a ball for Cutter until his arm ached. When evening came, he made a round, stopping at each site to thank every camper for putting up with what he hoped would soon be over. To a man they echoed what Sarge had told him; they didn't need to know exactly what was going on, just that he was up against a civilian power broker.

When he got back he fed Cutter first, figuring he'd be hungry after all that time chasing that now filthy tennis ball. Then he threw together a meal for himself, silently wondering if it might be his last. But the moment the thought formed he remembered who was looking out for him, and he had the feeling anyone who tried to get past Rafe Crawford would be in for a surprise, and not the good kind. Still, he grabbed up his own weapon of choice and placed it beside the chair, angled so it looked like part of the supporting structure.

Now that it was dark enough—which happened later here than anyplace he'd ever been—he switched on the new floodlights he'd attached to the side of the van. They starkened the shadows, but threw everything within their considerable reach into full, bright light. Something he would normally not care for—he'd even apologized to all his fellow campers for the glare that was to come—because he enjoyed the look and sound and smell of nighttime most places, but especially here, with the scent of evergreens that would stay the same this winter, when most other trees were bare.

Plus, he would have preferred his eyes be adjusted to the dark, but the reason for the lights took precedence, so he would just have to depend on Cutter for that early warning. And that didn't particularly worry him; he might still be a bit skeptical about some of the talents they claimed the dog had, but there was no denying he was a damned good watchdog.

As the clock crept onward, he began to wonder if this was going to happen at all, at least tonight. Maybe the Lydens needed more prep time. Maybe they'd had to call in outside help. Maybe—

*Maybe, maybe, maybe... That all you got, Crockett?*

He laughed out loud this time, sending a silent thanks to his lost comrade, who even now was helping keep him sane.

He went inside and grabbed the book he'd been reading, something he'd borrowed from the Foxworth headquarters shelves. He remembered his grandmother reading this detective series when he was a kid, and he'd been curious. Halfway through the first book now, he was beginning to see why she'd loved it so much.

Leaning back in the chair, book in hand, feet up on the edge of the currently not in use firepit, he hoped he presented a casual and unthreatening vibe. Cutter plopped down beside him, close enough for the occasional stroke. The dog seemed relaxed, but Jordan knew he was ever alert, and his nose and those ears missed nothing.

He was deep into the story when Cutter's head came up sharply, and a low growl issued from his throat, startling him out of it. Jordan looked at the dog and saw his ears swivel toward the east, the downhill slope to the road.

A moment later a voice sounded in his ear. Rafe.

"Heads up, Crockett. Car just parked down on the road, and one man got out. Appears to be alone. Dark clothes, about the right height and weight, but couldn't get a facial ID. Walked into the trees."

"Yeah," Jordan said. "Cutter just alerted."

"Copy," came another voice he recognized as Quinn's. "On it."

That was Teague, who was back at Foxworth headquarters to handle the next stage of the plan. He was glad the man was there. Between him and Hayley, Emily was well protected. And that was what mattered most to him.

Silence followed. Jordan realized after a minute or so he was holding his breath and consciously let it out. The silence continued for another minute, then Teague's voice came through again.

"Confirmed. It's not his personal vehicle, but it's registered to a Lyden company."

"Roger," Jordan said, not even wondering anymore how they had such easy access to information.

So this really was it. He drew in a deep breath and slowly let it out. Then again. And oddly, a deep sense of certainty settled upon him. It was Hart. As if he could see the man skulking through the trees toward him, he knew it. There was no way the coward would risk anyone else finding out the truth of what had happened to Eddie.

He wondered if the guy had had any problem with running home to Daddy and telling him what had happened. Or maybe he hadn't told him, maybe he had fed his family the lie. Given them the line about wanting to find Jordan because he was worried about him. It didn't seem like anything the Lydens would care about, but it might make for some good PR. And the thought that

Hart would lie even to his father fit. After all, he lied to himself, told himself he was heroic and worthy of a high place in the world, all the time.

But surely it would have taken somebody with Lyden-size power to bury the truth. While the Army didn't have much evidence—Hart had seen to that. At such close range the rounds had gone right through Eddie, and Lyden found the slugs in the desert dirt and policed his brass, all while Jordan had been desperately trying to save Eddie's life—they did have his statement. Surely the military wasn't that far gone, that they'd bury the truth themselves. It had to be his family who had quashed it. A few phone calls, some pressure brought to bear...

"You're ten times the hero he thinks he is," he murmured to Cutter as the dog continued to let out those low, threatening, deep-throated growls.

And then Cutter was on his feet, his attention focused unwaveringly on the trees to their left. The low growls became fierce snarls and a couple of loud barks, and Jordan did as Quinn had told him again.

"Got it, dog. I know he's coming," he said softly.

*What I don't know is if I can pull this off.*

He was no actor, he knew that. Yet he was going to have to act his brains out to be convincing. Yes, they'd planned it all out beforehand, what to say that was mostly likely to work, and ways to tweak it depending on variables or unexpected twists and turns.

*Maybe he'll just come in, gun at the ready, to take me out.*

He almost wished for that, for at least then it would be over quickly. He had no doubts the moment it was clear Lyden intended to shoot, he'd be dropped in his tracks. Snipers like Rafe Crawford didn't miss.

Cutter was clearly on edge. To be honest, so was he, but whereas he was nervous, he was fairly sure the dog just wanted to be cut loose to go after the approaching threat.

"Wait," he said quietly. "We've got to wait."

Clearly reluctant, the dog settled down into a crouch, the snarls fading back to those low, quiet growls.

"Jordan, you're on?"

He blinked. That was Hayley's voice. "Yes," he said.

"Target has arrived, it'll have to wait." Quinn that time.

"It can't," Hayley said.

There was only a split-second pause before Quinn said "Go." That was how much faith he had in his wife.

A moment later Jordan heard another voice. Emily. Speaking his name, and three more words.

"I love you."

For a moment everything else faded away. There was no danger, no approaching enemy and suddenly no fear. And he said the only thing he could. "I love you, too."

"We're clear." Hayley again.

And that quickly, in the space of less than thirty seconds, everything shifted, settled. He'd get through this. Somehow. And when it was over...

He found himself smiling, in spite of everything.

Cutter made an odd little sound, and when he looked, the dog was watching him with an expression that looked almost like approval. But immediately after they made eye contact, the dog was back on duty.

Thanks to Cutter, Jordan knew where to look, since the animal was zeroed in on those trees. And he thought even he heard the brushing of a branch against...something. Cutter clearly knew the man was close; he was fairly quivering in anticipation. Jordan stood up, wanting to be on his feet when Lyden stepped into the clearing.

*Unless he just takes a shot from the cover of the trees...*

"I've got him," Rafe said in his ear, as if he'd somehow sensed Jordan's thought. "He makes a wrong move, I'll drop him."

A sudden image of the man, night-vision gear in place, the approaching threat clearly in his crosshairs, calmed Jordan. Foxworth was the best run operation he'd ever seen. The Army had nothing on these guys.

He walked over to double-check something on the van, then came back toward the firepit, as casually as he could manage with Cutter hunkered down there strung wire-taut.

"Easy, dog. But thanks."

Cutter shot him a quick glance at the last word. Gave a soft little woof.

And Jordan nearly laughed at himself for being so comforted because he had a dog on his side. A very special, even unique dog.

But the biggest comfort of all came from the amazing fact that he had the most incredible woman in the world waiting for him.

# Chapter 33

When the moment finally came and the approaching man stepped out of the trees and into the light enough to be recognized, Jordan was able to at least start out as planned. He looked over, tried to act surprised and prepped himself to sound casual. And as respectful as he could manage, although it turned his stomach a little.

"Lieutenant Lyden?" He worked up a decent—he hoped—smile. "Wow, good to see you, sir."

Lyden stopped in his tracks, his brow furrowing. He looked startled, even drew back a little. Glanced warily at the dog, then back to Jordan. He looked much as he had the last time Jordan had seen him, physically, although the dark hair had grown out into a carefully trimmed, businesslike haircut. The ears still stuck out a little, and his neck was still a little short for his height.

The only thing added was a little weight. The only

thing missing was the chronic fear bordering on terror that had always been in his nervous, darting eyes.

Because he was home now, with his wealthy family to back him, protect him, coddle him.

*The only thing he's got to fear is the truth, and the only one who carries that is you.*

"Crockett," Hart Lyden finally said, as if he weren't quite sure, as if the friendly greeting had derailed his thinking. Just as planned.

Gavin de Marco's instructions played through his mind. *He'll expect you to want him dead on arrival. So greet him as if he's a long-lost brother in arms. Make him have to stop and rethink.* Jordan remembered it hadn't taken much to do that before, and apparently that hadn't changed even here, back in the nest. He and Eddie had always joked you had to rethink more often when your thinking was a mess in the first place.

"What are you doing all the way out here?" He smiled wider now, as if to show he was joking when he said, "Slumming?"

"I… Of course not. I just… I like to check on fellow vets, make sure they're doing okay."

*Fellow vets. Right, jackass.*

But the script seemed to be working and so, encouraged, Jordan went on as planned. "That's good of you, coming out to check on us homeless guys. I figured you'd be busy being a high roller again by now."

If he'd said it the way he felt it, it would have been dripping with scathing sarcasm. But he didn't.

*You're going to have to act. Like you know you're not in his league, his class. He's a Lyden, and you're properly awed. Play up the difference between your station in life and his. You're just a stereotypical homeless vet, while he's bound for glory.*

He'd winced inwardly at that particular bit of coaching, probably because while he knew de Marco meant it as a tactic, it hit a little close to the bone.

"You look as if you're doing all right," Lyden said, looking at the van. Jordan supposed it did look like one of those six-figure jobs, if you didn't know he'd done it all himself.

"Not as well as you, but then we all knew that. We're just grunts. You were the one destined for greatness." He gave it his best smile, hoped he hadn't overdone it. "We used to say that one day we'd see you giving a speech from the White House and be able to say, 'Hey, I served with him!'"

Lyden was starting to look like someone who had stepped onto what he'd thought was a solid surface that was now starting to give way beneath him. As if he'd been certain of how this would go, and it wasn't going that way at all. That narrow brow of his was furrowed even deeper now.

*There's a reason de Marco is who he is.*

"How long have you been here?" Lyden finally asked, after another wary glance at Cutter, who was on his feet with his gaze glued to the man.

"Just got here yesterday." He put on his best light bulb moment expression. "Hey, there was some reporter here then. Was that how you found us?"

"I... Yes. We saw the report."

We. As in the Lyden family, soon to be dynasty? He fought back the repulsion and pasted on his best impressed smile. "And you're here already? That's great, sir. It's good to know that you won't forget us when you're in a position to help."

"Of course I won't. I plan to do everything I can to help the plight of veterans everywhere."

It rolled off his tongue like a campaign speech, and Jordan was nearly certain he'd already been rehearsing it.

*Like you had to rehearse this next part?*

"And you'll have the résumé to do it now," he said, trying his best to make himself sound impressed. "Just like you planned. Smart, sir."

He held his breath, hoping he hadn't taken a step too far, hoping that Hartwell Lyden's ego was as overblown as he thought it was.

"It is working out as planned," Lyden agreed, and for the first time Jordan saw a trace of a smile. "Service to the country always looks good on a political résumé."

"So it was an investment in the future, not a desire to go out and fight enemies," he said, nodding as if in understanding agreement, and a little awe.

"Of course." Lyden's nose wrinkled. "No one who could do better would *want* to do that kind of thing."

Well, that was step one, getting him to admit that was why he'd done it, why he'd joined up in the first place. He steeled himself, ordered his stomach to stop churning because the worst nausea inducement was yet to come. He poured on a little more of the welcome wagon brew, trying to gauge just how much Lyden relaxed. The longer he blathered, the more it was noticeable. He just had to hope it would be enough.

A new voice spoke in the earpiece. De Marco. "I think you've got him at ease enough. Go for it."

He sucked in a deep breath. And went for it. "I'm really glad you're here, Lieutenant."

"You are?" Lyden still looked confused, but leavened

with suspicion. Jordan was a little surprised they'd let him come alone to handle this.

"Yeah. I wanted to apologize, for how messed up I was that day. I got everything tangled up in my head, you know? I wasn't used to being under fire, not like you combat guys were."

Lyden puffed up a little. "It does take a certain mental discipline not to fall apart."

*Right. Fall apart so much you grab a weapon by the trigger and shoot one of your own.*

"I see that now, now that I'm back home. It was silly to think you had meant to shoot Eddie."

Lyden gaped at him, clearly stunned. "Meant to shoot him? You thought it was intentional?"

*Almost there...*

"I know, crazy. Why would you, of all people? He meant nothing to you."

"Hmph." A touch of the disdain Jordan remembered had slipped into his tone and manner. It made Jordan want to follow through on the wish he'd had since he'd seen Lyden's face, to take him out at the knees. "I'm a Lyden. He was a nobody."

*Just like I was. And still am.*

He made himself focus, just as de Marco spoke again, steadying him. "You've got him Jordan. One more tug, and you've landed this shark."

"I'm really sorry for any trouble I made for you. I should have known better." He let out a wry laugh. "As if anyone would have believed me over you anyway."

"No, they wouldn't. Especially not when my father got through with them."

"And I realized later, once I wasn't so scared any-more—" damn, this crawling made him want to puke

"—that it had to have been an accident. You didn't mean to shoot Eddie, he just happened to be in the wrong place, moved at the wrong time. And you were in a shoot first, make sure later mode." *Unable to tell a backfire from a gunshot, and piss-poor with a gun anyway.* "So, accident, right?"

"Of course it was an accident," Lyden snapped. "Why would I *want* to shoot him? He was just a mechanic."

For a moment Jordan couldn't react. Couldn't quite believe it had worked.

"You did it," came de Marco's voice in his ear. "Nice work. Move on fast now, keep him talking while we make sure we've got it."

Jordan felt so many things boiling up inside him. He wanted to release them all, but doubted that would be wise; it wouldn't accomplish much to have gained that confession and then end up in jail himself for jumping Lyden like the lying swine he was. Besides, Lyden didn't seem to have realized what he'd just done. Of course, he also didn't know about the modifications made to the van yesterday, either. But he'd better move on before the idiot had a chance to think.

Jordan pressed on, waiting on a razor's edge for that earpiece to sound again. But he spoke mildly, as if he were only making an observation, "Yes, that's all he was, a mechanic. Not like he could get in the way of your future plans." Lyden's gaze narrowed slightly, as if he heard the implied insult in the words but the casual tone made him unsure if it was intentional. "So," Jordan went on the same way, "what's first? City or county office? Or are you going to skip right on past that to statewide? Nothing to stop you, right?"

He looked confused now. Jordan went on quickly.

"I'll have to find out how long I have to live here to vote, won't I?" *Early and often, as the old joke that wasn't so funny anymore goes, and against you.* "Oh, wait, you can probably tell me that, can't you?"

"Thirty days," Lyden said. "You can register after you've lived here thirty days." For a moment he sounded exactly like a candidate trying to win over a prospective supporter. Jordan heard a laugh in his ear, realized it was de Marco. That had to be a good sign, didn't it, that the great, world-famous attorney was laughing?

The improbability of it all almost made him laugh out loud, too.

"It's on its way, Jordan." Teague's voice this time. "It's already hitting the big sites. Our friends posted the video, and reposts and sharing started almost immediately."

"Good to know," he said, choosing words that could serve as an answer to both statements. "Make sure to send us all some campaign literature. We're always happy to vote for someone who served with honor and distinction." *Which eliminates you.* Then, his gaze now steady and zeroed in on Lyden, he asked, "So what *did* you plan on running for first?"

He saw Lyden's brows twitch again at this emphasis on the past tense.

"We haven't decided yet."

"You mean Daddy hasn't?"

That sparked a reaction. "What's that supposed to mean?"

"It's a family operation, isn't it? The whole Lyden machine?"

Teague's voice again, sounding delighted. "It's exploded. And one of our friends who happens to be within watching distance of the Lyden mansion said it just went from dark to lit up like a Christmas tree. It's all yours now, Jordan. Rafe?"

"Copy," came the voice so calm it seemed the man must be nerveless. "Still have him." Then, with a tiny hint of amusement. "In case you want to get reckless, Jordan."

He did. He truly did. He looked at the man who had killed Eddie, the man who had stolen such a huge part of the life of the woman he loved. And this time he didn't even try to stifle his chuckle. And it quickly grew into a full-on belly laugh.

Lyden looked irritated at first, but it almost as quickly grew into anger. "What's so damned funny, Crockett?"

"You, you clown hat. You really thought you were going to get away with it, didn't you? That you could kill a man worth a thousand of you through your own stupidity and incompetence, and just walk away."

"You just said yourself it was an accident!"

"While you denied you did it at all...until now."

Lyden sneered then. "And I always will. And I'll get away with it. Because like you just said yourself, nobody would believe you over me."

"They don't have to. You're going down, Lyden. Hard, and for good. Pretty soon everyone will know what useless, cowardly slime you really are."

He'd hit the man's breaking point. Lyden reached behind his back.

"Gun," came Rafe's voice, as freakily calm as it had been all along.

"I know. Hold," he said, to both Rafe and Cutter.

"Until I can't," the sniper answered. The dog snarled in protest, but held.

Lyden apparently hadn't even heard Jordan's words. He was busy fumbling—as he had that day—with a weapon. He pulled a small handgun out of his belt and aimed it at Jordan. He clearly intended to use it. Jordan was almost disconcerted by how calm he felt. Maybe Rafe was rubbing off on him.

"Been wondering why you didn't do that in the first place, back when Eddie was bleeding out on the ground after you shot him."

"I almost did," Lyden said, his voice sounding a little like Cutter's snarl. "I should have."

"Maybe killing both of us would have been twice as hard to cover up, huh?"

"Dad was pissed I didn't."

"Well, he's going to be even more pissed now."

"He won't care about you. He just told me to clean up the mess." He raised the gun, although his hand wasn't particularly steady. "And everyone will believe you're just another suicide."

"You might want to rethink that," Jordan said. Lyden stared at him, as if the casual tone confused him. "You see, I added a couple of pieces of equipment yesterday. The lights—" he smiled then, widely, as he gestured back at the van "—and two cameras."

He saw Lyden's gaze shift, saw him spot the two devices. As if acting out of some animal instinct—although that was sort of an insult to Cutter—he swore harshly and ran toward the cameras, the gun now raised as if to smash them.

The moment he moved, so did Jordan. He grabbed the crowbar he'd put by the chair, straightened, spun and swung all in one continuous motion. Cutter, taking Jordan's move as assent, leaped toward the man. The end of the crowbar smashed into Lyden's ribs in the same instant Cutter's jaws clamped on the wrist of the hand that held the gun. Lyden screamed as he dropped the weapon. He went to his knees, Cutter still gripping his wrist.

"Yeah, if I was as lousy a shot as you I'd use it as a blunt instrument, too," Jordan said. "But it doesn't matter now. It's over, Lyden."

"Nice move," Rafe said in his ear, sounding amused again.

"Get this dog off of me! I'll have you arrested for assault! You'll go to jail, Crockett."

"I doubt it. Foxworth has those videos already, and they're multiplying on social media like the locust you are."

"Foxworth?" Lyden sounded startled; it was clear he knew the name. "What do they have to do with—" He was cut off by a rather odd buzzing sound that Jordan realized was the man's phone.

"You'd better get that," he said with a crooked grin. "It'll explain everything. But I guess you can't do it with your arm in a vice, can you? Cutter, guard."

The dog obediently but clearly reluctantly released Lyden's arm. But he didn't move an inch, and the steady growl that issued from his throat kept the man watching him nervously as he grabbed for the phone.

A moment later Jordan could hear the sound from the video that Foxworth had sent—he didn't know how they'd gotten the number and frankly didn't care—the playback of everything that had just happened here. Lyden was staring at the small screen, and even from here Jordan could see how well the new floodlights had lit up the scene.

The phone started buzzing again, multiple times, and Jordan laughed at the look on Lyden's face as call after panicked call started to come in. The Lyden machine was in overdrive.

"Ten thousand views in less than five minutes," Teague gloated in his ear. "And that's just one site."

Jordan relayed that statistic to Lyden in much the same tone of voice. "It's already everywhere, Hartwell. Everything you said, did and admitted to here is out there now for the world to see. And there's no stopping it. There's not a spin doctor in the world that can turn this around. And if anything ever happens to me, or to anyone connected to me—" *I love you, Emmie* "—you'll be the prime suspect."

"You bastard!" Lyden screamed. Cutter's growl became a snarl again, but he held.

"You're done, *Lieutenant*." He spat it out at the man who didn't deserve the rank. "You'd be lucky to be 'just a mechanic.' But you don't have the skill for it. And every time you feel like whining about what's left of your miserable life, I want you to think about why. That you brought it on yourself. Because this was for Eddie."

He stood there, staring at the man now in the dirt, held there by a fierce dog who showed no sign of relenting.

"Well done." Coming from Rafe Crawford, it was a compliment he'd treasure.

He heard a sound from the trees behind him, knew it was Quinn. The man came to a halt beside his dog. "And just in case you have any idea that you or your family can bury this," Quinn said casually, "Foxworth will always be around to make sure it's dug up again. No matter where or how you try to hide it. Even the Lydens won't be able to cover this one up."

He turned to look at Jordan then, and echoed Rafe's words. And this time the "done" part truly resonated.

Done.

It was over. They really had done it.

For Lyden, it was over.

For him, it wouldn't be over until he was with Emily again.

# Chapter 34

Emily knew Hayley was driving as fast as she could, but it still wasn't fast enough.

She wasn't really complaining, she'd known Hayley had needed to be at the Foxworth headquarters to help Teague make sure the video got spread far and wide. But now that it was done, and after a few minutes spent looking at the ballooning spread of the truth about Hartwell Lyden and the mad scramble of the family to quash the story—sort of like trying to call back a bomb that had already gone off—she thought she might just fly apart into a thousand pieces if she couldn't see Jordan soon.

Almost in that same moment she heard that beloved voice coming over the car's audio system, which was tied in with the Foxworth phones. "Hey, Emmie, you want to spit on this piece of debris before it's carted off?"

He sounded so...free that she was grinning the mo-

ment he said her name. The nickname only her family
used. And that still held, because he was her family now.
In the best possible way.

"Who's carting him off?" she asked Hayley.

"Quinn called in Sloan, who made some calls. She
knows who's left in the Army who still cares about the
right things and will stand up to the Lydens. And she's
already called a certain senator who, as an honestly honored vet himself, stood with her then. If I know her, the
investigation has already been reopened. He'll be the
Army's until that's done."

"Good enough," she said, then reached up to key the
speaker as Hayley had shown her. "Don't need to," she
said to Jordan. "You did the perfect job for both of us."

Quinn's voice came through. "Hayley, you two en
route?"

"ETA eight minutes. Or less, if Emily has anything
to say about it."

"Good. Rafe and I are going to move Lyden to JBLM.
Sloan's local contact will meet us there."

She was so anxious to get to Jordan it took Emily a
moment to translate the acronym to Joint Base Lewis-
McChord, the military installation just south of Tacoma.

"Let the investigation begin," Hayley said with satisfaction.

"Jordan?" Emily asked.

"They'll want to talk to him, obviously, but we'll get
him there later. We sort of figured Emily would want to
see him first."

"Coming right along there, Mr. Foxworth," Hayley
said with a grin that was obvious in her voice.

When they arrived, Hayley made the turn and headed
up the hill. They weren't even within sight of Jordan's

spot when she heard Cutter's welcoming bark. And when they got there the car hadn't even come to a complete stop before Emily was out and running, just as Cutter started running toward Hayley. She laughed out loud as the dog threw her an acknowledging yip as they passed going in opposite directions. She thought she'd never felt so light, so free, in her entire life.

As Jordan turned and looked at her, his face wearing a similar expression, she thought she just might be able to fly the rest of the way. At last she was in his arms, he was holding her, kissing her, and she dared to let herself believe in tomorrow. And all the tomorrows after that.

Later, back at the headquarters, Emily snuggled up next to Jordan on the couch as they watched the news reports unroll. The moment Cutter had opened the front door for them—romping like a pup who appeared the total opposite of the fierce guardian he'd been "on duty"—Teague had told them he'd been recording all of the outlets, to take a seat and he'd get the popcorn, because they were going to enjoy this.

And they did. They even laughed a couple of times at the various Lyden representatives floundering to cover it up and failing utterly. When one ambitious citizen journalist managed to corner the senior Lyden and ask what this did to his son's plan to run for office, the old man glared and denied there was or had ever been any such plan.

"So," Rafe drawled as they finally shut down the flat-screen TV, "you not only got some justice at least for Edward Bishop, you saved the rest of us from having to deal with that…thing in office."

"You're welcome," Jordan said, grinning.

The change in him was nothing less than amazing, and

Emily had the feeling she was only now seeing just how much this had been weighing on him. Not that it had all been joyous—there had been a moment, when a photograph of Eddie had unexpectedly popped on-screen during a report, when the loss had threatened to swamp her all over again. But Jordan had been right there, hugging her the instant it appeared, sharing the loss with her, and she regained her equilibrium much faster than she otherwise would have.

They spent one last night in the comfortable bedroom at Foxworth, finding the pull between them as strong as ever. More so, in fact, now that the hovering shadow had been removed. They both knew there were a lot of details coming up, that Jordan would have to be part of the investigation that would change everything, but for now, they simply reveled in each other, the new happiness flavoring every move, every touch.

Oddly—or perhaps not—Cutter did not insist on staying this time, but rather happily went home with his people. He knew his job was done, Quinn told them.

And even Rafe left them with a rare grin, saying they were on their own.

They made the most of it.

The next day Gavin de Marco arrived early, just after the Foxworths, and Emily had to admit she enjoyed Jordan's stunned look when he realized the man would be accompanying him today to a meeting with a couple of Army representatives and, via a video call, a certain senator whose name engendered respect from any true veteran. A little later Sloan arrived, announcing she would be going as well, since she had a personal connection to the senator—he'd been the one who had helped her in her fight for justice for her late Navy SEAL husband.

That fight had made her name well-known in the same circles as well, and her voice would add weight to their fight to make the truth known.

And then the woman Emily remembered from those countless televised hearings looked from them to Cutter, then back with a wide grin. "Another success, huh, dog?"

Jordan blinked. "You, too?" he asked.

Sloan nodded, her long bangs sliding forward with the movement. "John was dog sitting, and they were out on his usual daily run when Cutter suddenly changed course. He literally led John to me."

Emily was smiling as she glanced at Hayley. "A sheriff's detective is your dog sitter?"

"Wasn't our call," she answered cheerfully. "It was our honeymoon and he was going to stay with Teague, but he decided differently. He planted himself next to John's car and refused to move."

"That dog," Jordan pronounced, "is scary." A grin flashed again. "But in a really good way."

In the end Emily insisted on going along to the meeting. She not only wanted to be there for Eddie, but for Jordan. Plus she wanted to be around all these incredibly dynamic people. She also wanted to know right away how it went. Since she hadn't been a witness to what had happened she hadn't expected to be an actual part of things, but both Sloan and her now friend—and former Army colonel—Senator Bienvenido insisted she at the least be in the room.

She got to remotely meet the senator, one of the few she regarded highly, who respectfully expressed his condolences on her brother, and promised her it would not be swept under the Lyden rug. He also decided she had every right to sit in on the proceedings, which she hadn't been prepared for, but with Jordan at her side she got through it anyway. It was tough, hearing the story of Eddie's death again, but when it was done she felt a sense of finality.

*We've done all that could be done, little brother. Rest in peace now.*

She supposed the sapped sort of feeling she had now was from the ebbing of the adrenaline that had been coursing through her at some level ever since Jordan had dropped into her life. Or maybe it was simply that having him—in all sorts of ways—had drained away her tensions. She smiled inwardly at her own thought.

It was late afternoon before they got back. Jordan began to gather up what things of his had ended up at the Foxworth headquarters, readying, she supposed, to go back to the camp. She had a few things of her own to collect, but first she had to ask him something.

"Jordan?"

"What?" He turned, some of that underwear he'd made that wisecrack about in his hand. The underwear she had indeed gotten her own hands into. She had to smother another smile. That was happening a lot these days.

"I need to go home to attend to some things. Will you come with me?"

He blinked, then smiled much like she imagined her own would have looked like if she'd let it out. So she did. "I'd like that," he said. "I'd like to see…where you live."

So they ended up on the road together, and as she drove toward home Emily couldn't stop wondering what it would be like to take off in his van with him, heading somewhere she'd never been with him, exploring with him. Then she realized she was already doing that, in a very personal sense.

She only realized she was smiling again when he spoke. "You look happy. Glad it's over, huh?"

She glanced at him as she made the turn onto her narrow, rural-looking street. "I am," she said. "But I was thinking more about beginnings than endings."

She saw him swallow, and his voice was low and a little unsteady when he said, "Me, too."

"Maybe we can talk about that. Moving on from this, I mean. I know it's only been—"

She broke off suddenly as her little cottage came into view.

"What?" he asked.

"That car in my driveway—"

"What?" he repeated, but his tone was entirely different, amped up and tense, and she realized where his mind had gone.

"It's nothing to do with the Lydens," she said quickly, and he relaxed and let out a relieved breath. "It's my father."

# Chapter 35

The simple words were a punch to the gut for Jordan. Her father. Eddie's father.

He was feeling so many things he couldn't sort them out, and was tempted to jettison the lot and get the hell out of there.

Run.

Even the thought made his stomach churn. He wasn't that guy. He wasn't his parents, he wouldn't run. He'd faced down Hart Lyden, hadn't he? No, he wouldn't run. Even if this was a meet-the-family thing.

Especially not with Emmie beside him.

As they pulled in behind the not-brand-new but well-kept—*so sue me, I notice that stuff*—larger SUV with the logo for Bishop Tool on the door, a man came down from the porch and started toward them. Jordan felt an odd tightness in his throat as he recognized Eddie's lanky build and long stride, and it increased when the man got close enough for him to see the shape of his jaw and his nose, the mirror image of his best friend.

"Damn, Eddie looked like him," he whispered.

"He did," Emily confirmed, reaching over to clasp his hand for a moment. "And he will be delighted to meet the man who tried so hard to save Eddie's life."

*But how about the man who's sleeping with his daughter?*

"Emmie!" the man exclaimed as she got out of the car and ran to meet him, throwing her arms around him as if it had been a year, not two weeks, since she'd seen him. But then he supposed it felt like a year, after everything that had happened. Jordan opened the door and got out of the car, but stayed where he was.

"You're back early," she exclaimed happily.

"Business was done and I missed you. I was just leaving you a note," Mr. Bishop said.

She leaned back, looked at the piece of paper in his hand and laughed. "Dad, you're hopeless."

"I already tried texting you," he protested.

"Oh. Sorry, I forgot I had my phone muted." Even from here he could see her take a deep breath. "A lot's happened while you were gone."

"Has it? I've been too involved in negotiations to keep up with anything, and then I was on the plane." Jordan had thought the man hadn't noticed him yet, but his next words told him otherwise. "Something to do with the young man who's with you?"

She turned then and, with a smile that somehow eased all his tension, waved him over.

"Dad, this is Jordan. Jordan Crockett. Jordy, my dad, otherwise known as Benjamin Bishop."

They were already shaking hands when something

changed in the older man's expression. "Jordy? Eddie's friend?"

"Yes, sir."

The handshake became a tug, and the next thing he knew he was enveloped in a hug almost as fierce as the one he'd given his daughter. "Thank you," Ben Bishop said.

"Sir?" He said it questioningly but respectfully.

Mr. Bishop pulled back and grasped his shoulders as if he wanted to hold him in place for an inspection. He was blinking a bit rapidly, and those eyes, also so like Eddie's, bore into him. "Thank you for trying to save my son."

"I… He was my friend. My best friend."

He left it at that, since no more words came to him. But Emily didn't have that problem.

"There's so much more to it, Dad. I know you never listen to news while traveling, so…well, just come inside. I'll make coffee. Or maybe something stronger. You may need it."

Jordan was glad of the distraction of looking around Emily's home as they went inside. He'd already noticed the carefully tended garden, full of colorful summer flowers and some plants whose leaves had color of their own. It reminded him of his grandmother's garden, where he would usually find her if she wasn't in the house.

Inside was a bright, cheerful place, full of blue and white with a dash of yellow here and there. Sky, clouds and sun he thought suddenly, surprised at himself; he usually didn't think about such things.

"I think a glass of wine might be in order," she said and headed for the kitchen.

"We rarely drink. Is it that bad?" Mr. Bishop asked as he gestured Jordan into the living room and a seat on the couch. Then the other man sat in the armchair opposite.

"It's…a long story," he said. "And complicated." *And it depends on how you feel about Emily's choice to let me into her life.*

But he knew they had much to get through first, and when she came back with three glasses of a red something—he was hardly a wine connoisseur—she set them down, walked over to a carved wooden box on the coffee table and took something out. An envelope. She pulled out the contents, and Jordan recognized immediately that it was his letter to her. She glanced at him, as if for approval of what she was about to do. Just two weeks ago he would have struggled with that decision. But now it was over, done, handled as best it could be. So he nodded.

"It started with this," she said quietly, handing the letter to her father. To Eddie's father.

And then she sat down beside Jordan, close enough that it drew her father's gaze, which made Jordan twitch a little. But she simply told her father to read, and they would go on from there.

It took them a long time to get through the story of everything that had happened. And when it was done, and all the questions answered, Mr. Bishop sat, head bowed, in silence for a long moment before he looked up again, at Jordan.

"That thank-you I gave you before wasn't nearly enough, Jordan. You not only tried to save my son's life, you gave us the truth of his death and made sure the person responsible will pay in a manner most odious to him."

Jordan's mouth quirked. "He's not going to have quite the future he expected." Then he sighed. "I know it doesn't bring Eddie back, Mr. Bishop, but…"

"I think," Emily's father said seriously, "you had best

call me Ben. Because I suspect something else happened during all this."

Jordan froze. How had he known?

As if he'd asked aloud, her father answered, "I know this because I haven't seen my girl look this happy in… well, ever."

Emily blushed. She actually blushed. And Jordan couldn't help himself, he grinned. And instead of being nervous, he suddenly felt the confidence of a man who'd just seen a happy future he'd never expected to find unrolling in front of him.

Jordan gave a last swipe with the rag to clear out the excess oil, then hit the switch. The sander fired right up again, and he gave a nod of satisfaction. The kind of tools Bishop made were not what he was used to working on, but his brain was making the switch from one kind of machine to another fairly quickly. And if he'd built this one right, he'd have added a new functionality to this power tool that it hadn't had before—the ability to reach into tiny spaces and smooth out anything from wood to metal, depending on the head attached.

*Sometimes I'm not sure my head's attached. It keeps wanting to float off into some happy ether.*

He caught himself looking around the Bishop workshop in wonder. His entire life had shifted. He was out from under the Lyden shadow, he had a job he enjoyed, working for a generous man he liked and respected already…and above all he had Emmie. His pulse kicked up just thinking about her, as it always seemed to.

As if he'd somehow conjured her up with his thoughts, she was there. And her father was with her, which put a damper on what he would have liked to do. Ben Bishop had welcomed him into both his daughter's life and the business his family had built, but that didn't mean he'd want to witness the deep, long kiss he wanted to plant on Emmie's luscious mouth.

The senior Bishop gestured him into the small room that served as the office for the workshop, although it didn't get used as such that often since Frank Cramer, the foreman of sorts, preferred his table in one corner of the shop where he could better keep an eye on things.

"I needed to speak with you about something," his new boss began.

Worry spiked, simply because this was all so new, and Jordan wasn't used to having so much good happen at once. He didn't think he'd messed anything up, but maybe—

"I've been talking to the Foxworths, and to your Sarge," Ben went on, surprising him. "And they're supportive of my idea. Now I just need you to agree to help."

"Of course," he said instantly.

Ben smiled. "Without even knowing what I'm asking?"

"After everything you've done for me? Including not running me off with a shotgun?" he added with a glance at Emily. "Absolutely."

"Good. I want you to turn this room into an actual office and spend some time in it."

Office? Him? "Uh…doing what? Sir?"

Ben smiled at him. "Coordinating Bishop's new outreach program. Sarge told me some of the guys who muster out have trouble adapting back into the civilian world, and that getting that first job is sometimes an issue."

Jordan nodded; he'd seen it a few times. Heck, he'd experienced it, not sure what to do with himself or how.

"I figure that first entry on a civilian résumé is the

hardest, so Bishop wants to help with that. And I want you to be the liaison between us and returning vets who might need a little help with that first step."

Jordan blinked. "Me?"

"Who better? Oh, and our first applicant will be here this afternoon. I think you know him. Guy named Marcus Arroyo?"

Jordan was feeling a bit buzzed, but he smiled and nodded. "Yes, I know him. He's a good guy."

"Is that a yes, then?" Ben asked, smiling back.

A yes to helping out, like Sarge did? To doing that kind of good, after the corruption that the Lydens brought?

"No," Jordan said, taking the man aback a little. "It's a yes, sir," Jordan said, putting all the respect he felt into it.

And when Emmie threw her arms around him, looking up at him with pure joy in her face and glowing in those lovely eyes, he did what he'd resisted in the beginning. He kissed her as if his life depended on it.

Because it did.

# *Epilogue*

Emily didn't know if this was a regular thing for the Foxworths, inviting clients to their home, but she felt honored either way.

"You know," she said as she and Jordan sat in the comfortable, welcoming living room with the big fireplace and the windows that looked out through the trees with a glimpse of water beyond, "that if there's ever anything we or Bishop can do down the line, you have only to call."

"All we ever ask," Quinn said as he handed her a glass of wine and Jordan the beer that matched the one he was having himself. Hayley brought out a tray full of luscious looking and smelling treats, from some crispy roasted potatoes with a variety of toppings to chicken wings to shrimp with dipping sauce, and something she couldn't quite figure out until Hayley explained.

"It's a BLT, without the bread."

Emily saw it then, the curly leaf of lettuce holding

chunks of tomato and onion, strips of bacon, all topped with blue cheese. And she smiled in delight, since she loved the traditional sandwich but rarely indulged.

"That's brilliant," she said.

"That's Quinn," Hayley said. "He invented it when we were out of bread and he didn't feel like going out to get it. He's quite good at that."

Something in the other woman's eyes and smile gave Emily a pretty good idea of why Quinn hadn't wanted to leave the house. She knew because she'd seen that same look in her mirror a few times lately.

Jordan had spent most nights at her place, in her bed. Which she now thought of as their bed. And when she found him one morning wandering through the garden, stopping to look at the various plants and even bending down to smell flowers here and there, she knew she'd be asking him to move in completely sooner than she'd even hoped. It had all happened so fast that, now that things were calm, she was a little nervous. But her father had reassured her, saying he was a good man, and that he'd known her mother was the one for him inside of five minutes.

Next week, at her father's insistence, they were going to take Jordy's camper and head for the coast, for a week of simply being together. The first of many such trips, the man she loved had promised her. Wherever she wanted to go. To which she'd answered that where didn't matter, as long as he was there.

"Where's your resident troublemaker?" Jordan asked with a grin that made her heart do that little flip.

"Cutter? He's off making his rounds," Quinn said. "He should be back any minute now."

At their looks, Hayley explained. "He checks the

neighborhood regularly, makes sure everyone's all right. They all seem to like it, so we let him do what he's obviously decided is his job."

"He's a different sort of dog," Emily said, moving the acquisition of a canine of their own up on the list.

"So, the veteran outreach program is on?" Quinn asked after they'd gobbled down a few of the finger foods.

Jordan nodded. "We've already got two on board."

"Good work," Quinn said. "We're here if you need anything."

There was a sound at the other end of the room, and she looked that way in time to see a doggy-style door flap open and the dog recently under discussion trot in. He stopped, looking at them. Then, suddenly, he vanished down a hallway.

Emily glanced at Hayley, whose brow was furrowed as she said, "Well, that was odd."

A moment later the dog was back, trotting toward them, something dangling from his mouth. Quinn was the first to react, grinning, and Hayley began to laugh. The dog nudged Emily's knee as he passed, then went directly to Jordan and sat in front of him, practically on his feet.

"And here we are," Hayley said. "Back where it all started."

Emily felt her throat tighten, her chest fill as she watched Jordan gently take what the dog had brought him.

"Thanks, buddy," he said softly, reaching out with the other hand to stroke the dog's head. Then, as Cutter went over to plop on the floor between his people, Jordan shifted his gaze to her. "I don't need to cling to them anymore."

"But we'll keep them, forever. Because they brought us together."

He nodded, as his fingers closed around the dog tags that had brought Foxworth into his case.

And the woman he loved into his life.

\* \* \* \* \*

*Catch up with everyone at the
Foxworth Foundation with previous books
in Justine Davis's Cutter's Code miniseries:*

Operation Witness Protection
Operation Payback
Operation Whistleblower
Operation Mountain Recovery
Operation Second Chance

*Available now from Harlequin Romantic Suspense!*

## #2259 COLTON'S YULETIDE MANHUNT
*The Coltons of New York* • by Kacy Cross

Detective Isaac Donner wants to catch the notorious Landmark Killer in the splashiest way possible—if only to prove to his father he has the goods to do it. But his by-the-books partner, Rory Colton, isn't ready to risk her life for a family feud. Her heart is another matter...

## #2260 DANGER ON THE RIVER
*Sierra's Web* • by Tara Taylor Quinn

Undercover cop Tommy Grainger stumbles upon a web of deceit when he rescues Kacey Ashland, bound and drowning, from the local wild rapids. Could the innocent-looking—yet oh-so tempting—elementary school teacher be tied to an illegal contraband cold case that involves Tommy's own father?

## #2261 A DETECTIVE'S DEADLY SECRETS
*Honor Bound* • by Anna J. Stewart

When Detective Lana Tate comes back into FBI special agent Eamon Quinn's life, he'll do anything for a second chance and to keep the woman he's always loved safe. Soon their investigation threatens not only their lives but also whatever future they might have together.

## #2262 WATCHERS OF THE NIGHT
*The Night Guardians* • by Charlene Parris

Forensics investigator Cynthia Cornwall is brilliant, introverted—and compromised. Her agreement to keep Detective Adam Solberg off his father's murder case has put her life in danger, job in jeopardy and heart in the charismatic, determined cop's crosshairs.

# HARLEQUIN
## PLUS

Try the best multimedia
subscription service for romance
readers like you!

---

## Read, Watch and Play.

Experience the easiest way to get
the romance content you crave.

Start your **FREE TRIAL** at
<u>www.harlequinplus.com/freetrial</u>.